THE THREEPERSONS HUNT

BOOKS BY BRIAN GARFIELD

Fiction

Death Wish
Deep Cover
Gangway (with Donald E. Westlake)
Kolchak's Gold
Line of Succession
Relentless
Seven Brave Men
Sliphammer
Sweeny's Honor
The Hit
The Last Bridge
The Vanquished
The Villiers Touch
Valley of the Shadow
Vultures in the Sun
What of Terry Conniston?

Nonfiction

The Thousand-Mile War: World War II
in Alaska and the Aleutians

THE THREEPERSONS HUNT

by Brian Garfield

Published by

M. Evans and Company, Inc. NEW YORK, NEW YORK 10017

This is a novel and all characters and events are fictitious. Principal locales are real but several specific places (like the settlement at Cuncon) do not exist in fact where this novel places them. There is a real White Mountain Apache Tribal Council and it has a real chairman but his name is not Frank Natagee and no resemblance is meant to be suggested. The same is true of officers of the Arizona Highway Patrol, the Indian Agency Police Force and the Arizona State Prison at Florence. The dispute over water rights described herein is suggested by recent events but in many particulars it is fictitious and should not be taken to represent actuality.

M. Evans and Company titles are distributed in
the United States by the J. B. Lippincott Company,
East Washington Square, Philadelphia, Pa. 19105
and in Canada by McClelland & Stewart Limited,
25 Hollinger Road, Toronto M4B 3G2, Ontario

9 8 7 6 5 4 3 2 1

For ZM,
without whom

Blue Mountain Spirit of the East,
In your house of the blue clouds
Where the blue mirage soars,
There is the life of goodness
Where you live.
I sing of good things there.

Yellow Mountain Spirit of the South,
Your strength is of yellow clouds.
Leader of the Spirits, holy Mountain Spirit,
You are nourished by the good of this life.

White Mountain Spirit of the West,
Your strength is of white mirages;
Holy Mountain Spirit,
I am happy with your words
And you are happy with mine.

Black Mountain Spirit of the North,
Your strength is of black clouds;
Black Mountain Spirit,
I am happy with your words
And you are happy with mine;
Now it is good. *Enju.*

—*Apache Indian song*

CHAPTER ONE

A DARK column of cumulonimbus blew in across the desert from the Pacific Coast. It gathered condensation above the hot plains and when it reached the mountains of the eastern Arizona midlands it broke against them and there was rain.

The volume of precipitation made flash floods in the mountain ravines. Each trickle became a rivulet that joined other rivulets until dry canyons roared and creeks thundered over their banks.

The thunder and rain passed on but the floods continued for an hour or more behind them before the thirsty earth sucked them in.

A white Ford station wagon squatted crosswise in the dirt like a toy left askew by a child who had lost interest in it. On its roof a red high-intensity light revolved and flashed. It was an Indian Agency car: *White Mountain Apache Reservation Police.*

The cop who went with it stood beside the thatched

wickiup and kept his eyes on Sam Watchman's face when Watchman slid his Highway Patrol cruiser to a stop in the muddy ruts. There were seven or eight wickiups in various stages of architectural dishabille, two of them falling down: when a wickiup got beyond the patch-repair stage the Apache simply built a new one to live in and used the old one for storing firewood until it decomposed.

There were several corrals and pens; there was a windmill with its tank; some little vegetable patches drenched and drooping behind the wickiups; a few old cars and pickup trucks; a dozen Indians in black hats or squaw dresses, observing Sam Watchman's arrival with suspicion; a barbwire fence, three strands that ran around a ten-acre meadow—the far gate stood wide open; scrub-brush hills beyond the meadow and the darker timber of the White Mountains still farther. You could see the shadow-streaks of falling rain over the peaks thirty miles away.

Over on the open tailgate of a ruined grey pickup truck sat an Apache giant in a plaid shirt, a young man the size of a grizzly bear with a face you could strike a match on. His bootheels dangled almost to the ground. He was smoking a cigarette and drinking beer out of a can, and watching everything.

Watchman got out of the cruiser. The Indian Agency cop came forward, his transparent rain-slicker flapping in the wind. The air was like freshly washed glass and the wind had a good smell to it.

"*Pasó por aquí*," Watchman said. *He passed by here.* It was not a question. He saw in this scene everything that was supposed to be in it except horses. The place was a horse ranch but there were no horses.

The Agency cop had small eyes high in his face and twisted gristle for a nose. He didn't look quite forty. "One cop," he said. "I send a squeal and they send me one cop. Hell you must be a Texas Ranger."

Watchman knew the joke. It was one of those "true"

legends from the Old West. Somewhere in Texas they'd had a riot in some frontier town and the constable had telegraphed the Texas Rangers for help. A single Ranger had arrived on his horse and the constable had been aghast.

"Only one Ranger?"

"Only one riot, ain't there?"

"You see him?" Watchman asked.

"No. But he was here."

"How much of a jump has he got?"

"Maybe two hours."

"Horseback," Watchman said. "Took the whole herd, did he? Smart."

"Real smart," the Apache policeman agreed. "They had thirty head here. Call me Pete Porvo."

"Sam Watchman."

The village Apaches looked on with brooding stares while Watchman shook Pete Porvo's hand, walked over to the fence and looked at the meadow. The corral gates were wide open too.

Porvo caught up with Watchman at the fence. "No point getting dogs on this. Hounds wouldn't know what horse to follow. Anyhow he was here in the rain, there wouldn't be no scent."

"They told me he was stupid."

"Joe knows horses. He knows guns. I reckon he knows this country as well as any man alive. Put him in a city he's pretty dumb. But up here?"

"That's why he came back here," Watchman said. He turned his face straight toward Porvo. "You know him pretty well?"

"Hell—it's a small town, this Reservation. This ain't Window Rock."

Either this was a shrewd psychic guess or Porvo had been prepared. Window Rock was the Navajo capital and there was nothing about Watchman that could identify his tribe to the eyes of a stranger.

Probably they'd told him on the car radio. *We'll send you our Navajo trooper. He's on his way up there anyway.*

But Watchman let it go. He squinted toward the mountains. "Would he go up there? Or stay down in the hills?"

"He knows it all. I'd just be guessing."

"Guess, then."

"He'd stay down closer to where folks live, I expect. Ain't nothing for a man to steal up in the piny woods there."

That could be right. If it was, Watchman thought wryly, it cut down the search area from two million acres to one million. It was a big Reservation.

Porvo said, "He'll turn those horses loose one at a time. After a while they'll come home by themselves. Ain't no point trying to track him in the meantime, if that's what you was thinking."

Watchman shook his head and started to walk back toward his Arizona Highway Patrol car. He stepped around the puddles. Porvo trailed him, screwing up his eyes against the blaze of noon sun that had reappeared behind the storm.

Three Indian men stood in front of the biggest wickiup. Watchman stopped and said to Porvo, "Any of these folks see him?"

"You seen him, didn't you Eddie?"

One of the Indians nodded slightly.

Watchman tried a smile. It didn't have any visible effect. "You try to stop him?"

Eddie let one eyebrow rise a quarter of an inch—it was the sum of his reply.

Porvo said, "You don't try to stop a man got a rifle pointed at you."

Watchman swiveled on both heels. "What rifle?"

Porvo turned to Eddie. "You get a look at it Eddie?"

It was an effort for Eddie to speak; he had to conquer a reluctance, a resistance to the uniform and the stranger. "Guess I did."

"Well?"

"Saddle gun," Eddie said. "Lever. I think maybe thirty-thirty."

"Where the hell did he get it?" Watchman felt a little anger. "That's all we need, him batting around up there with a rifle."

"Prob'ly figured he needed one," Porvo said with oblivious logic.

"You know where that puts him legally?"

"I'm just a country cop. Where's it put him?"

"Dead or alive," Watchman said. "He's a fugitive on a capital-crime conviction. He's armed—anybody can shoot him on sight. They were right after all. He's stupid."

"Man," Porvo said softly, "ain't nobody around here going to shoot Joe Threepersons. These are his people."

"He steals some more horses, his people are likely to start losing patience with him."

"Oh I don't imagine he'll steal any more horses," Porvo drawled with an odd little smile. "Prob'ly next time he'll just ask for a horse and the man'll give it to him. You kind of wasting your time, you know. You ain't going to get Joe."

"Whose side are *you* on, Porvo?"

"Come right down to it, I guess I'm on Joe's side." Porvo met his eyes guilelessly.

"He's a convicted murderer."

"It was a white man he killed. You know, hell, you're an Innun yourself."

"I'm a cop," Watchman answered. "So are you, if you ever get around to remembering it."

"I ain't no Uncle Tomahawk."

Watchman got the topographical map of the Reservation

out of his car. He spread it out on the hood. Water had beaded on the wax finish and made dark discs through the back of the map. He leaned on his hands, studying it.

Porvo laughed quietly in his throat. "Man if you need a map of this country you ain't never going to find him."

2.

A county sheriff's car made a roadblock across the highway. A deputy sat on the front fender in the blaze of early afternoon sun. There were dark sweat patches all over his khaki shirt.

Watchman drew his car up by the county car's bumper. The deputy squinted through weather-whacked blue eyes. "How do."

Watchman nodded. He didn't get out of the car.

The deputy said, "You got traffic duty?"

"Detective division."

"Looking for that killer?"

"He's on horseback. You may as well call this off."

"I'd have to check with my dispatcher."

"You do that."

"Anyhow," the deputy said, "he ain't going to show himself around here. Even a lizard knows enough to stay out of this sun."

"You could have been down on the desert. Fifteen degrees hotter down there."

"Yeah. Ain't I lucky now." The deputy bestirred himself, slid down to his feet and walked toward the door of his car. When Watchman drove off the deputy was reaching inside for his radio microphone. In the mirror Watchman saw the deputy's hat brim turn, indicating his interest in Watchman: *What's that Indian doing in a state trooper's uniform?*

‡ 14 ‡

The sun made the world brittle and blinding. Ahead of him U.S. 60 ran straight up the plateau. Perspective narrowed it to nothing and beyond that in a lavender haze stood the summits. The rain had gone on. Tufts of cloud hung here and there in its afterwash.

Tiny in the distance a truck came toward him from the east, appearing and disappearing at intervals with the rises and dips in the road. It skimmed forward on top of the heat mirage, which made ponds of the paving. The sun beat hot reflections off its windshield. Presently it loomed, tossing a mane of oil smoke. Watchman gripped the wheel when the truck went by: its passage shook his car and the wind of its wake made his wheels shimmy on the damp road. When its diesel stink was out of his nostrils he began to breathe again.

The road two-laned up through piñon and juniper hills that looked like orchards because of the size and separation of the small trees. A barbwire cattle fence ran along beside the road on the right. There wasn't all that much decent graze up here; it took fifty acres to support one steer in this kind of country but the Apache tribes had plenty of acres. Not as many as the Navajos but then there were five thousand Apaches on this Reservation and there were maybe a hundred and fifty thousand Navajos up on the Window Rock. It made you wonder.

He found the turnoff. A pair of ruts forked away from the highway, went through the fence across a rail cattle guard and disappeared into the hills. He went that way, bouncing in the ruts.

The dirt track bisected the route Joe Threepersons had probably followed on his stolen horses. Ahead of him the foothills started to crumple and heave toward the dark forested high country; the land wasn't as harsh and arid as his own Navajo country but it had its own kind of drama.

He drove slowly across three or four miles of wagon track. The undercarriage of the Plymouth was taking a beating from the rocks. In the damp earth he saw tracks of cattle, deer, javelina, bobcat, coyote, jackrabbit, lizard and snake. Evidently no human foot had trod this ground since the invention of the beer can. A hawk drifted above the trees some distance to the south. Two Herefords browsed in the brush near the track; they watched him drive by, chewing, swishing their tails at flies.

The noise of his approach startled a little gather of whitetail deer that bounded away in alarm. He kept watching the earth for signs of the recent passage of a herd of horses. He didn't expect to track on foot but at least he might get an indication of the fugitive's direction of travel.

By the odometer it was six and three-tenths miles from the highway to the point where he found the spoor of the stolen horse herd. Too many of them to make an accurate count possible. Now of course the question was whether Joe Threepersons was with the herd. He might have split off on his own in some other direction, riding one horse.

But he hadn't. If you knew horses you knew that. These horses were still traveling east in something like a straight line. If the man had turned them loose they'd have begun to wander, they'd have milled around and browsed a while and then they'd have headed home.

Watchman left the car and took a little walk to see what he could learn from the tracks. The earth had dried to a crumbly, cakey texture except where the trees shaded it; here it was still moist in places and some of the hoof-prints were quite clear. He was able to single out a set of prints that represented one horse zigzagging back and forth behind the rest of the herd: its prints were imposed on top of the others and it was the only animal that made so many switchbacks and turns.

This was the track of the fugitive Indian's mount: Joe

Threepersons was riding behind the other horses, driving them, zigzagging to chouse strays back into the herd and keep them all moving. All except one horse which he had let go on purpose. In fact he'd probably driven it away; otherwise it would have stayed near the herd.

Undoubtedly he planned to keep doing that, reducing the herd one animal at a time so that no one would be able to tell which one carried him. At the moment it was easy enough to single out the tracks of his own horse but it would be dark presently and by morning he'd have so much of a lead that there'd be no point trying to follow the tracks from here. Tomorrow it would rain again—it was that season—and the tracks would wash out then.

Watchman had known all that before he'd decided to come over here for a look. He had come anyway because at least it narrowed the district where Joe Threepersons would probably end up. Ahead were the foothills, the timber country that fed the tribe's sawmill, and the main Reservation settlements at Fort Apache and Whiteriver.

To a White Mountain Apache like Joe Threepersons this Reservation was what "home" was to Robert Frost: the place where when you go there they have to take you in. Pete Porvo was right: if you had to have a map you wouldn't find him.

So what am I doing here?

Following orders? Being a good German? Acting like a stalking horse for the white masters? Lisa had asked him why he stayed in the department and kept taking their insults and he'd told her, *I'm just trying to earn my gold watch.* But there wasn't a whole lot of truth in that.

Another time he'd tried to explain it to her: *I come from a long line of white Indians. It gets to be a habit. My great-grandfather rode scout for General Crook, he was an Army Indian. Helped them track down Geronimo.*

For his great-grandfather there's been a kind of logic

to it: Navajo and Apache were bitter enemies in those days, never more so that after the 1860s when the Navajo were tricked, trapped and massacred by Kit Carson's armies so that forever afterward the Navajo nation had been subjugated and humiliated at gunpoint into Reservation bondage while, not far to the south, the Apache tribes continued for twenty years to run free and proud. The Navajo hated the Apache for their freedom; and so the Navajo scouts had gone to war against the Apache even when it meant fighting shoulder-to-shoulder with white soldiers. It was the only war the whites would let them fight, so they fought it. It was better than no war at all.

My grandfather and my father were Agency Police on the Window Rock. My grandfather rode a while with Burgade's Rangers. My father fought in the Aleutians and out in Kwajalein and Okinawa with the Seventh Division. So you see it's an old and dishonorable tradition in my family, fighting for the white man. When I was in the Army it was peacetime but they sent me overseas to Seoul for a year, so I took a flag of Navajo design and planted it on Korean soil and claimed it for the Navajo nation.

He'd done his tour of duty with the Military Police and then he'd gone to the university at Tucson on the GI Bill. A Highway Patrol recruiter had visited the campus the spring before graduation. So here he was in a uniform with a Sam Browne belt and a big hat and a six-gun in a clamshell holster on his hip just like a movie cowboy, and he had had ten years of chasing speeders down the highways and untangling bloody wreckage and living on café chili and coffee. And now they'd sent him to track down a young fugitive Apache who was up there slamming around somewhere in those hills with a .30-30 rifle that could go off any time: an Apache who was trying to cross an emotional minefield and might just be in a frame of mind to take some people with him.

Watchman resented it with the feeling he had been

wound up and pointed in Joe Threepersons' direction and turned loose for the entertainment of the white bastards who'd revel in watching two Indians square off, the same way they delighted in watching cockfights and prizefights between black men and Mexicans.

3.

Watchman was down on one knee inspecting the hoof-prints when the whacking boom of an explosion froze him in alarm.

Rifle shot; he recognized the sound a second later. Its hard echo beat across the hills.

The report was directionless. Watchman crouched back against a ball of scrub oak. His head turned quickly, he tried to watch everything at once. There was no way of knowing whether that rifle was shooting at him or at something else but he could hardly ignore it.

He unsnapped the holster and palmed his service revolver. The adrenaline pumping through him made his hand shake.

The rifle boomed again and this time the bullet made a crease in the earth twenty feet to his right; it whined away like a flat stone skipped across a pond.

He heard the nearby *crack* of the next one. It broke some twigs out of the scrub oak beside him.

He threw himself belly-flat behind the scrub oak and fired two blind shots in the general direction he thought the rifle had spoken from.

Instinct prompted panic but his experience steadied him. There were two possibilities. Either the rifleman was a terrible marksman or he hadn't meant to hit Watchman. Either way it meant he wasn't likely to get killed right here and right now.

He edged his face forward past the clumped stems of

the oak to peer back toward the road ruts where the shots had come from.

This time he saw the muzzle-flash. The bullet shook the scrub oak.

That was two in a row the rifle had put into the oak; so the odds changed. Not a poor marksman; they were warning shots.

Flat on the ground he considered his horizons. There was a dip behind him, twenty feet away—a shallow crease in the land that had probably been a torrent two hours ago. He began to slide back toward the gully; he triggered three .38s toward the place where he'd seen the muzzle flame, rolled into the gully and slithered in the mud and a rifle bullet chopped the air overhead.

Now what the hell?

He was fumbling to reload. Two cartridges dropped from his hand and he left them in the mud.

You've got no right to scare a man this way. He whacked the cylinder closed and fired a couple of potluck rounds. The revolver slammed against the heel of his hand in recoil; the racket had his ears ringing. The stink of cordite fouled the air.

There was a shot but it wasn't aimed anywhere in his direction—it didn't have that sort of *crack*. He searched the brush but his view was restricted by the scattered fat trees. He caught the reflection of sunlight off something metallic and he was rattled enough to turn his sights that way before he realized it was only sun-glare bouncing off some part of his own car.

He moved ten feet to one side to change his field of view through the clumps. There was another rifle shot. Again it wasn't aimed in his direction. It had a muffled explosive sound as if it were being fired away from him.

He moved again but still couldn't see anything. There was a third rifle shot and then a fourth, these last two quite close together. Thoroughly mystified he crawled up over the lip of the gully into a cluster of piñons and slithered between them, his uniform soaked with mud, prising the branches apart with his left hand and poking the revolver out ahead of him.

Then he heard briefly the crunch and scrape of someone moving through heavy growth; after that the padding of footfalls in the soft earth, a man dogtrotting. The sound dwindled quickly.

4.

He edged cautiously back toward the dirt track and found the place where the rifleman had squatted down to shoot at him. Deep heel-indentations and pointed toes: cowboy boots. Everybody around here wore cowboy boots, that didn't mean a thing.

Quite obviously the man was gone. When Watchman got to his feet he heard the distant revving of an engine being started. The roar settled down to a chug and went whining away in a low gear.

He put the revolver away in its clamshell holster and started running back toward his car in disgust.

Whoever it was had followed him up the highway in a car. So it wasn't Joe Threepersons.

The Highway Patrol cruiser squatted like a derelict on its rims. Watchman walked around the car and stared unhappily at the four bullet-shredded flat tires.

He broke a leafy twig off a scrub oak and rubbed it between his palms to clean them. Then he contemplated the 6.3-mile walk back to the highway.

You're being a pretty stupid Indian. He tramped over to the car. The bottom of the door scraped the ground when he dragged it open.

It hadn't occurred to the rifleman to disable the police radio. Watchman switched it on and hoped he hadn't parked in a dead spot and put the microphone close to his lips.

"Niner Zero. Niner Zero. I have a Code Ten-thirteen."

"Dispatch to Niner Zero. Go ahead on Ten-Thirteen."

In an embarrassed mutter he explained where he was and the girl on the radio desk had to ask him to repeat it. Finally he got it across to her and asked her to make contact with Trooper Buck Stevens and ask Stevens to bring him a few items. When the awkward dialogue concluded he sprocketed the microphone and reached for his coffee thermos.

He left the door open in the heat; he settled back on the seat, caked with mud, and pulled his hat brim down over his eyes. It would take a while.

Sitting in a half-doze he reviewed the events that had sentenced him to this.

CHAPTER TWO

THE WALLED Arizona State Prison was surrounded by several acres of cropland contained within an eight-foot-high Anchor fence topped with nine parallel strands of barbwire strung in a configuration which in cross section resembled an arrowhead. There were no watchtowers on the fence.

From the corner where the north road intersected U.S. 80-89, the fence ran south along the shrubbed shoulder and travelers on the highway could glance out of their car windows and see small groups of prisoners working the farm fields, guarded by correctional officers who worked in pairs on horseback, armed with riot shotguns and hunting rifles.

The prison had been built just after the turn of the century to replace the infamous and medievally rancid Territorial Penitentiary at Yuma. The present facility stood midway between Phoenix and Tuscon on the arid outskirts of Florence. It was antiquated and inevitably overcrowded. Its administration was as enlightened as could be expected —the state's penal budget was insanely low—and conditions inside were "average" by national comparisons. It was the state's Maximum Security Prison but at frequent intervals it had provided assurances that it was not escape-proof.

Only three highways led out of Florence and these were susceptible to rapid interdiction by cars of the Pinal County Sheriff and the Arizona Highway Patrol. Once a man broke out of Florence prison he had little choice but to strike out on foot into barren country where summer heat clung to the ground like melted tar and the pursuit was an amalgam of helicopters, Jeeps, packs of hounds, horsemen and Indian trackers. Yet prisoners kept breaking out and usually one or two fugitives got shot to death by overzealous manhunters but that was regarded as being part of the game because it was a country in which Westerns were very popular and it was no disgrace to die with your boots on.

Most of those who attempted to escape were chronic losers, the ones serving terms of twenty-to-life whose chances at early parole had been destroyed by circumstance, luck or their own behavior.

Fully half the population of the cells spoke no English or next to none. Some were Chicanos: Mexican-Americans who spoke Spanish. Others were Indians who spoke minimal Spanish, no English, and bits and pieces of native American dialects understood by no one outside their own villages. Unable to communicate with their lawyers they had been convicted and sentenced.

Language did not end the problem. The regulations of Anglo law made little sense to Indians whose own laws were based on logic instead of statute, reason instead of prejudice, and compensation of victims instead of punishment of criminals. An Indian who caused another Indian an injury that laid him up was required by tribal law to take upon himself the victim's job and support of his family until the victim was ready to do his own work again. An Indian did not understand laws that sent him to prison while his victim's family starved because there was no one to harvest the crops or care for the animals.

The Indian in Florence prison came to understand that he could not expect sanity or reasonable justice in an Anglo judicial-penal system. It was therefore sensible to get out of the place and run into the desert where a man could make his own justice with the earth.

Five prisoners were involved in the July 5 escape. Three were Chicanos and two were Indians: one Papago and one White Mountain Apache.

The break had taken place late in the afternoon. It was the day after the holiday and by their own later admission the two guards were hung over. Evidently the prisoners had taken this into account in planning the time of their break.

The five were not close friends or comrades-in-crime; it was just that they happened to be the five individuals who had been assigned to that particular work detail on that particular afternoon.

The Weather Bureau's recorded high-temperature for the day, reached just after two in the afternoon, was 104 degrees Fahrenheit. By half-past-four the temperature had not dropped more than two or three degrees and the two horseback guards had posted themselves under the spindly trees that threw a bit of shade alongside the employees' houses, just within the high fence.

The five prisoners were weeding. The rows were planted in sweet corn but the stalks were not yet two feet high; there was no problem of visibility and the horseback guards were reputed to be expert marksmen.

The five prisoners worked five adjacent parallel rows so that the guards could watch them without distraction. Each prisoner dragged a large burlap sack into which the pulled weeds were stuffed. Ordinarily the guards walked their horses around close to the prisoners but it had been a very hot week and these were not especially troublesome prisoners. By the late afternoon when the prisoners were down at the far end of their rows, the guards were separated from them by the full width of the field and the prisoners were separated from U.S. 80-89 by only a twenty-foot strip of ground and the Anchor Fence.

At first it was not clear whether the beige 1968 Chevrolet came along as part of an outside plan or whether the prisoners simply waited until they saw a car approaching from the south, then went over the fence and commandeered the car by standing in the road in front of it and forcing it to stop or run them down.

They went over the fence by tossing their burlaps across the barbwire and vaulting the nine-foot barrier by boosting one another and by monkeying up the woven-wire Anchor steel with fingers and boot-toes. It was no great athletic feat; the burlap protected them from the barbwire and the only real risk came from the rifles of the two guards under the trees. But the guards had the sun in their eyes and the prisoners were in constant motion once they set their plan in operation. The guards reacted slowly and when they did their shooting was poor; all five of the prisoners got away.

The beige Chevrolet stopped, the convicts squeezed into it, doors slammed, the car moved away to the north.

It was several minutes before the facts were sorted out and several more before alarms were issued. By then the escape car had had time to get ten miles from the prison. The warden alerted enforcement agencies and roadblocks were set up on the Pinal Pioneer Parkway to the south, on the highway below Florence Junction to the north, and on

State Highway 287 between Valley Farms and the Casa Grande ruins to the west.

Units of the County Sheriff's office and the Highway Patrol met for a briefing at the prison at seven o'clock and the hunt went into operation by seven-fifteen. Local police within the town were already searching all streets and driveways and garages for the missing car; three beige Chevrolets were investigated but all of them were owned locally and quickly cleared of suspicion of involvement. Two ranchers arrived at the prison in horse-vans with packs of hunting hounds, and a helicopter like a bloated mosquito hovered near the prison yard, the setting sun throwing a sharp reflection off its Plexiglas bubble.

Scout planes made ground-search patterns and at Florence the operation was coordinated in the warden's office by the warden, the senior Undersheriff, and Captain Fred Custis of the Arizona Highway Patrol.

Late in the twilight a search plane reported a light-colored car apparently abandoned in a desert draw about a mile off U.S. 80-89 up toward Mineral Mountain. The site was some sixteen miles northeast of the prison and Captain Custis immediately dispatched two Jeeps and a Dodge Power Wagon filled with hounds.

Some time was wasted debating the feasibility of throwing up a cordon of men around the area—the fugitives were on foot now and had only some two hours' jump on the pursuit; they had to be somewhere in the hills within a ten-mile radius. But the logistics were prohibitive and so was the cost; it was decided to entrust the hunt to the dogs. Still the officers were edgy because if the car belonged to confederates of the convicts it was possible the convicts were now armed. A deputy radioed Florence the license number of the car and the information was put through to DMV Phoenix but it would be a while before they would ascertain the identity of the car's owner.

One of the deputies affixed a red battery-lamp to the

collar of the leading hound and the dogs were turned loose to follow the spoor, which was given by items of clothing from the escapees' prison cells. The dogs ran baying into the hills and the officers in their Jeeps chased the bobbing red lamp, five men to a Jeep, armed with pump rifles.

The escape car had been abandoned here because the country began to buckle and heave almost immediately beyond it; this was as far as a car could go. The Jeeps ran with full headlight beams but it was hard going; the deputies almost pitched out on some of the hills and several times the dogs got too far ahead and the trainers had to whistle them in. Frequently the headlight beams swept wildly across the sky like air-raid searchlights. Probably the fugitives could see them coming but it couldn't be helped: a Jeep with a broken axle was useless.

At nine-fifteen the baying changed in volume and tone and the trainers knew the dogs had closed.

The Jeeps stopped on a hillside and one man remained on guard, moving the Jeeps periodically to play the headlights against the opposite slope where the dogs circled a high clutter of boulders.

The police fanned out to cross the canyon on foot, carrying flashlights and weapons, moving slowly with their muscles braced against half-expected bullets. But the convicts weren't shooting the dogs and this led the police to believe that perhaps after all they weren't armed.

When the police approached within flashlight range they found the convicts in a tight knot around a middle-aged couple and the blade of a pocketknife was pressed against the woman's throat.

The man and woman were being held by four convicts— a fact which only became important later. The immediate problem for the police was how to handle the situation and it looked like a stalemate. The convicts had two vulnerable and innocent hostages. They wanted free passage out, they wanted one of the Jeeps.

One of the deputies went back across to the Jeeps to radio Florence for instructions. On receipt of them he returned to the flashlit tableau and stalled for time with a series of arguments which were sensible but did not reach receptive ears.

The police might not try to stop the convicts as long as they kept their hostages, the deputy said, but this would not prevent the police from shadowing the convicts everywhere they went and if the convicts tried to harm the hostages to discourage their followers, the police would kill them.

At this point a rifle spoke. One of the deputies had slipped up the hill to one side and taken careful aim on the most exposed of the four convicts, a Mexican-American named Ruiz. The orders were to wound, not to kill. In this case either the shooting was imprecise or the deputy exceeded his orders; the convict Ruiz received the bullet through the bridge of his nose and dropped dead.

The other three convicts huddled close behind their frail human screen. The pocketknife drew a drop of blood from the woman's throat but the convicts were not yet ready to destroy their only means of protection. They began to scream demands at the deputies and step by step the deputies gave ground, retreating across the canyon toward the Jeeps with the convicts in strange pursuit. From the darkness another rifle shot exploded but this one missed and after that the convicts began to move the hostages back and forth around them so that there was too much risk of hitting them.

Guided by the Jeep headlights the warden, the Undersheriff, Captain Custis and their retine of pilot fish arrived in a Land Cruiser and the Dodge Power Wagon. There was a whispered conference. Over on the dark hillsides several deputies were practicing psychological warfare by loudly working their bolts to throw cartridges into the chambers of their rifles.

The warden knew his convicts. He could see they were uncertain. He felt that time and resistance would abrade them into surrender.

The warden walked out into the blaze of headlights and offered to exchange himself for the civilian hostages. The offer was refused.

In sibilant Spanish the warden told the prisoners that they were cowards, that they had no *macho*, no *cojones*, that they would cook in hell like frying bacon for all eternity because of the unforgivable mortal sin they were committing against innocent bystanders. He spoke at some length and not without eloquence, and because the convicts listened to him he felt he had them.

In the meantime the dead Ruiz was carried over to the Power Wagon and the dogs were set to sniffing out the trail of the fifth escapee—the missing one—but they scented no spoor.

The warden was an effective talker, his Spanish was first-rate. He spoke of mercy and leniency, he tried to impress upon them that if they voluntarily released the hostages he would see to it that federal kidnapping charges were not pressed against them and that they would be liable for trial only on a charge of jailbreak; since they were all lifers the conviction would add nothing to their sentences.

Unfortunately this information had an effect opposite to that which the warden desired. It reminded the convicts of how little they had to lose. They seemed to be arguing and the warden suspended his sermon.

The three prisoners decided it was not fair to kill the innocent. They therefore shoved the two hostages away from them. In the same motion they made their runs.

The three convicts ran in three directions toward holes in the surrounding cordon and although the rifles began to chatter none of the convicts was hit in the first volley; the deputies had to avoid shooting the hostages and their own companions across the circle and therefore they had to aim low, and shooting at the feet of a running man requires an extraordinary degree of marksmanship.

The second volley caught one of the convicts point-blank. Four bullets entered his body almost simultaneously from four directions and he fell, critically wounded.

Another convict made it to the cordon but by the time he reached it the hole had closed. He was swatted across the face by a swinging rifle. It broke his jaw and knocked him down.

The third man, the Papago, was a good sprinter and made it through the lines and was thirty feet beyond when a bullet broke his spine and dropped him.

One deputy was wounded in the foot by a stray bullet and there was a tired sigh as air leaked out of a Jeep tire.

Of the four convicts only one ultimately survived—the man with the broken jaw. One was already dead; the other two died of injuries within forty-eight hours of the incident. The surviving convict after intense questioning in the prison hospital was tried, convicted and sentenced to an additional twenty years, the sentence to run concurrently with his existing life term.

2.

Two-and-a-half days later it began for Sam Watchman. He drove into the lot against the morning sun with his hat brim pulled down to his nose in lieu of a sun visor. He left his dusty Volvo in a slot that said OFFICIAL CARS ONLY, VIOLATORS WILL BE TOWED AWAY AT THEIR EXPENSE. It was seven o'clock and hotting up for a scorcher in Phoenix.

Rush-hour traffic crawled past the front of the AHP

building, enough sunlight hitting the chrome to blind a pedestrian. Watchman kept his hat brim down until he was inside the glass doors.

There was a hush of ducted air. At the desk the bald sergeant was interviewing a complainant, looking him over closely as if inspecting him for bodily signs of Communism or felonious character. The sergeant waved Watchman through without giving any evidence he had ever looked up to see who he was.

A bilious green hallway lit by wire-netted bulbs; he passed the canteen room where two patrolmen were drinking coffee and a third was on the phone: "What's the squeal? . . . All right, who catches? . . . Shit, all right." When Watchman continued on his way the patrolman was reaching for his hat and kit.

Captain Fred Custis had a corner office with a view of the parking lot. From the desk he gave Watchman a bleak glance across his steepled fingers.

The size of Custis was a tribute to the breweries and his white mustache was stained to amber by cigar smoke. He decided to be hearty. "How're they hangin,' Sam?" Then he tugged out a crumpled handkerchief and blew his nose. "God damn summer cold."

It looked as if it had been two days since the captain had been near a razor. His uniform looked lived-in. You had to credit his industry. He would work an eager twenty-four-hour day and that was mostly the reason for his success in the department; certainly it wasn't his brains.

He uttered a grinding snort to clear his nasal passages and scraped a sleeve across his mustache.

Watchman said, "You told me to report in for assignment."

"That slot where you parked just now. I was watching. It's for official cars only—can't you read?"

"I'm an official, Captain."

"Your car isn't. I ought to send Dancey out there to put a summons on your windshield. Ought to have the damned foreign crate towed away."

"I'll move it, Captain." In a minute he was sure Custis would ask him sarcastically if he couldn't afford a native American car.

The desk was covered with green linoleum and the walls were illustrated with framed citations and news-photo clippings, crowded together like medical diplomas in a doctor's office. Most of the pictures featured Custis with his pale-eyed, clenched-teeth public smile, holding a prisoner by the elbow or looming above a podium or shaking hands with celebrities.

Captain Custis blew his nose. "How would you like a lateral promotion?"

It pricked Watchman's interest and he brought his eyes back to Custis.

"Sit down a minute." It wasn't a courtesy; Custis didn't want to have to look up at him. Watchman sat.

"Lateral to where?"

"Investigations Division."

There had to be a catch and Watchman waited for it.

"Of course it's temporary until we see how you work out over there."

Ten years ago Custis had been on the line working a cruiser out of Phoenix and Watchman had been a rookie and circumstances had assigned him to Custis' car. They hadn't liked each other the first day and nothing had changed since then. Custis was a good cop from the old school but people like Watchman didn't fit into his concept of Good Guys. Now Custis was offering Watchman not only an olive branch but a plum and it had an odd smell.

Custis had the writing board pulled out from one side of his desk and there were papers and photographs on it. He stood up, singled out one of the photographs and tossed it spinning across the desk and began to spread the rest of the documents out on the desk.

Watchman reached for the glossy. It was a print-out that showed a pair of mug shots, one profile and one full face.

This one had a round face and looked a little soft around the cheeks—his body probably carried fifteen pounds more than it needed to. But a mug shot betrayed no more character than a death mask and there was no way to ascertain what the man's face would look like when it was animated or how he moved or what his voice sounded like or how he used his hands.

The face was somewhere between twenty-five and thirty-five. It was the face of an Indian and the only real distinguishing mark was the cauliflowering of the left ear. A disfigurement like that would be a dead giveaway in a lineup, but first you had to find him.

Within the photos the movable lettering of the chin rest identified the man: "J. Threepersons."

"Him," Watchman said.

Captain Custis screwed up his face and there was a moment of suspense and then he sneezed, not getting the handkerchief to his nose quite in time.

Afterward he wiped his mustache. "As of eight o'clock this morning it's your case."

Custis pushed two more papers across the desk—the fingerprint chart and the description sheet—and stood up. "You're to get a make on him. Find, fix and apprehend."

"All by myself?"

"You have all the mighty resources of the nation's crime-busting institutions at your fingertips," Custis said in his dry way of attempting humor. "There's an APB out of course. The mug shots have been circulated. In theory every police officer in the southwest is looking for him. But you're the one who'll be on the case exclusively. He's important enough to warrant a one-officer cover but he's not important enough to justify taking a whole squad of line detectives off work on more active cases. The bulletins have the Warning-This-Man-May-Be-Armed-And-Dangerous tag on them but I don't really think he's the type to go on a murder spree."

"What type is he?"

"Just a no-account Apache." Custis looked up from under his white eyebrows. "Don't get stiff on me like that. The chairman of the Tribal Council up at Whiteriver used exactly those words to me. One Apache calling another Apache a no-account Apache. So take it up with him, not me."

"You wouldn't have called the chairman of the Tribal Council if you didn't think the subject would head home. What did they tell you up there?"

"Said they hadn't seen hide nor hair of him. I told them to put their Agency Police on it but I don't trust those clowns to find their way to the bathroom."

"Then you figure he's hiding out on the Reservation."

"It's the only home he knows. Only place he'd feel comfortable."

"So you single out the only Indian in the department to go look for him."

"I figured maybe you'd be able to think the same way Threepersons thinks."

"Do you know how much cooperation I'm likely to get up there? I'm a Navajo. Maybe we all look alike to you, but before the Anglos came down here and unified the Indians by giving them a common enemy, Apaches and Navajos used to shoot each other for sport. If the Apaches are hiding him out they might not talk to a white man about it but they'd sure as hell not talk to a Navajo."

"That's ancient history. It's all one big happy family now."

"You've been talking to anthropologists." Watchman

used a tone on the word that he might have used in pronouncing the word "Custer." "Maybe you go up to Flagstaff or Gallup for the big intertribal ceremonies and watch all that oozing brotherhood. That's fine on white man's turf, Captain, but right now we've got Hopis and Navajos murdering each other over the rights to a few useless acres of land and the Apaches are laughing themselves silly every time somebody gets killed there. A Navajo going onto the Apache land, that's more of a foreigner than a white man."

"I guess you don't want the job then."

"I didn't say I was turning it down."

"You just want to know what's in it for you. Well I can answer that and the answer is, not much. It's a lateral promotion, no pay raise. You'd be made temporary detective grade, but that's not a civil service title and there's no tenure. I don't make permanent personnel assignments in that division, that's Lieutenant Wilder's job, and anyhow if the job was permanent you'd have to take the examinations and pass them. If you handle this job all right and Wilder likes your performance, I expect he'll give you a crack at the exams. That's all I can promise."

Custis didn't have to finish the implied statement: *But at least it's a change from pushing a Plymouth around the boondocks giving out speeding tickets.*

Watchman gave it very brief thought. "This was really your own idea, was it?"

"I talked it over with the A.G."

Then it had been the Attorney General's idea and that made more sense. Up at the state capitol they were more sensitive to the effects of public relations. Setting an Indian cop to catch an Indian fugitive would have a nice ring to it and it would get the department a good bit of mileage in the papers.

"And you really think he's hiding out up on the White Mountain Reservation?"

"I wouldn't bet my badge on it. It's just a hunch. What would you do in his shoes?"

"I'd have to know something about him first."

"Talk to Wilder, he's got the details. I'll pencil you in and let him know you're on your way over there." Custis sat down, indicating that the interview was ended, reaching for a ballpoint pen. His face was screwed up in distaste but perhaps that was only the nasal agony of his summer cold.

3.

Lieutenant Lloyd Wilder was a few years younger than Watchman, a hotshot with several university degrees in police science. Watchman had known him at a distance for several years and casually for six months, as one gets to know an official of a different branch who works out of the same small building. Wilder was amiable and up-to-date and had a very fast way of talking, like a salesman half afraid someone would try to interrupt his pitch.

"He was doing ten years for second-degree murder. The original charge was first-degree but his lawyer copped a plea. He'd served five and a half, he'd have been eligible for parole seventeen months from now."

"Then why bust out if all he had left was easy time?"

"That's one of the questions I'd like an answer to. Okay, here's as much background as I've been able to get on him—I may get more coming in, this is kind of short notice. I gather you never met him?"

"No."

"I did, once. When the county cops arrested him I happened to be on my way back here from Albuquerque. I chauffeured him up to the County Jail at St. Johns. I remember it because he was a curious character. Usually you arrest a man for murder he's either morose as hell or violent as hell. This guy seemed as cheerful as if it was the first time in his life something had gone right for him."

"What's that supposed to mean, Lieutenant?"

"I don't know what it means. All I can tell you is, I never saw a man quite so happy to go to jail."

"Who'd he kill?"

"Man named Ross Calisher."

"White man?"

"Yes. Calisher was vice-president and operating manager of a big ranch up in Apache County where Threepersons worked as a line rider."

"He was working there when he killed Calisher?"

"That's right."

"What was it? Family dispute?"

"Something like that. It came out that Calisher was making time with Threepersons' wife and Threepersons called him down for it. It wasn't one of those unwritten law killings, it didn't take place in the bedroom in the heat of anger. Calisher was killed in his own living room with his own gun, but Threepersons still had the gun in his pocket when they arrested him the next morning."

"Now that's pretty stupid."

"Nobody said he was a genius."

"What about Threepersons' wife? You put surveillance on her?"

"I would have if she were still alive. She died, just a few days ago. Ugly car accident on the Black Canyon Freeway at the Camelback intersection."

"She died before or after the breakout?"

"A day or two before."

"Maybe that's why he busted out."

"It's possible—God knows how anybody's mind works. She had their kid in the car, a little boy. Eight or nine years old."

"He still alive?"

"No. Both killed instantaneously. She lost control of the car, went across the divider and hit a loaded semi head-on. The truck driver's in the hospital with about forty broken bones and a fifty percent chance."

"I remember Buck Stevens talking about that one."

"I was talking to Stevens this morning at the briefing. You stand pretty high in his books. You want him for a partner on this job? I can check it out with the captain. . . ."

"If it's all right with you. He's a good cop." The words were ordinary but it was the highest compliment Watchman knew how to pay a colleague.

He studied the mug shot again. It didn't tell him anything new. "What was his wife doing in Phoenix?"

"She lived here. Had a little house in one of those developments up in Sunnyslope. She had a job running an Indian curio shop out on. . . ." Wilder had to look it up in his notes ". . . . Bethany Home Road. Place called the Katchina Boutique."

Watchman made a face. "Apache woman?"

"San Carlos Apache." Wilder put a cigarette in his mouth but didn't light it; it wobbled up and down as he spoke. "She got the job here after he went to prison. Here—have a look."

The photo showed a surprisingly good-looking young woman with an infant in her arms. She hadn't gone to fat; she had the good looks of youthful radiance but she also had fine bones and a face which contained more self-assuredness than you expected to find in the features of a line rider's wife.

"This was taken before the murder?"

"Two or three years before it. I guess he borrowed somebody's camera to take that picture. Indians don't go in much for cameras, do they?"

"Not much."

"I haven't got a picture of Calisher here, but he was a stud. Threepersons wasn't the first man he put horns on. In fact there's some woman's husband down in Texas still serving time for attempted murder, for trying to beat Ross Calisher to death."

Wilder took the cigarette out of his mouth. "This is a phony. I gave up smoking." He put it down in a clean ashtray. "Calisher used to be World's Champion rodeo cowboy and then some uncle of his hit a big oil strike and Calisher started hanging around with rarefied people. That's how he got the job managing Rand's operation."

"Charlie Rand?"

"You know him?"

"No. I've heard of him."

"Well Calisher was Rand's foreman. Naturally when he got killed, Rand leaned real hard on the County Attorney to get a first-degree conviction. But Threepersons had a pretty good lawyer."

"An Apache line rider? Where'd he find a good lawyer?"

"Politics. Rand owns one of those big cattle and timber operations right along the edge of the White Mountain Reservation. You know about the water-rights squabble up there?"

"A little."

"Well there's maybe a dozen big operations up there, white-owned, but Rand's the biggest and the rest don't count. It's pretty much Rand against the Apaches. The fight's been going on for I don't know how many years. Rand has a high-powered battery of lawyers so the Apaches have a high-powered battery of lawyers. One of them defended Threepersons. Dude called Dwight Kendrick."

"It rings a bell. He's handled a lot of Indian rights cases."

"Seems to know his way around a criminal court well enough, too. He managed to get the charge reduced to second degree."

Watchman sat with an ankle across a knee, his hat perched on his upraised knee. He fingered the four dents in its crown. "Anything else I need to know?"

"What do you want to know? You can take these files with you."

"I do have one question. The captain seems to think Threepersons is hiding on the Reservation. Is there any evidence or is that just his theory?"

"Actually it was my theory and he picked up on it. No, there's no evidence. It's just that Threepersons spent his whole life on the Reservation or just outside of it. Where else would he go at a time like this?"

"Any sign of how he got out of Florence in the first place? I don't mean the prison break, I mean afterward."

"No. Nothing at all. We're still working on it."

"Then for all we know he could still be in Florence."

"Not unless he's a mole. We've done a house-to-house."

"He'd know how to lie up in the brush."

"The dogs would have found him."

"Not if he got his hands on a bottle of vinegar."

"You think he's that bright?"

Watchman said, "I don't know the man. What do you think?"

"He didn't impress me as being very bright. But you could have a point—that's the kind of tidbit they pass around the mess table in slam. He could have picked up that information and remembered it when he passed somebody's kitchen window. But I don't set that much store in it myself. A well-trained hound won't be discouraged by a little vinegar."

Wilder pushed the papers together into a stack, the notes and the files on Joe Threepersons. He put them in a manila accordion-file envelope and wrapped the closer string around its disc, and passed it over to Watchman. "Anyhow I'll ask the Florence police to give it another once-over. I doubt he's still there, it's been too long." A glance at his wristwatch: "They busted out of there sixty-three hours ago."

"It's a pretty cold trail and we don't seem to have any leads at all. Don't expect miracles."

"I never do." Wilder sounded weary.

"Where do I hang my hat now?"

"It's a road job. You don't need a desk, do you? I hope you don't, we haven't got any to spare. Damned building's bulging at the seams."

"You'll pull Buck Stevens in this morning?"

"If I can get the captain's okay. I'll get on it right away." Wilder gave him the benediction of a meager smile. "Good luck anyway. I suppose I should say that. I don't really expect you to find him unless he makes a stupid mistake. That's what usually nails them." He spoke like a man moving toward cynicism, as if he'd lost his faith in good police work.

"How important is it? Finding him I mean."

"On a priority scale of one to ten it rates about an eight. It wouldn't rate that much except he's getting a pretty good press—one widower Indian at large in spite of dogs and everything else the Establishment can throw against him. It'll give the department a black eye if he stays loose too long."

And it'll look a lot less like an underdog getting ground up in the computerized meat grinder if an Indian's the one who nails him. That was the unspoken kicker but they both knew it and it made Wilder break out his sad little smile again.

Wilder's intercom phone buzzed. Wilder picked it up but held the mouthpiece cupped in his palm while he spoke to Watchman. "You need anything else?"

‡ 42 ‡

"Not right now." Watchman got out of the chair and Wilder lifted the receiver, talked and listened, then reached for the outside telephone and answered it. With his hat in one hand and the Threepersons file in the other, Watchman got to the door but Wilder's voice arrested him:

"Wait one, Sam."

Wilder went back into the phone: "Give me that again." He penciled something on his calendar pad.

There were more grunts and murmurs and finally Wilder cradled it and ripped the page out of the pad. "A break. City P.D. found a hot wagon along the Grand Canal early this morning. They just got done tossing it and labbing it and guess whose prints are all over the damn thing." The sad smile. "I did say he wasn't too bright, didn't I."

Watchman looked at the scrawled jottings. "Stolen out of Florence last night."

"So the son of a bitch was hiding out in town all the time."

"Okay," Watchman said, "but how did he know when the dragnet was lifted?"

"Maybe just luck. He knew we couldn't keep the town bottled up forever."

"Do you believe in that kind of coincidence? Look at the timing—he had to come out in the open and steal that car within a few hours after we called off the roadblocks. How did he know?"

"Maybe he had a radio with a police band."

"And knows all the signal codes by heart?" Watchman shook his head. "And he wouldn't be traveling around in a prison uniform, somebody'd have spotted him. So he got himself a change of clothes."

"I think we'll make a detective out of you all right."

"What I'm saying is he must have had outside help."

Wilder said, "Your job to find that out."

Watchman went to the wall map and traced the line of the Grand Canal on the inset city map of Phoenix. "Along North Sixteenth," Wilder said. "Mean anything to you?"

"Two blocks from the Federal Indian Hospital. Where'd they take his wife after the accident?"

"City morgue I imagine. Case like that, there'd be an autopsy, they'd check for alcohol or drugs in the system."

"But would Joe Threepersons know that?"

"That's another good question. You find out, all right?"

"Here's another one. Why leave the car here?"

Wilder said, "That one I can make a stab at. You don't hang onto a hot car any longer than you have to. You ditch it and steal another one. If you keep changing cars nobody has time to catch up with you because it takes time to post a car onto the hot list."

"If he's that smart he'd be smart enough to wipe his prints off, wouldn't he?"

"He would unless he wanted them to be found. But we may be giving him credit for too much smarts."

"Why would he want them found?"

"To make us think he's still in Phoenix." Wilder smiled again. "You can read anything into it you want to, Sam, but the only way to find the answers is to go out and do the legwork."

Watchman swung toward the door but stopped with his hand on it. "Am I uniform or plain?"

"You can suit yourself. If you go plain you'll have to use your own wheels, but you can voucher the mileage."

Watchman considered it. A lot depended on what types you had to interview. Some were put off, closed up, by the uniform; others were scared enough to open up.

Waiting for Stevens to come in off patrol he sat in the canteen with coffee and the file. It didn't tell him much. Joe Threepersons had confessed to the murder of Ross

Calisher; the confession had been obtained lawfully with his attorney present.

Subject had been born at Cibecue on October 5, 1941; it made him some two-and-a-half years younger than Watchman. Raised mainly at Whiteriver and nearby communities on the White Mountain Reservation. Mother died 1947, father died 1962. One brother, born 1934, died 1953 in South Korea. One sister, Angelina, born 1944, evidently still alive.

Bear that in mind, he thought. They were only three years apart in age. How close were they? Would the subject expect his sister to hide him out?

Subject had been educated after a fashion at mission schools on the Reservation; evidently he hadn't been much good at school—at fifteen he had gone to work for one of the white-managed cattle operations at Whiteriver. In 1959 he had gone into the Army for two years with a nine-month stint in West Germany, two months of which he had spent in the stockade—his first recorded criminal conviction. (Assault on a noncommissioned officer.) It appeared he had frequent problems with his temper. Returned to Arizona in August 1961, and the record showed three arrests for drunk-and-disorderly and one for drunken driving, all in the space of the next seven months. It wasn't unusual. A lot of them came home from the Army, took one look at the Reservation and spent their back pay on whiskey.

In June 1962 subject had been arrested in Showlow and was subsequently convicted of assault on a police officer. Sentence suspended. At the time he was employed by the tribe's lumber and sawmill operation; capacity unspecified, but probably ordinary laborer. There was another arrest for D-and-D in Globe—September 1962—and then the file showed no further arrests until the Calisher homicide in 1968.

Rap-sheets were not character studies but things were

visible between the lines. There was recorded the marriage of subject and Maria Poinsenay, a San Carlos Apache girl, on December 3, 1962, and it was significant that after the wedding there were no further arrests on the subject's record.

There was an oddity about the wedding. A Christian ceremony had been performed at the Baptist mission at Cedar Creek, where briefly subject had gone to school in 1954/55, and that was unusual because it was the groom's bailiwick, not the bride's. Also the newlyweds had not gone down to San Carlos to set up housekeeping among the bride's relatives and this was another break with tradition.

The record showed the birth of a son, Joe Junior, "on or about" October 18, 1963, with baptism performed at the mission early in November. At this time subject was described as a resident tribal member of the White Mountain Apaches but a paid (and taxed) employee of Rand Enterprises, so evidently he had got the job on Rand's cattle ranch within a few months of his marriage. He had held the job, it appeared, without trouble until September 4, 1968, the date of his arrest on the murder charge.

Buck Stevens arrived at eight-thirty and Watchman looked up from his ruminations. "Busted both legs getting here, didn't you."

Stevens had a rowdy grin. "You on the warpath again?"

"What coop they find you in this time?"

"Sam, your whole trouble in life is you never learned the importance of the coffee break."

Watchman shoved the Threepersons file at him. "Here, read this in the car. Let's go."

"Where to?"

"Uptown."

Watchman filled him in on the broad outlines on the way to the parking lot. Stevens had not turned in his cruiser

‡ 46 ‡

and they used that, Watchman driving while Stevens opened the folder.

He let Stevens read without interruption; he concentrated his attention on the traffic. Phoenix was turning into a second-rate imitation of Los Angeles, smog and all.

Finally Stevens laid the dossier on the seat between them. "I hear the son of a bitch is a mean hand with a rifle."

"Where'd you pick that up?"

"I don't know. Somebody around the squad room. Everybody was talking about the jailbreak that day. I guess you weren't around."

Watchman had been on traffic duty west of Gila Bend that day; he'd only heard about the break on the radio.

"You know that guy Porter, used to partner with old Gutierrez? He comes from up there in Apache County someplace—Showlow, I think. He used to go to all those turkey shoots at the rod and gun clubs up there. He says if Joe Threepersons was entered in the shoot, nobody else had a chance."

"Now that's news to comfort a man."

Watchman fitted the cruiser through a narrow space between trucks and squirted ahead a block and searched for the next gap in the traffic.

Suddenly Buck Stevens said, "It's that God damned sister of hers," reviving a conversation Watchman had thought dead four days previously. "We should have strung her out over an anthill."

"Shut up," Watchman said.

Lisa . . .

"I wish it had worked out with you two."

Watchman gave him a bleak glance and ran the amber light. "In just a minute you'll be picking up your teeth with two busted arms, white man."

Stevens had a brash grin, a lot of teeth. "Sam, right

now you're so easy to goad it almost ain't even fun any more."

"Then quit it."

"You ought to get it out of your system before you keep it bottled up so long it starts to rot." Stevens crossed his legs with one knee against the dashboard. "You know you've changed some since I used to know you up north."

It went both ways. Stevens had filled out in the past six months. He was getting just a bit of a belly on him from the roadside hamburger lunches, the French fries and root beers. In another five years he'd be a cop with a big gut on him but right now he still had youth, the amiable rookie look.

Stevens had partnered in Watchman's car on the final lap of his training program until a rifle bullet had taken him off patrol last October. When he'd come back on duty in January the department had rewarded him with a one-man car at the Willcox division and Watchman hadn't seen him again until a week ago when Stevens had finished his tour of duty at Willcox and got his transfer to Phoenix.

It was nothing against Buck but he had won the headquarters assignment with less than a year's service while Watchman had spent ten years on back-road boondock beats; promotions and good assignments came a little faster for blond Anglos than they did for a dark-faced Navajo whose features were as bone-craggy as those of a Frederic Remington warrior.

Stevens said, "You look like you've been sucking lemons."

"Button it up, will you?"

"Hey this is Buck, remember? Old paid-his-dues Buck, your faithful white companion?"

"I thought I taught you to step away from a snake that looks mad. You don't keep prodding it with your finger."

"It wasn't me that made you mad, it was Lisa. Quit

taking it out on me. Hey we traveled some miles together, or maybe you forgot. Sam you used to be a friend of mine." Stevens took a breath and met his eye. *"I'm* still a friend of *yours."*

Watchman made no reply. Shortly thereafter Stevens uncrossed his legs and looked at the street signs at a passing intersection. "Where we headed, anyway?"

"We'll check out the area where he ditched the Ford. Maybe somebody saw him around the hospital."

"Sounds like a dead end to me. What if somebody did see him? So what?"

"I'd welcome suggestions."

Two red lights later Stevens said, "Yeah, well let's check out the hospital."

4.

In a dour frame of mind Watchman emerged from the hospital and squinted against the midmorning blaze. Stevens said, "Zero. Now what?"

"For once in my life I'm going to take Captain Custer's advice." He started the cruiser and put its nose out into Sixteenth Street.

"The Reservation?"

"Aeah."

"Then why are we heading back for the HP building?"

"Pick up another cruiser. You can keep this one."

"To do what?"

"Poke around Phoenix. Take the mug shots with you, ask around. For all we know he's still in the city—he left the car here. Check out his wife's house, that curio shop where she worked, any friends she had around there. Maybe she said something to somebody. Maybe Threepersons was snooping around her house before he ditched the Ford—maybe somebody saw him. Hell, be a detective."

"Sure." Stevens patted a yawn. "I guess it's a way to pass the time."

They drove without conversation toward the center of the city but finally Stevens picked up the Threepersons file and thumbed through it the way a bank teller would count money. "Don't they know all this paper's a fire hazard?"

"Way back there was an old chief who noticed how the white people thought paper had some mysterious power. If a white man loses his papers he's helpless—you hear white preachers say nobody gets admitted to Heaven unless there are writings about him in a great book. That old chief was a wise man."

"You guys never had any writing at all, did you."

"Didn't need it. That old chief said words that are true sink deep in a man's heart and stay there."

"How's anybody know what this old chief said if nobody wrote it down?"

"There was some anthropologist. He had a tape recorder. You ever see an anthropologist without a tape recorder?"

"I don't know. But I never saw a cop without two and a half tons of paper."

"Look Buck, I'm sorry I jumped down your throat before."

"No charge."

"I just don't want to talk about Lisa right now. Whole thing's still too raw, you know?"

Stevens had kind eyes when he wasn't hiding himself behind wisecracks. "It's only I was worried a little that maybe you got sore because I got the headquarters beat so fast."

"You can't help it you had the misfortune to be born blond. You'll just have to learn to live with your handicap."

It wasn't bitterness; he wasn't sure how to define it. If

there was blame it wasn't Buck's. Watchman had been looking at his boondock beats and was beginning to realize he wasn't sure how long he was willing to go on accepting it.

He'd had an offer from Diego Orozco's private agency in Phoenix. The pay was half again his present salary and it meant he'd have a permanent base of operations instead of being transferred from ghost town to ghost town every year. But the work wasn't movie-private-eye stuff, it was industrial espionage and tracers: repo cars, missing persons, errant spouses.

There'd been a feeler of interest from the Federal narcs but that would mean dealing with human garbage all the time and he wasn't zealous enough for that line of work. Ambition had never burned many holes in his pockets. He had a tendency to drift; he knew he'd let it all ride a while until one day something deep in his viscera made the decision for him. When the time came he'd know.

5.

Wilder had two bits of information for him, one from the city police. The rear license plate of the stolen Ford had been smeared with mud. "I'd call it a mark of hasty professionalism. An amateur wouldn't think about the license plates at all. A pro with the right connections would change the plates. But a guy who knows the ropes, if he's in a hurry he'll mud them up a little, enough to change the shape of one or two digits. Judging by our profile on Threepersons I don't think he'd have thought it up by himself."

Watchman said, "What's the other item?"

"He's got a sister."

"I know. What about her?"

"She lives in Whiteriver," Wilder said. "Alone."

Watchman looked at him. "She's twenty-eight."

"I can't help that, Sam."

Watchman went into the canteen and bought a cardboard cheese sandwich from the machine and a container of coffee. It was pushing ten o'clock and if he didn't hit the road the whole day would be destroyed; it was a good three hours' drive up to the Reservation.

He swallowed the last of the cheese and dropped the Styrofoam coffee cup in the trash liner and went out to the lot.

Someone came out of the building and stopped to peer around and when Watchman put the car in motion the uniformed figure loped toward him waving a sheet of paper.

It was Wilder. Watchman pulled up beside him. "What form did I forget to fill out?"

"Glad I caught you. They thought you'd already gone." Wilder handed him the paper. "Just came in the mail. Here's a copy of the envelope."

Two Xeroxes. Watchman took them. "A Xerox of an envelope?"

"I sent the originals down to the lab. But read it."

The envelope was addressed to the Highway Patrol with a little typed notation at the lower left: "Attn. Officer In Charge Of Threepersons Case." That made Watchman look at the postmark. "Globe, Ariz., July 6, P.M."

Dear Sir,
With reference to the escaped convict Joe Threepersons, this is to inform you that he was not guilty of the murder that he was in prison for.

Watchman turned it over but it was only a Xerox and there was nothing on the back of it. He looked at Wilder. "What the hell."

"Yeah."

"Joe didn't write this himself."

"Okay, detective, why didn't he?"

"One, he was still bottled up in Florence when this was mailed in Globe. Two, I doubt Joe knows how to use a typewriter. Three, I doubt he'd be able to spell, let alone compose a letter in business style."

"Go to the head of the class. What do you make of it?"

"No signature. I thought anonymous tips like that usually came on the phone."

"Usually they do. But we get letters. Maybe it's somebody with a recognizable voice. A speech defect or something."

Watchman thrust his hand out the car window to give the Xeroxes back but the lieutenant said, "You keep them, it's your case. We've got the originals down in the lab. I'll let you know if anything turns up by way of fingerprints. We'll find out what kind of machine it was typed on, but I doubt we can spend the time to find out who wrote it. Could be some crackpot. Most likely is."

"Or somebody with enough interest in Joe to try and persuade us to go easy on him."

"Yeah, it could be the sister. Maybe she's a trained business secretary or something."

"Living on the Reservation?" Watchman folded the Xeroxes. "I'll find out when I talk to her."

"It makes sense," Wilder said. "I mean she might figure we'd be less inclined to shoot him on sight if we thought there was a chance he was innocent."

"Is there?"

"A chance? Come on, Sam. He had the gun in his pocket and he made a voluntary confession. Far as I know he never tried to rescind it."

"Then it's kind of strange, this letter."

"But it's got you wondering, hasn't it."

"Aeah."

"I suspect that's what it was supposed to do, Sam."

6.

Driving up toward the mountains, east out of Phoenix along U.S. 60, you pass a dirt road below Superior that curls south from the highway into scrubby hills. It is marked "APACHE TEARS ROAD." Watchman passed the sign at sixty-five.

In the 1880s the Apaches had a stronghold on top of a sheer cliff below Superior. They staged attacks from there on Pima towns and white settlers until the blueleg Cavalry surrounded the stronghold and besieged it. When the Apaches ran out of ammunition the braves elected to leap from the cliff rather than suffer the indignity of capture. In the morning their women buried the dead at the foot of the cliff and their tears drenched the earth and instantly froze into dark pebbles of pure volcanic Obsidian glass. That is the legend. Today the lapidaries sell the Apache Tears as costume jewelry. Most of them come from pockets at the foot of Apache Leap Mountain.

Watchman took the bypass ramp around the town of Superior. He drove on up through the discolored slag piles of Miami and into the chrome, plastic and neon town of Globe, with its miners' saloons and used-car arenas and drive-in root-beer stands.

Out of Globe the highway makes a wide turn into more hills studded with scrubs: greasewood and paloverde and manzanita, here and there the spines of yucca, century plant and cactus.

The road climbs and climbs until without warning the earth falls away: beyond hangs an empty space. But beyond the space the earth resumes and continues to climb. The color of the Salt River Canyon is a sun-bleached greyish tan accented with richer darknesses of eroded rock strata and clumps of growing things. There are glimpses, four thousand feet below the highway lip, of river froth at the bottom.

The highway runs down to the bottom in switchbacks along the cliff shelf. At the top the crow-flight line from rim to rim is not more than ten or twelve miles but a driver has to spend more than an hour negotiating the heroic passage down, across and up.

The river marks the boundary between the San Carlos Reservation and the Fort Apache Reservation. On the north side, after a bridge, there is a lonely gas station that sells ice cream, soda pop and water cans for cars that have boiled over trying to make the steep twisting climb.

Watchman filled up at the station and put the receipt in with his expense vouchers, and began the climb. He hit the residue of the early afternoon's rain about halfway up: slippery patches where the water had brought the oil in the pavement to the surface. He took it easy getting to the top and that was when the radio squawked into chatter and informed him that the Agency Police had found Joe Threepersons' spoor at a clan-cluster of wickiups not far ahead of him.

CHAPTER THREE

A T THREE o'clock two cars came tandem down the rutted track: a Highway Department panel truck preceded by Watchman's Volvo with Buck Stevens at the wheel.

Stevens emerged grinning fiercely. "If you're fixin' to spend the night out here maybe you ought to make a circle with the wagons. I hear there's a lot of hostile redskins in these parts."

"You want a fat lip, white man." But Watchman gave him half a smile.

"I brought your clothes. That's a pretty shrewd idea, disguising yourself as an Indian." Stevens' guileless smile hid none of the sarcasm.

They talked while Watchman changed into mufti: Levi's and a plaid shirt and his rundown mountain boots, and a stockman's hat that drooped at the brim. The crew from the yellow panel truck were jacking up the cruiser and changing tires one by one.

"You realize you've only been on this job six hours and you've already gone over budget," Stevens said. "You know what it cost to get that truck out here with four new tires?" He plucked a stalk of yellow grass from the ground and poked it into the corner of his mouth. It was the color of his hair. "Man stopped me down the road a few miles."

"Roadblock?"

"No. Some cowboy, asked me if I was the trooper assigned to the Threepersons case. He said there's a man down at the horse camp wants to talk to you real bad."

"What man?"

"Charles Rand."

Watchman rammed his shirttails into his Levi's and cinched up the belt. "May as well have a look at him. He might be able to help."

2.

It looked as out of place as a Cunard liner in the midst of a Portuguese fishing fleet. It was a big silver-grey Rolls Bentley polished to a deep shine. From half a mile away, driving down toward the horse camp, Watchman was able to recognize it.

Watchman had left Buck Stevens with the Highway Department crew. When the cruiser was reshod he would drive it back to the barn. Watchman drove the rattling old Volvo into the yard of the Apache horse camp and parked it beside the towering Bentley. The Agency Police car was still parked where it had been before; Watchman had the feeling Officer Porvo had been ordered to wait here for Charles Rand's arrival.

There was a small group out in the meadow talking —three Indians and three Anglos. They had seen Watchman arrive and they were walking in toward him.

Even at a hundred yards he recognized Charles Rand easily from magazine photographs. The suntanned big face went well with the wide white hat and the white shirt. Rand wore no jacket but his slacks were obviously part of a suit that had cost as much as the average Apache made in six months. He was neither extraordinarily tall nor especially heavy but he carried himself as if he were. He didn't strut or swagger; he was more prideful than that. His shoulders rode wide, pushed back like a lieutenant general's; he rolled when he walked.

The two Anglo cowboys with Rand had the narrow-hipped stride of rodeo riders and they both carried rifles. The two Indians were men Watchman had seen earlier in camp—probably head men in the clan—and then there was Patrolman Pete Porvo with his small high eyes drilling into everything they touched.

Rand came forward ahead of the others. Watchman met him at the open corral gate. He dredged the ID wallet out of his hip pocket and flapped it open to display his badge but Rand hardly glanced at it.

"I'm with the Highway Patrol."

"I'm against it, personally." But Rand smiled. The outdoor eyes crinkled to show he was joshing. He had a slight Texas prairie twang in his voice. "I hear he shot the tires out from under you."

"It wasn't Threepersons. Whoever it was had wheels."

"Then he's got help." Rand's lips made a thin line, under pressure. He turned his gaze toward the hills. "Son of a bitch."

The others caught up. Watchman was looking at Pete Porvo. The Apache policeman's face had closed up—with guilt, or with innocent resentment; it was impossible to tell which it was.

Rand said, "I'd like to get a crew out on his trail before he decides to use that rifle he's got. You got any objections?"

"You'd have to talk to the Apache Council about that. It's their land."

"They're not going to lift a finger and you know it." Rand was staring at Porvo now. Porvo reacted with a quick grin that came and went almost instantly: a rictus of unease.

Rand turned his shoulder to the Agency cop and said to Watchman, "Walk off here a little piece with me," and strolled toward the Bentley.

Watchman went along with him. Rand was fitting a pair of big-lensed sunglasses into place, hooking them over one ear at a time. "Look. Suppose I brought half a dozen, a dozen men over here and put them under your command. You've got jurisdiction here."

"Sorry, Mr. Rand."

"My men are eager to help."

"Sure they are. But you tell me a better way to stir up hard feelings on the Reservation. Having a gang of your cowboys stomping all over it with guns in their hands? Thanks just the same, but I'll pass."

At the door of the Bentley Rand stopped to face him. There was no chauffeur; Rand would be the kind of man who did the driving himself.

"You're Navajo."

"That's right."

"How's that going to affect the way you conduct this hunt?"

"My job's to find the man, not make excuses. That answer you?"

"I'll reserve judgment until I see you perform. So far you're off to a piss-poor start."

Watchman smiled. "I guess I am."

"I asked Phoenix to send a manhunt out and they oblige me with one Navajo. It's got a stink of politics to it and I've always had a first-rate sense of smell. I'm putting you on notice—understood?"

"I think we ought to straighten one thing out, Mr. Rand. You don't wear the right uniform to give me orders."

Rand's teeth showed. "Sure as God made little green apples, mister, the right word from me and you can get blown clear out of your job. You're obliged to pay attention when I talk to you, hear?"

Watchman said nothing. Rand blustered on a little while until he heard himself. Then he stopped, slightly embarrassed but continuing to regard Watchman disdainfully. "Down in Phoenix they figure nobody cares what happens to a no-account Indian. Well I just want it clear this is one Indian who's got enemies in high places. I want him brought down and I want it done fast."

Watchman asked gently: "Why?"

The sunglasses hid Rand's reaction. After a moment he said, "Let's just say I've got a grudge against him. It was my foreman he killed."

"That was a long time ago."

"My foreman's just as dead as he was then."

"Come off it, Mr. Rand."

The Texan put his hand to his mouth and dragged down the corners of his lips as if clawing grit from the crevices.

"All right, look. I've got a property up there that shares thirty miles of boundary with this Reservation. I run beef up there—hell I feed the population of a fair-size city every year. It's not the biggest industry I've got, but I'm still the Texas cowman my daddy made me and this ranch counts heavy with me. You understand what I'm sayin'? Then this worthless Apache kid comes busting up here, ramming around the Reservation, stirring folks up, and before you know it there's going to be an incident. Now I don't want an incident. I can't afford one right now. I want this boy stopped before he can create one."

"I'm just a country boy myself, Mr. Rand, and I don't see the connection between your cows and Joe Threepersons' incident."

"Then I'll spell it out. This tribe's got litigation against me, they're trying to destroy my beef operation by drying up my water supplies. Now that case could go either way right now. But suppose there's a big splash of publicity about some poor unfortunate lone Indian that's being hounded for weeks and weeks by merciless white racist authorities. You see what that does? I can't afford to let the bleeding-heart press get all het up right now on this killer-boy's account. That kind of sentimental horseshit weighs too heavy with some of those Federal judges. They claim they're objective but that's a lot of crap—they're just like everybody else in the government, they're petty bureaucratic hacks and they're eager to get pushed around by public opinion. Here I'm running more beef on that little old ranch than this whole tribe manages to feed on two million acres, and now they want to take my water away from us so we can *all* starve. And everybody keeps whining about lo the poor Indian. Poor Indian hell. I'm not about to give up what's mine for the sake of a bunch of hardscrabble losers that had this country for a thousand years and couldn't even grow a blade of grass on it."

Watchman peeled back his sleeve to look at the time and Rand took the hint. "All right, I didn't mean to ride my hobbyhorse. But you wanted to know why it's important to get that killer fast and get him quiet. I've told you."

"I intend to find him as fast as I can, Mr. Rand. But I'm not up here to do special favors for you."

"You find him, that's all. I don't care who you do it for. And make sure he doesn't find you first. You wouldn't be the first man he killed. He's a son of a bitch with a rifle."

"So I hear. If you were to send those men of yours after him—where would you tell them to start looking?"

"Now that's the first smart question you've asked me. All right, I'd prowl Whiteriver. I'd send my boys into every tumbledown wickiup in town. That's where his worthless friends hang out—that's where his sister lives. He'll be around there, scrounging food like a pariah dog."

"Then I'd better get at it. Unless you had something else to say to me."

"I'll say this much. You'll likely have to kill him, if he doesn't kill you first. He's a real old-fashioned Apache. I don't know about the Navajos but these Apache still hang onto the old war virtues. Of course they're not allowed to practice them any more and that's why they spend more time drunk than working, but they value those old-time notions. When it comes to a boy like Joe Threepersons, he's likely to figure it's better to have a lost cause to fight for than no cause at all. He's not going to quit and give up the first time he sees a cop get close to him."

"I'm beginning to admire this guy," Watchman said.

"Look out he doesn't give you a chance to admire his marksmanship. All right, I won't hold you up. But I'm keeping a close eye on this—you just remember I've got access to a few ears down in Phoenix."

Watchman expected his superiors wouldn't let him forget it.

He gave Rand a crisp nod—Rand didn't offer to shake his hand—and swung toward the Volvo.

A long time ago he'd given up arguing with men like Rand. Underneath their veneer of anthropological knowledge there beat the hearts of Custer's kind. Whites like Rand were spoilers who couldn't leave the land alone; their real attitude, which none of them would admit out loud, was something on the order of *If God meant them to be white men He'd have made them white in the first place.*

Sure. And if God meant us to fly in airplanes He'd never have invented the railroad.

The squabble between the Apaches and the Rands wasn't fundamentally legal. It was a conflict of ways of thought.

These Indians made poor farmers because to plow the ground was to stab the bosom of White Painted Woman. The Sioux Crazy Horse had said, "One does not sell the earth upon which the people walk."

Pete Porvo was watching from the corral gate when Watchman turned the car around and drove out.

3.

The plateau highway had reddish pavement as if the surrounding red earth had bled across it. Up in the foothills a welcome-to-Apacheland billboard said in detachable bright-red letters "FIRE DANGER EXTREME."

He came down a bend past the Assembly of God mission at Cedar Creek, and then past the little Baptist mission where the subject had been schooled and married, *Pastor Geo. S. LaSalle,* and up a little grade with the serrates of hazy mountains making lavender teeth on the horizons. He was 175 miles out of Phoenix and it was half-past four when he came downhill on the approach to Fort Apache past the cluster of cheap new Mutual Aid Houses.

The occasional windmill . . . a grass valley, a stream with cottonwoods, then Fort Apache, the old Army buildings crumbling where they hadn't been shored up for use as part of the Theodore Roosevelt Indian Boarding School (Bureau of Indian Affairs).

On up the road toward Whiteriver he passed the sawmill of the Fort Apache Timber Company, then the dusty rodeo arena and a good stand of shade trees. The mountains crowded in closer and he rolled into town past the imposing single-story building that housed the headquarters of the White Mountain Tribal Council. Beyond it squatted the Whiteriver trading post and the town's gas station, WE DON'T LOAN TOOLS.

Along the dirt roads that spider-webbed out from the center he could see kids on donkeys lassoing dogs for practice. A fat woman in a pink squaw-dress waddled out of the trading post and climbed into the driver's seat of a badly sprung pickup. Loose horses and colts browsed along the road shoulders.

Watchman parked in front of the trading post. Four Apaches on the trading post verandah watched the Volvo from under their high-domed hats, and behind Watchman a car approached with a gravel-crunching rumble of slow-rolling tires.

It was Pete Porvo's white Agency car. Watchman stepped out of the Volvo.

The agency prowl car pulled over and Porvo left the engine idling when he got out.

"I wasn't following you. Just had to come this way myself, that's all."

"Sure," Watchman said. "They told me I'd find Joe's sister up here."

"Angelina. She ain't seen him or heard from him." Muted sensations of dislike floated off Porvo like heat waves. He added, "I believe she drove up to Showlow this morning. Be back tonight around eight, eight-thirty—she works over to the roadhouse nights."

"Thanks."

Porvo laid one arm along the roof of his car and pointed toward the council house. "You might want to talk to Mr. Kendrick, he's the one handled Joe's case at the trial."

"He's here now?"

"Got an office over there. That's his Corvette parked around back." Porvo slid down into the seat and spoke through the V-notch between the windshield and the open door: "I come up with anything, where'll I find you?"

"I'll be poking around here a while."

"We ain't got anything in town you could call tourist accommodations," Porvo said overcasually, and pulled the door shut.

Watchman stood there, the sun warm on his face, watching the prowl car shimmy away faster than it needed to.

The men on the porch watched him with undisguised suspicion. They also knew. The moccasin telegraph had done its work.

He went inside the trading post because it was always the center of communication and gossip.

It was cool inside and a lot bigger than the branch trading post at Chinle where he'd grown up. Cowboy hats hung from the beam above the cash-register counter. On a pillar above a calendar which notified debtors that it was July 8 there was a carefully printed misspelled sign, BUILDING SUPPLES. Three females in bright patterned dresses stood browsing the notions shelves like the Three Bears: a fat woman about Watchman's age and a girl about thirteen with an infant girl in her arms.

It was one of the last old-style general stores, part supermarket, part feed-and-grain, part clothing emporium, part hardware, part Woolworth's. Some wit had hung a little wood box on the wall with a three-inch slot in its lid: DO NOT PUT MONEY IN THIS BOX.

There was a smell of leather harness. Watchman bought a pack of spearmint gum.

"You know Joe? Joe Threepersons?"

The girl behind the cash register was in her shy teens and she only shook her head, not meeting his glance. But there was a man at the bulletin board whose face swiveled when Watchman spoke. Watchman took his change and broke open a stick of gum. "You know Joe?"

"Maybe I heard of him," the man said, and went outside on bowlegged boots with the heels run down on the outsides.

The four men on the porch were watching the door

without blinking. Watchman let them have their look at him. "I guess you heard I'm looking for Joe Three-persons."

Nobody made any answer of any kind. Watchman said, "There might be a reward," and stepped out into the sunlight and walked toward the council house.

A breeze moved dust across his path and a boy on a horse choused a seventy-dollar cow down the street. Watchman felt the prod of the flat S&W .38 automatic against his spine where it rested under his shirt in the thin Myers holster; it was inconvenient there but it was out of sight and he didn't want to alarm people. He had to remember not to sit back too fast in wooden chairs or the thing would thud like a bomb.

It was half-past four and the shadow of a cloud moved across the town. Over the hills north of the trees he could see the shadow-streaks of a rain squall. But heat misted up from the earth and before he entered the council house he stopped and armed sweat from his forehead. Back on the trading post verandah the four Apaches were still watching him. It wouldn't have surprised him if one of them had turned to spit at the ground.

4.

The girl at the reception counter looked comfortable in her fat but her face was stern. *"Enju?"*

"I don't talk Apache, sorry." He produced his wallet. "Highway Patrol."

"Oh yes, about Joe Threepersons. I'm afraid the Chairman isn't in just now. . . ."

"Maybe in the morning?"

"Of course. Shall I make an appointment?"

"Don't bother, I don't know where I'll be. I'll take my chances. Mr. Kendrick in his office?"

"I think he is." She pointed down the hall.

"You know Joe pretty well?"

"No," she said, but it wasn't a closed-off negative. "He's older than I am, he didn't live here any more by the time I was old enough to notice boys. My brother went to school with him, though. At the Baptist mission."

"Your brother around?"

"You'll have to wait till next year. He's in Spain. He's in the Air Force."

"Anybody else around here that knew Joe very well? Any relatives besides his sister?"

"Well you might try his . . . uncle, Will Luxan." The hesitation was caused, probably, by her uncertainty at translating in her head: there was no exact synonym for *uncle* in the Athapascan tongues, of which Apache and Navajo were dialects. The relationship was more specific in the Indian languages: *mother's-brother* or *father's-brother*.

"He lives in Whiteriver?"

"You know the Shell station up by the roadhouse?'"

"No, but I can find it."

"He owns the station. He lives in the house right behind it."

"I didn't know Joe had such prosperous relatives."

She didn't have anything to say to that. Watchman said, "What's your name?"

"Lisa Natagee," she said and it shot his mind into another orbit so that he had to bring it back by force. *Lisa . . .*

He went without hurry down the hall and found a door near the end with a wooden plaque screwed onto it, LEGAL DEPARTMENT. He stopped with his hand on the knob and looked back along the corridor at the girl who was fitting a card into a plastic Wheeldex. Her head was bowed with concentration so that the black hair had swung forward to hide her face. He thought of his own Lisa in slender fair-haired images and took his eyes off the overweight black-haired girl at the desk, and went into the law office.

5.

Faded blond hair fell limply over Dwight Kendrick's ears; he was an imposing bear of a man, huge and pale with great butcher's shoulders and an improbably lean waist, as if he spent a good part of his life lifting weights in gymnasiums. It was hard to judge his age; he had to be at least forty. He had a penetrating but superficial voice and that was a little surprising in view of his spectacular court-room reputation.

Kendrick's fingers were very long and thin and moved like sea fans as he spoke, opening and closing with carnivorous sensuality. "I don't know what the hell they expect. The unsavory record of the Indian Bureau—Christ they make the first American the last American at the trough. Nothing extraordinary about Joe, I can tell you that much. It's only what you've got to expect when you raise a man by filling his head that his own people are dirty savages whose extermination is required for the purification of the democratic republic. Of *course* he's got a temper. Of *course* he behaves irrationally. What the hell else can they expect of him?"

"We don't all behave the way he behaves," Watchman murmured. "But right now I'm more interested in where I might find him."

"I'm sorry," Kendrick snapped. "I don't think it's incumbent upon me to help you crucify Joe." It wasn't as if everybody else didn't also call Threepersons by his first name but Kendrick pronounced it with a kind of offhand familiarity which implied ownership. It grated on Watchman.

Kendrick sat back, crossed his legs at right angles and laced his hands together behind his head. "Look, I imagine legally he's still my client. Certainly if he were to come to me I'd continue to act in his behalf—I'm not the kind to betray a man just because he's in some kind of trouble. Now you're supposed to be an officer of the law, you ought to know as well as I do that there's a privileged relationship here. Even if I knew exactly where you could lay your hands on him, I'd be under no obligation to tell you." Kendrick generally looked away at neutral objects while he was talking but at intervals his pale eyes would flash up to make sure he had been understood.

"If you knew where he was," Watchman replied, "I hope you'd have the good sense to advise him to turn himself in."

"What for? Another dose of white justice?"

"The longer he stays loose the worse it'll go for him."

"Suppose he stays loose forever?"

"Do you think he's smart enough?" Watchman said, and studied him for a response.

Kendrick smiled a little as he might smile to a small child who had asked him a question about the universe, but Watchman got no audible answer to his question and so he tried another. "You're supposed to be an officer of the court. You're supposed to have some kind of duty to advise him to give himself up."

"All right, I'll admit I've been playing a little game. I don't know where he is. I haven't heard from him. It was all a harmless exercise to find out how tough you'd get about it. Frankly I find it rather rancid that they'd pick out their token red man to handle this assignment. It stinks of television politics to me. I don't know why the hell you put up with it, if you've got any guts at all."

"Mr. Kendrick, I'm a police officer, it's my job to enforce the laws."

"I would have assumed that with an assignment as delicate as this one they must have given you the option of turning it down."

"I didn't see any reason to." The interview was getting out of hand, the interrogator becoming the interrogated. He made an effort to get it back where it belonged. "It would help if you could tell me about him. Who his friends were, where he used to hang out."

"I'm sorry. Actually I never knew him all that well, he was only a client and I'd never met him prior to his arrest. But even if I could help you I'm not sure I would. Joe's got enough cards stacked against him. I understand Charlie Rand's been on the horn to Phoenix several times already, trying to get them to mobilize the National Guard to track him down or some such idiocy."

"You know Rand, do you?"

"We're eyeballing each other across a legal fence. I'm handling the tribe's case against him."

"What's it about?"

"Don't you read the newspapers?"

"I'd just as soon hear it from you. I keep remembering Joe Threepersons used to work for Rand. It was Rand's foreman who got killed.'

"It's cheap pettifoggery, that's all. I don't think it's got anything to do with Joe or that old murder."

"The case was pending, even way back then. Wasn't it?"

. 'It was. But Joe was only a cowhand."

"He's an Apache and he was working for a white man who seems to be regarded as the Apaches' number-one enemy. I find that a little hard to understand for openers."

"Quite a few of his red brothers work for Rand. It's not unusual. In a labor market like this one you go where the jobs are. Rand's hiring and he doesn't ask questions about your politics."

"Isn't that a little risky—for him?"

"He's a tough son of a bitch, or he thinks he is. I guess he likes to think he's welcoming the challenge."

"This squabble's over water rights on the boundary of the Reservation, isn't it?"

Kendrick's eyes raked him. "In a nutshell, the Bonito River supplies the water along that side of the Reservation. There's a string of recreation reservoirs along the river and the tribe draws irrigation water out of them. Some years back Rand and his neighbors started drilling deep wells on their side of the line and they dug on a slant so that the wells bottomed out straight under the riverbed. It's diverting a lot of acre-feet from the Apache water supply and the tribe's having trouble finding enough water to irrigate the farms, and half those recreational facilities are closed down because the lakes are nothing but mud puddles. We've been trying to obtain an injunction to re-strain Rand and his cronies from pumping out those wells. So far the Court of Appeals seems to be in Rand's pocket —Rand's lawyers claim there's no mention of water rights in the Fort Apache treaty. And they say even if there were, it wouldn't affect this issue because Rand's wells are on his own private property. Naturally we're claiming an analogy with mining law where you're not allowed to drill slant-shafts under your neighbor's claim. We're also arguing that water rights are implicit in the treaty even if they're not specified. We've got plenty of precedents and we'll win it, and Rand knows that. He's just being obstructionist."

Kendrick lit a cigarillo and blew smoke at his match. "We're getting a little off the subject of Joe Threepersons, aren't we?"

"Maybe. But the better a picture I've got, the better a chance to find him. Did Joe have anything to do with any of these wells?"

"He wasn't a driller if that's what you mean. I suppose he must have ridden past them a thousand times on his rounds. He was a line rider, his job was to keep the fence in repair and look out for livestock in trouble."

"Where'd he live?"

"Line shack at the northwest corner of the ranch."

"With his wife and kid?"

"Of course. They were only two or three miles off the highway to Showlow. It wasn't a bad little house, I visited it once to interview his wife. Rand treats his employees pretty decently, he's no cotton farmer."

"You talk as if you admire the man."

"I respect his good points. It doesn't pay to underestimate your opponent."

"You happen to know if anybody's living in that line shack now?"

"Somebody must be. It's twenty miles from the ranch headquarters—too far to commute on horseback. There's always somebody posted out there. Rand has four or five line shacks. Christ he runs better than a half million acres."

"All of it cattle?"

"About half. He grows feed corn and alfalfa, and there's a lot of timber."

"And that's what he needs the extra water for?"

"I gather it is. I'm no expert on farming."

"Joe worked up there for better than three years. Did he have any especially close friends who might still be there?"

"You'd have to ask around. I don't know many of his friends. He's got a sister here in town, and an uncle by the name of Luxan."

"Anybody else?"

"Not from me," Kendrick said. Watchman heard the knock at the door and turned in his chair to look that way, and Kendrick lifted his head: "Yes?"

It was a young Indian with long hair held back by a

multicolored headband. His suit was tailored and hadn't come from stock and the patterned Justin boots were polished to a vicious shine. Late twenties, Watchman judged, and full of vinegar.

"I think we're about to nail down the figures on Hawkes Lake," the intruder said as if Watchman weren't there.

It seemed to excite Kendrick. "About God damn time. How soon, do you think?"

"Tonight, if my boy comes through." The young Indian looked at Watchman.

"Come on in, Tom. This man's name is Watchman, he's from the state police. My assistant, Tom Victorio."

Victorio's grip was quick and firm and quickly withdrawn. Kendrick said, "Tom's a bit of a firebrand but he does the work of five lawyers and I expect to see him practicing before the Supreme Court before he's finished."

It didn't appear to embarrass Victorio. Kendrick waved the cigarillo at Watchman. "He's on Joe Threepersons' trail."

Watchman said, "Somebody's trying to convince us he was innocent of the Calisher murder. What would you say to that?"

Kendrick's eyes widened a little. "Who told you that?"

"Anonymous. We don't know."

"But it wasn't Joe himself."

It was a statement, not a question. Watchman said. "What makes you say that?"

"Joe confessed at the time of the murder. That was what made it so hard to get the charge reduced."

"Then you don't think there's anything to this."

"Look," Kendrick said, "I'm in no position to come right out and state flatly that Joe was guilty. I was his attorney—still am, for that matter."

Watchman said, "But you can't state flatly that he was *not* guilty."

"On the strength of an anonymous tip to the police? I'd need a lot more evidence than that, wouldn't you?"

"I was just wondering if you might have any other evidence to back up the tip we got."

"The tip didn't come from this office," Kendrick said. "That's about all I can tell you about it." He jabbed the cigarillo toward Tom Victorio. "I've about shot my wad on the subject of Joe Threepersons. Why don't you take Mr. Watchman down to your office?" A quick shift to Watchman: "Tom knew Joe better than I did. Which is not to say they were friends."

"I wouldn't take the son of a bitch on a Christmas tree," Victorio said. "You find him, you're welcome to him."

6.

Victorio's office was a cubbyhole. Squeezing inside, Watchman said, "Then you wouldn't like to buy the idea that he might have been innocent."

"I wouldn't know anything about that. I wasn't around here when he killed Calisher. I was still in law school. But if somebody told me Joe was innocent I'd have to laugh a little. Joe was born guilty."

"Of murder?"

"He beat up on a lot of people. Calisher happened to be the first one who died from it."

"He didn't beat Calisher up. Calisher was shot."

"So?"

"It just makes you wonder," Watchman said. "He always liked to use his fists, didn't he."

"He's one hell of a shot with a rifle."

"But he never shot at a man that you know of, did he?"

Victorio said, "Not that I know of, no."

"Then why all of a sudden the gun?"

"According to the testimony it was because the gun was handy. Calisher had it on the wall. He had guns all over the wall."

"I thought you weren't there."

"I was at the trial. That was months after the murder."

There was hardly room between the shelves of law texts for the tiny desk and two chairs. A work lamp hung from a cord above the desk. The small window was set high and the sky beyond was obscured by a tangle of mesquite branches. The wooden nameplate on the desk said THOS. JEFFORDS VICTORIO, ATT'Y. Watchman said, "That's a handful of a name."

"I've thought about changing it." Thomas Jeffords had been the white man who'd made peace with Cochise.

"You hate Joe," Watchman said. "Why?"

"Look, if it wasn't for that stupid fool and his temper, Maria Poinsenay would be alive right now."

"Maria Poinsenay—that's Joe's wife, her maiden name."

"The son of a bitch talked her into marrying him when the whole tribe was against it."

"Why were they?"

"Wrong clans for marrying," Victorio said. He adjusted the lapels of his suit jacket when he sat down. "Look, you want to find him? Have yourself a look around old Will Luxan's place. Will Luxan never could stand Joe but that never made any never-mind to Joe, he'd probably head right back to old Uncle Will like a homing pigeon."

"Luxan's his mother's brother?" Ordinarily in the clan and family arrangements that relationship was not a particularly close one.

"Actually they're not related. Will Luxan was an old buddy of Joe's old man. Luxan comes from someplace way over in New Mexico but he's lived here maybe forty years. He sort of got adopted by Joe's grandfather. Later on he married into the tribe. They call him *Tio* Will but he's nobody's real uncle. Incidentally Joe's old man was a San Carlos, he moved up here when he married into the clan here."

"So Maria belonged to Joe's father's clan and that's why they weren't supposed to marry each other?"

"Yeah. What are you, Hopi?"

"Navajo."

"Then you've got the same setup."

"More or less. You think there might be a chance Joe would head for his in-laws' in San Carlos?"

"I doubt it. They never could stand him."

"You must have been soft on Maria Poinsenay," Watchman said; he wanted it out in the open.

"She was pretty deep in my guts, yeah."

"But she married Joe."

"Joe married her. He was a big hero back from the Army and I was way the hell down in Tucson at law school."

"Are you San Carlos?"

"No, I'm White Mountain but there's branches of my clans down on the San Carlos and I used to work down there summers. I met her the summer before Joe came back from the Army."

"But then you had to go back to law school and he moved in on her."

"Man, I wish I knew how in hell he ever forced her into it."

"Forced her?"

"Well I mean she wasn't *stupid*. Picking *him* over *me?*" It was evident Victorio still had a few things to learn about the ways of the human heart. Self-consciously he adjusted the hang of his suit jacket.

"Tell me about Joe. What's he like? How does his mind work?"

"It doesn't. He's a reacter. Lets his feelings push him around like a wind pushing a tumbleweed." Victorio seemed pleased with the image; he paused to savor it. "He was always getting into fights over nothing at all. Getting drunk and beating up on people if they looked at him cross-eyed."

"All that stopped after he got married, didn't it?"

"I guess Maria kept him in line. Like I said she was pretty bright. She'd know how to keep him out of jail." Rage began to simmer at his lower lids again.

Watchman said, "She died on the highway and the next day Joe broke out of Florence. Now there's got to be a connection."

"Sure. He got the news and went berserk. It's not the first time. It never took much to make him fly off the handle—you never saw a temper like that son of a bitch has got. I've still got a scar on my arm where he went through my shirt with a busted beer bottle."

"What was the fight about?"

"You'd have to ask him. I was having a beer minding my own business and all of a sudden he was all over me."

"Were you both dating Maria then?"

"I had the inside track. Maybe that was what set him off. God knows what goes on inside that pea-brain of his."

Watchman didn't ask who'd won the fight. Victorio didn't look like much of a brawler.

Watchman said, "All right, let's say he went berserk. That prison breakout was pretty well planned, but let's assume he was just lucky. He's a little crazy and he can't stand prison any more so he busts out. Then what?"

"All I can tell you is try Will Luxan. Joe always thought the world of Uncle Will. Other than that I've got no ideas. For all I know he's halfway to China now—either that or trying to rig up a bomb to blow up the prison with. I wouldn't put that past him."

"It sounds a mite fanciful."

"When Joe gets mad he hits anything within reach."

"I'll bear that in mind. Who else knew him well?"

"Oh all kinds of people, I guess. Jimmy Oto, he's still around Whiteriver. They used to hang out together at the roadhouse just after Joe got out of the Army. That old mealymouth LaSalle over at the mission might give you an item or two, but whatever he tells you, use a grain of salt. The old bastard's still somewhere in the Victorian age, he'll tell you all about the plight of the noble savage. You talked to Angelina yet?"

"His sister? No. I understand she's in Showlow."

"She'll be back by after-supper drinks time. She works at the roadhouse. You ought to treat her with the kind of respect you'd show a skittish mustang filly."

"Why? What's wrong with her?"

"In that family they're all a little crazy in the head. Joe's brother was killed in Korea going up against a whole Red Chinese battalion single-handed with a Browning automatic rifle. He got the Medal of Honor for it but he also got dead."

"What does Angelina do over there? Wait tables?"

"A little of everything. She sings a song now and then, she serves beer and setups, she runs the cash register. Sometimes she just sits in the corner. Hell I don't know. The place belongs to Will Luxan and I guess he'd keep her on whatever she did. He kind of feels obligated to the family."

"I understand she's not married."

"She married a white man back, oh, six-seven years ago. It didn't take, they got divorced maybe six months later. She'd be a good-looker if she put some weight on, but every man I know of that's tried to date her up ended up with a black eye sooner or later. Anyhow nobody wants to marry into that clan, they haven't got two pesos to rub together. Joe and Angelina, they're the last of the line."

The thought made Victorio grin. "And high time too."

Then his smile coagulated. "Listen, I'd kind of like for Joe to get found, so if you need a hand you just let me know. You'll find it's a taut town up here, most folks don't like to hear any questions about anything at all from outsiders. I'll see if I can help offset that a little."

"Thanks," Watchman said. Then he went out.

7.

Watchman had the feeling there was going to be no way to untangle the Threepersons chase from the water dispute. Water was the basis for survival in this country—and Joe Threepersons was astraddle the whole mess: an Apache who'd worked for the Rand interests, a Reservation Indian who'd been convicted of murdering the Rand foreman.

This Reservation fell away from northeast to southwest. From the high escarpment of the Mogollon Rim it plunged through timbered mountain country of streams and lakes; down through scrubby hills; across these valleys where Whiteriver and Fort Apache squatted in the dust; out along red-clay plateaus, then down the steep pitch of the Salt River Canyon. Beyond that river was the San Carlos which was a separate Apache Reservation of an area some two hundred thousand acres larger than the Fort Apache Reservation; but the San Carlos was poor land mostly, if not desert then something close to it. The fortunes of the Arizona Apache tribes were dependent mainly upon the natural wealth of the White Mountain high country: the timber, the grass and above all the water.

But across the Reservation boundary the Anglo ranchers had drilled their wells, depleted the water-table and cut off the flow into the string of reservoirs that not only gave the Apaches a lucrative recreational enterprise but stored up water for all the farm country below. Without irrigation from the lakes, the farms would blow away like Okie acres in the dust bowl.

By now half the Apache lakes were cracked mud flats with shallow ponds in their centers. Stunted fields of corn and greens stood withered under the sun and if the newspapers were right it would be the worst crop year in twenty-five years on the Fort Apache Reservation, come harvest time.

The Rands claimed the Indians weren't making good use of the water when they did have it. It was true enough. Watchman had seen it on the Navajo Reservation and it was the same thing here: the grandsons of Cochise and Geronimo were not farmers, they hadn't been born to the soil and even under expert agricultural guidance they still managed to ruin half the land they farmed by neglecting to terrace it, by refusing to rotate crops and by stripping it for planting so that the midsummer cloudbursts inevitably scraped off all the topsoil and left the Apache farmer with nothing but eroded rock shelves and sand and clay. But they were learning. It took time: you didn't make farmers into Indians in two generations and it wasn't realistic to expect the reverse to happen any faster.

In a land of scarce rainfall water meant everything: without it land was valueless and therefore water was more valuable than the land itself. But in the century of the Indian Bureau the water rights of the western tribes had been reduced steadily and both the rights and the water had evaporated.

The Anglos who believed in things written on paper had the words in their favor. The treaties by which the Indians occupied their Reservations had been drawn up a century ago in a time when it had not occurred to anybody to specify any relationship between the land itself and the water that fed it. Water rights were not mentioned in the treaties or the government-tribe agreements or the Acts of Congress which shaped the legal boundaries of Federal-Indian relationships. It was on the strength of these omissions that the Rands based their arguments: there was no mention of Indian water rights in any of the treaty agreements and therefore, if rights were not mentioned, then there were no rights.

To Rand the issues were financial. To the tribe they were life-or-death. It was possible the Calisher murder had nothing to do with water rights but the complications which now ramified from it had everything to do with them. The tribe would aid and abet Joe Threepersons not merely because he was a member of the tribe but also because his enemies and the tribe's enemies were the same. And if by hampering white justice the tribe could help put Charles Rand's tail in a crack, the tribe would make a lot of sacrifices to see that happen.

What it meant, in the end, was that Joe Threepersons was going to be damned hard to find.

CHAPTER FOUR

1.

T HE WIND blew the smell of exhaust across the apron of the Shell station.

It was a two-stall garage with one pit and a stall without a lift, a concrete floor with a grease-clogged center drain. A can of kerosene stood in the front corner with a potato stuck over its spout. There was only one man on duty and all Watchman could see of him was his bowed back and legs. The man's head was out of sight under the yawning hood of a half-ruined Ranchero.

Fifty yards north of the station stood the roadhouse, the Broken Arrow, set back behind its dusty parking lot. It was a big rectangle sided with brown boards; there were no windows at all. The name of the place was painted in a faded crescent across the movie-set false front and an illuminated Coors Beer sign overhung the front door. The place

had a forbidding aspect, like a slaughterhouse: the grim
solid walls without windows gave the impression someone
was ashamed of what went on inside.

It had to be fairly new because it had only been legal to
sell whiskey on Reservations for a few years but the
Broken Arrow looked as if it had stood there as long and
as immutably as the mountains behind it.

Watchman got tired of waiting and went inside the stall
to show himself.

"Be with you in a sec." The man was touching a bare
finger to the engine block—testing the cylinders by the old,
but still best, method. If an engine is missing on one
cylinder, touch a hand to each cylinder. The one that isn't
hot is the faulty one. But you need tough skin.

"I'm all alone here right now. Sorry to keep you waiting."

"It's all right. I'm looking for Will Luxan."

The mechanic looked up over his shoulder. A chinless
youth with inquisitive eyes. "He just left. He's either over
at the Arrow or you find him home, house back there in
the trees."

Watchman thanked him and asked him to fill the Volvo
and check under the hood when he had a minute. He left
the mechanic in communion with the Ranchero engine and
walked across the pebbled dust toward the roadhouse. The
sun was dropping toward the Salt River district and on the
red macadam road the inbound traffic was heavier than it
had been. The automatic jabbed his spine when he went
up the porch steps to the brown door.

The Broken Arrow had red lenses in the ceiling and fake
oil lamps along the walls and old posters of Jeff Chandler
and Jimmy Stewart fighting the Indian wars. It was a low-
budget imitation of a nightclub with short picnic tables
and benches in place of booths, and rickety wooden stools
along the bar. There was a little bandstand raised eight
inches off the floor at the far end of the room beyond the

end of the plank bar which ran two-thirds the length of the right-hand wall. The place was redolent of stale beer and tobacco smoke. It was too dark to tell how clean or filthy it might be.

Gradually his eyes adjusted and peopled the room with five-drinkers at the bar, two men at a back table, a one-armed Apache tending bar and a girl at the register in a long black dress with a white imitation-lace apron.

She had very wide cheeks and the vivid lipstick didn't suit her. Watchman asked her about Luxan and she pretended she hadn't heard him. He asked again and she said, "He ain't here."

"Then I'll try his house." He began to turn away.

"No . . . "

"Why? Isn't he home?"

Her face closed up, intransigent in bitterness. "You just got to bother him, don't you."

"You think he's got something to hide?"

"Oh for God's sake." Irritably she kicked the long skirt away from her feet with a backward flick of her heel. She couldn't have been much more than eighteen.

"What makes you think I'm going to make trouble for him?"

"I heard about you," she said.

"What did you hear?"

"Nothin'." The surly downward glance; now she was a fourteen-year-old, the cabaret costume and lipstick forgotten because she was rattled.

"What are you to Mr. Luxan?" He threw in the *mister* to reassure her.

"Daughter. What difference that make to you?"

"Well I don't mean your daddy any harm."

"That ain't the way I heard."

"Take my word for it." He left the place, thinking at least she had spunk; sense always came later.

2.

In Indian society there was fierce competition for status and prestige; success was important and was measured in symbols or in possessions. Ambition was not frowned upon but greed was—you found no moneylenders within the tribes and that was what enabled white traders to get rich because they were the only ones who charged interest for money borrowed.

The size of Will Luxan's house was a surprise and he hadn't made that kind of money by amassing capital and lending it out. Therefore he was a man of imagination and a hard worker. The house was half again the size of any house Watchman had seen in the town proper. It probably had four bedrooms and more than one bathroom.

It was washed in pink stucco and had a red roof of half-round tiles. A degree of care had been used in situating it; the big old trees that crowded up close against it had been there a lot longer than the house had. Luxan had his own private cottonwood grove here.

Four cars browsed in the driveway, none of higher rank than a three-year-old Pontiac sedan. There was a basketball on a patch of grass in the yard and a swing hung from a cottonwood limb, made of a length of rope and an old truck tire. A nondescript but well-fed puppy wagged its tail at Watchman. From the profusion of cars and other evidence he judged Luxan had a sizable number of children.

A boy of eleven or twelve answered his knock and Watchman asked if Mr. Luxan was home. Through the open hallway he could smell beef cooking. The boy told him to wait here and Watchman winced at the boy's show of dislike. Evidently the moccasin telegraph had him confused with the boogie man.

Luxan's appearance was anticlimactic. He wore baggy

pants cinched by a belt at the top, like a mail sack; he smelled of the gasoline he had used to wash the grease off his hands. He was a big man, at least sixty years old, twenty pounds overweight and hair shot with grey. A sprig of hair stood up disobediently at the back of his head, glistening with the water with which he'd tried to stick it down.

Luxan came outside and pulled the door shut behind him. It was a slight and he meant it to be noticed. "I know why you are here."

His speech had the liquid gutteral *r*'s of the older Indian generation. He was a man who would not think it archaic to state that he had talked with the sun and the earth and the river and they had told him not to cooperate with the white-Indian outsider.

Watchman said, "Grandfather, I'd like to help your nephew Joe."

"I am no longer an uncle to this one. I can't help you."

"I understand he always turns to you when he needs wise counsel."

"I have told him many years ago not to come here any more times."

"He might come to you now, Grandfather. He has no one else. His wife is dead."

"Yes I know that. She was witched, I hear."

"Where did you hear that?"

"It is what they say."

"Who would want to throw a spell on Joe's wife?"

"I don't know. But I heard she sure got real sick before she went out in that car."

"Do you think Joe will come back here now?"

"I don't know what that one might do." Luxan's face hardened like dark polished wood. "But he would be a fool to come here. He would know it is where they look first."

"Where else would he go?"

"The whole world of mountains and deserts is out there." Luxan's big lips went all shapes when he talked. His hair had distributed a powdering of dandruff on the shoulders of his dark satiny shirt.

Beyond the house Watchman saw a teen-age boy on a donkey driving three cows in toward the little corral in the woods. A magpie pecked at lice on the back of one of the cows.

Luxan said, "I can see what is in your head. If you wish to see if he is in my house you can come look."

It was a challenge and Watchman did not turn it down out of politeness. He followed the old man inside. Luxan moved with deliberate strength; age had not hurt his co-ordination.

The front room on the right was a living room, twelve by fourteen. The furniture was what you could buy in the trading post: inexpensive, functional. There were two old stuffed chairs in need of reupholstering. The room had no closets and no occupants and Watchman followed Luxan out of it across the hall into the other front room. There were two bunks and some children's wooden furniture. Watchman opened the closet and got the smell of old sneakers. He said, "I guess you're a good businessman."

"I work hard and I have a great many brothers-in-law."

There was another children's room, two double-deck bunks in it and a litter of clothes and wooden toys. Opposite it was a slightly larger bedroom with a straw tick on the floor. Watchman looked in both closets and the bathroom. Across the hall was another empty bathroom and then Luxan showed him the utility room with its oil burner and water heater, and after that the corridor emptied into a kitchen that ran the width of the back of the house.

The twelve-year-old boy and a younger brother sat at a

chrome dinette table playing checkers. A middle-aged woman with the lean handsomeness of a *grande dame* stood beside the stove chopping vegetables into a colander. A girl about fourteen, with the same face as the girl in the roadhouse but no lipstick, was reading a book at a small wooden table in the far corner. There was a small refrigerator and a sink and a lot of open shelves, and the whole back wall was windows looking out upon arid fields that rolled away beyond the fringe of cottonwood trees.

"It's a very fine house, Grandfather."

Luxan was the only person in the room who acknowledged that Watchman existed. All the others including Luxan's wife were staring at fixed points on the walls or the floors. The twelve-year-old boy was continuously raking the hair back from his forehead; with an impatient gesture he slammed a checker across the board and said, "King me," and cleared his throat because his voice was changing.

"Now I have told you and your own eyes have told you he is not here," Luxan said.

The older boy who had brought the cows in came through the back door and stopped in his tracks to lay a narrowed stare against Watchman. He didn't speak at all.

Watchman said, "It is possible you'll see Joe, or hear from him."

"It is possible." Luxan conceded nothing.

"He ought to give himself to me. It will be bad for him if we have to find him ourselves."

"He has made his trouble," Luxan said. "Let him get out of it by himself."

"Why have you turned against him, Grandfather?"

"I'll tell you, men get bad sometimes. Sometimes they're witched bad and sometimes they just get bad."

"And Joe got bad, and you wash your hands of him."

He wasn't sure Luxan understood the idiom. But Luxan

said, "Joe never wanted to help anybody, he was never any good to his own clan. He made a lot of fights and finally he didn't have any friends around here at all."

"That when he took the job on the Anglo ranch?"

"Around that time, I think."

"And you haven't talked to him since then?"

"I saw him one time, maybe two times when they arrested him that time. Before he went away to the prison."

"But not since then."

"I always told him he shouldn't get drunk from too much beer. But he stopped listening. When a man stops listening to his elders there isn't anything more they can do for him. He has his trouble, we all know this—but he has to find his own way out of it this time."

Puritanical righteousness and forgiving compassion made a strange admixture in the old man. Watchman thanked him and made his way out of the house, feeling no closer to the fugitive Joe than he'd felt twelve hours ago.

3.

Driving to the mission he passed the Agency cop Pete Porvo. Porvo's prowl car was headed the opposite way and he didn't wave when Watchman passed him; there was a nod but not a smile of greeting.

The mission was right on the road below Cedar Creek. Watchman braked to avoid hitting a pariah dog on the oil-smudged road. He turned around and parked facing Whiteriver and when he got out two women were watching him: an Apache, her baby riding on a cradleboard on her back, and a big Anglo woman in olive corduroy trousers too large for her buttocks.

"Mrs. LaSalle?"

"Yes? . . ."

"My name's Watchman. I wonder if the pastor's around."

"He just went to tape up the garden hose. You'll find him in the workshop." She shaded her eyes and pointed the way.

It was summer vacation and there were no children around the mission school. It was a little greener than the ones up on the Navajo Reservation but the mock-adobe architecture, the severity of it, was enough of a reminder to put the taste of brass on Watchman's tongue. These were the schools where Indian kids were flogged for acting like Indians instead of whites. The missionaries were maybe a little less weak and venal and corrupt than their predecessors but they still believed you had to drill private notions of greed into Indians before they could become Christians and be saved.

George LaSalle was binding fricton tape around the hose nozzle like a tourniquet. Watchman started talking and then listened, and found LaSalle to be a vigorous old zealot filled with a lot of prejudicial nonsense from the Rousseau lexicon of antiquated idealism: "I understand my Inyans, you see."

LaSalle evidently had been born unawares and his many years' experience among the simple savages hadn't taught him anything. He was the sort of white man who indulged in self-flagellating atonement for the sins of his ancestors against Indians but his atonement took the form of insensitive charities and terrible advice. The key to the behavior of men like LaSalle was their conviction that the tribes were their personal wards.

"I tried to set him on the straight and narrow, God knows. But that boy's a pipperoo, I swan. A jim-dandy horseman, by the way—I kept telling him, if he only applied himself he'd be a crackerjack rodeo performer."

LaSalle's eyes flicked at Watchman like a lizard's tongue.

The gleaming unhealthy skin was stretched over his bones almost to the point of splitting; he had a sepulchral face and wispy tufts of white hair. He waved the hose around as though he were a snake charmer.

"He was a stubborn boy, you know; I imagine he's still a stubborn boy. I use the word 'boy' advisedly—he never allowed himself to grow up."

"Not even after he became a husband and father?"

"Well to be sure I never saw him much after his baby was born, but all you need to do is take a look at the evidence. That was a pretty fast crowd they ran with up at Rand's place."

"What crowd was that?"

"Well I shouldn't be telling tales out of school, should I, but I must say it was I who advised him against taking the job up there. After all, he had a perfectly good position at the sawmill right here in Whiteriver, and he did have a degree of seniority there. I think *she* turned his head, though. One word from *her* and he was off wherever she pointed him. I realize it's old-fashioned nowadays to speak of women leading men astray, but I swan she was a juicy little thing, she turned a great many heads, you know."

"I'd started to get the impression she was a steadying influence on him."

"Hardly, I'd say. She knew that crowd quite well, you know—the Rand bunch, that is. Not Mr. Rand himself, of course, but the hangers-on."

"Like Ross Calisher?"

"Of course. She was the one who sweet-talked poor Joe into moving up to the ranch where he'd be closer to Calisher. She wanted him to learn rodeoing from Calisher. I kept telling him he could learn it just as well down here."

"I knew Calisher was a big-time rodeo cowboy, but was he still doing it?"

"He'd broken a few too many bones to stay active at it,

but you never saw the man but he wasn't surrounded by an adoring pack of would-be apprentices. Some of them were fairly accomplished, I believe; certainly it was impossible for a boy like Joe to get anywhere near him—there was too much crackerjack competition. The place was rather like a thoroughbred racing stable the way it kept turning out rodeo competitors. I'm sure that's why Rand hired Calisher in the first place. To him it was like buying a champion stud horse—and I assure you that's more than a loose analogy."

Watchman nodded. "Calisher was fast with the ladies."

"The place festered with it," LaSalle said obscurely. "Affairs all over the place, I understand—clandestine types in the bushes every night. The place had a rancid reputation, you know. I'm not sure if it still does. But I swan, the talk you heard . . . Naturally it was just the place to attract a woman like Maria Poinsenay."

"They tell me she was having an affair with Calisher—that's why Joe shot him."

"I warned him not to move there. You could see that sort of thing was in the cards. Loose morals, violence, a brazen crowd . . . it was inevitable. The atmosphere made it nearly impossible to avoid that sort of thing. They were all having affairs. Rand's own wife was having an affair with that lawyer, Kendrick."

"Kendrick? I thought he wasn't on speaking terms with Rand."

"When has that ever prevented such things from happening? She divorced Rand, you know—she's married to Kendrick now."

"When did that happen?"

"I don't know, several years ago."

"Before or after Calisher died?"

"I'm sure I couldn't tell you."

LaSalle had a vivid imagination fueled by the excitement of forbiden fantasies. He was typical of a good many missionaries Beneath his theatricality was a curious undercurrent of fear—perhaps an unhappy fear that his own failures were too obvious.

"If he came back here," Watchman said after a bit, "where would he go?"

"To hide, you mean. Well I'm sure I couldn't say. Of course there are a lot of shirttail relations—the clan structures being what they are. He has a sister here, you might try there."

"I plan to. Did he have any close friends his own age?"

"Not many who are still here. The younger ones tend to drift away. The old women are constantly complaining about it, how the young men have forgotten how to carry baskets for their relatives. It's only a saying, of course, but it holds a great deal of meaning."

"I know."

"More than half the young people move off the reservations nowadays. They work in non-Indian jobs."

Watchman was one of those; he didn't press the point. "His wife's family is still down on the San Carlos, is that right?"

"I suppose so. I doubt they'd be much help to you. They weren't on good terms. At any rate an Apache isn't allowed to talk to his mother-in-law except through an intermediary—he must avoid her, never be in the same house or even be caught looking at her. They still keep these customs, you know, even though we keep trying to enlighten them."

Watchman covered a smile. It was becoming more apparent that LaSalle didn't realize he was an Indian. Perhaps he was so accustomed to looking at Indian faces that he no longer made the distinctions. Watchman's statepolice identification had triggered all the reflex associations; and LaSalle was a man of fundamentalist faith, disinclined to exercise any curiosity.

"There is one young man still in Whiteriver who used

to be friendly with him. Not a very savory boy, I'm sure. He's called Oto, Jimmy Oto."

Tom Victorio had mentioned the name. Watchman said, "He works in town?"

"I don't think he works at all. Welfare case. He married a girl from the *Twagaidn* clan—they live in that cluster of wickiups several miles northeast of town. It's a poor section, even for this place."

"Were they close enough friends for Joe to go to him for help now?"

"They were like this when they were schoolboys." La-Salle held up two fingers overlapped together. "They were always up to their ears in horrible pranks. I had to discipline the two of them constantly. But I don't see much of Jimmy any more, and I'm sure I couldn't say whether they're still as close as they were. Remember it was more than ten years ago."

4.

Sunset. The squalls had moved on to the east and the western sky was vivid with a sprawl of color. He crunched into the parking space in front of the trading post and saw Dwight Kendrick rolling forward from the council house in his grey Corvette. Watchman walked over to the car and Kendrick gave him a civil nod.

"Pretty spectacular sunset," Watchman said.

"I wouldn't know. I'm color-blind. How are your investigations proceeding?"

"I wouldn't say they were proceeding at all."

"Well they all tend to develop bad cases of lockjaw with strangers," the lawyer said blandly.

"The sooner he gives himself up the easier it'll go on him. Somebody ought to tell him that."

Kendrick smiled coolly. "You're not very subtle, are you. The fact is I haven't seen him and I don't expect to. He'd be an idiot to come back here."

"I doubt he's got much choice. He doesn't know any-place else."

"He was in the Army."

"Where'd he do his basic training?" Watchman asked without real interest.

"Fort Ord, I believe. But that's a lot of miles from here."

"He'd know the towns around there, though."

"It might be worth a try," Kendrick said. He was gunning his engine; now he put it in gear and Watchman stepped back and watched the Corvette eel into the road.

He bought a sandwich in the trading post and made that his supper and washed it down with a can of ginger ale. From the booth on the porch he put in a station call to Buck Stevens' apartment.

"How's business, Sam?"

"Slow."

"You coming back?"

"I've still got to talk to his sister. I'll probably over-night in a motel, most likely Showlow."

"Then I'd better give you what I've got so far. Where are you, pay phone?"

"Yes."

"I'll call you back so you don't run out of dimes. What's the number?"

Watchman waited for the phone to ring and answered immediately. "Okay, go ahead."

"Yeah. Item. Maria Threepersons and the kid, Joe Junior. They had it pretty good up in Sunnyslope. I talked to some neighbors and had a look at the house—they didn't lack for first-rate furniture. There's even one of those above-ground swimming pools."

"Where'd they find that kind of money?"

"I'm trying to find out. Item, she wasn't just a clerk in that curio shop, she ran the place. Manageress, whatever. There's two girls working there now but they don't seem to know who owns the place. Curioser and curioser, right?"

"Go on."

"She moved to Phoenix right after Joe went to the pen. The curio shop opened right away, with her running it. She was putting up in an apartment court then but it was only a couple months, then she bought the house."

"Mortgage?"

"I'll find out tomorrow. Anyhow the color TV and stuff came damned quick. You get the picture?"

"Enough. She had a benefactor. Any signs of a boy-friend?"

"The neighbors were a little cagey. they didn't want to look like busybodies, but I got the idea she had some dates with local bachelors. Nothing serious. There was only one steady visitor and he didn't look rich, according to what they told me. An Indian."

"Apache?"

"Nobody around there ever talked to him beyond hello-how's-the-weather. Most of the neighbors assumed he was some relative of hers, but she never said. Kind of a good-looking guy, drove an old Volkswagen beetle, kind of beat-up, dark blue. No license number, of course, they're not snoops."

Watchman had seen a car that matched the description. It had been parked in the gravel patch between the trading post and the council house. It wasn't there now. Co-incidence? Maybe; there were plenty of blue VWs around.

"The picture I get," Stevens said on the line, "he was nice looking and he wore pretty good clothes but he didn't look like he was rolling in money. Informant tells me he never spent the night with her. He'd show up evenings maybe once every three, four weeks. Take her out to dinner now and then when she could get a sitter. The kid was in day school up there, by the way. Pretty good school."

"Private school?"

"Yeah. Now here's the kicker—that blue beetle was parked outside her place the morning she died. Just before she went out and killed herself, he was there. Or at least his car was."

"Or a car that looked like his."

"Well sure. But what the hell. Man you better believe I'm trotting this phone bill over to Lieutenant Wilder the minute it comes in. Okay, let's see. . . . Item. The neighbor saw the beetle take off that morning and it ran the red light at the corner. I just throw that in for free—no extra charge—suspicious character breaking the law left and right."

"Sounds like he was rattled." Watchman thought about it and said, "Look, in the morning you call the Phoenix coroner and find out about that autopsy on her."

"Okay. I'm not finished yet."

"Then keep going."

"All right, let's see. Item. Same neighbor-lady told me there was a prowler around Maria's house last night, drove off in a station wagon. Probably Joe Threepersons but she didn't get much of a look. She's got a hell of a nose on her, this woman. Lives right across the street."

"What did she mean by prowler? Did he break in?"

"Not that she saw. When she saw the guy he was peeking in the windows. Then he drove off."

"That had to be Joe. All right, what else?"

"That note we got? The anonymous tip? No fingerprints on it. The typewriter's an Olympia manual with pica type. Ordinary kind of paper and all." Stevens coughed away from the phone and his voice came back: "Thing is, the trail still stops with those stolen horses up there."

"For all we know he's in Johannesburg. Forty thousand

people disappear every year in this country and a lot of them never get found."

"You sound like you haven't turned up a damn thing up there."

"You could put it that way," Watchman said. "It goes that way, they tell me—we're supposed to get used to eating a steady diet of wild goose."

"Well hang in there, kemo sabe."

5.

When he opened the phone-booth door it extinguished the interior light and he saw them standing by his car.

Five of them. One was digging around in his mouth with a toothpick. They all looked like delinquents, overage and gone to seed. He recognized one of them, the very big one with a gut on him: he'd seen that one sitting on the tailgate of a pickup truck swigging canned beer, down at the horse camp where Joe Threepersons had run off with the herd.

The man was genuinely huge. The skin of his face was suspended from massive cheekbones and he probably weighed 280 pounds, part lard but mainly muscle.

They weren't exactly Nature's noblemen. The big one put the comb away in his pocket and held Watchman's eyes as long as he could without stirring up violence in himself; then the left side of his mouth flicked upward and he glanced at his friend with the toothpick.

It broke the tableau and Watchman started down the porch steps. An engine raced momentarily and to his right he glimpsed a familiar grey pickup truck parked at the roadside. The headlights threw a splash of illumination as far as the gas station but the pickup had only one taillight and that was burnt out.

The big man stirred. He wore a maroon shirt with balloon sleeves and tight chinos on his long legs, cinched up so that his belly made a precarious overhang.

Sicksweet exhaust fumed from the pickup. Watchman walked toward them conscious of the weight of the automatic against his spine, and conscious of how long it would take him to get at it if he had to.

"You want something?"

None of them spoke; neither did they back away. The squat one kept digging at his teeth.

Watchman put his weight on the balls of his feet and flexed his knees a fraction—he wanted to be loose because he might have to move quickly. He said, "If that's your pickup you'd better get that taillight fixed before somebody rear-ends it."

The big one slid his childishly challenging glance from Watchman's face to his boots and when he had completed that gesture he made a little movement of his left hand, out to one side, and the four men behind him walked away toward the pickup.

The big one said, *"Enju, yutuhu nda."* It was addressed to Watchman and it wasn't friendly. Having spoken he wheeled slowly toward the pickup. The other four had climbed into its open bed; the big one got inside and smoke spurted from the ramshackle truck.

The breeze tousled his hair. He watched the truck recede, defined in silhouette against the flood of its own headlights. It had been an immature warning; but was it because he was a cop—any cop—or was it because of Joe?

The crumpled folds of the mountains had turned black with shadow. Sky merged with earth along the uncertain twilit horizons. He walked around the Volvo but the hubcaps were intact and the car appeared undisturbed.

It had been an irritating day filled with wasted words but there was a pattern to it like the design of a Chinle blanket and he got into the Volvo and drove up toward the roadhouse in an alert frame of mind because he had a feeling Joe was here. Right around here somewhere.

You didn't explain such feelings; you ignored them or you rode with them. There was more to be learned from what people said than could be found in their words. It was their faces and voices and the way they looked away; it was in the way they used their hands and the way they breathed.

They resented him because he was the outsider but that still left too much out. They were overreacting to him. They were lying to him, almost all of them, and it was because the town had something to hide. Joe, probably. Joe, and something more. If it wasn't guilt it was suspicion, and not all of it was directed at Watchman.

There were layers of secrets; what made it strange was that it was an Indian town—such intrigues were expected in Anglo communities but that was because they weren't real communities, they weren't tribes. Indian skeletons were usually on view to all because there were no closets to hide them in.

But here dark spirits had been stirred up. And he was beginning to sense that if Joe wasn't dug up soon there would be an explosion of violent forces.

He parked in front of the Broken Arrow and grinned at himself for his melodramatic imaginings. But when he got out he locked the car.

6.

They were mainly pickups and dusty Chevys and Fords and that was why he noticed the Volkswagen. He couldn't determine the color in this light but it was a dark shade.

He found it unlocked and looked for the registration slip but it wasn't in the car; he made a note of the license number and went into the roadhouse.

The lights were no brighter than before but this time he didn't have to accustom his eyes to a change from bright sunlight. The place was well populated but not over-crowded. The same one-armed bartender and a helper now, and a man at the register in place of Luxan's teen-age daughter. The bartender was very fast, probably faster than most who had two arms—he had to prove something.

Watchman didn't wait in the doorway. It was too much like putting himself in a picture frame for inspection. He went to the near end of the bar and waited for a beer and when it came he carried it toward the back of the room. Men at the bar turned to glance at him and there was enough challenge in their eyes to show they knew about him. But it wasn't a gamut; their resentment only simmered.

The decibel level of talk had dropped when he had entered. The room had had time to size him up and the talk resumed its former level until Angelina Threepersons left the corner table and carried her guitar to the stool on the bandstand. Then some of them stopped talking and looked at her, anticipating her song. Some others kept on talking as if they'd heard her before and didn't think much of her act.

Watchman took a small table and tipped his chair back against the wall. There were a few Anglos in the place—three in a bunch at the bar and two others, singly, talking with Apaches at tables. They were probably local sawmill technicians and livestock managers but ten years ago you wouldn't have found them in a place like this. The old barriers had come down. Allowing an Indian girl to sing non-Indian songs would have been unthinkable in an earlier generation.

The girl tuned up, not hurrying; she bent her ear over the f-holes of the guitar and ignored her audience.

There was a mournful quality to her, as if her gauntness were the product of sadness. The lamps bleached her face of color; it was a tired face, striking, the bones as fragile as a sick child's but the mouth and eyes creased by life. Once he'd had to tell a nine-year-old girl her puppy had been run over. Before she'd absorbed it completely and started to bawl there had been an expression on her face, quizzical and disbelieving and yet saddened and enraged all at once. Angelina Threepersons reminded him of that.

When she started to sing he was surprised by the repertoire. They were Kristofferson songs—*Sunday Morning Coming Down* and *Bobby McGee* and *Help Me Make It Through The Night*—and she did them well with a country twang and a husky deep delivery. But she sang without looking at her audience; she was singing for herself. Her music went into Watchman's bones with melancholy lassitude.

A fat Indian got up from his seat to Watchman's right and carried his empty glass toward the bar for refilling; it left a gap through which Watchman saw two familiar faces—Dwight Kendrick's and Thomas Jeffords Victorio's. Kendrick swiveled his gaze around and it passed across Watchman casually and kept turning until it reached the girl on the bandstand; for a moment Kendrick pretended he hadn't seen Watchman but then he thought better of it, looked back and nodded. He said something and Victorio looked over his shoulder and lifted a glass of whiskey in Watchman's direction. It might have been an invitation but Watchman ignored it. He acknowledged the attention with one hand and returned his glance to the girl. A few minutes later he picked up movement in the edge of his vision and turned to see Kendrick and Victorio making their way to the door, and out.

After the third song Angelina carried the guitar back to the corner table and left it standing up on the seat of a chair. She walked to the bar. Her legs weren't particularly long but she had a languid way of moving, or perhaps again it was weariness. She was wearing a black cowboy shirt with pearl buttons and a sheathed red skirt that almost reached the floor. The points of her shoulders were pronounced, exaggerated by the masculine tailoring of the shirt. The bartender spoke to her and handed her a tray and she carried it toward the front of the room. Watchman followed her with his eyes. Her black hair, tied in a bun, bobbed among the tables.

He drained his beer and when she was on her way back with a tray of empty glasses he waved her over.

"Another beer?"

"A little talk. When you get a minute."

"You must be the Navajo."

"Highway Patrol," he said.

He reached toward his wallet but she spoke quickly. "I'd sooner not talk here." She looked back across the room but the bartender was talking to someone. She turned her face toward Watchman and her quick smile was pretty but it was mocking and left an uncertain aftertaste.

"Name a time and place," he said.

"Have you got your car here?"

"Beat-up Volvo right outside. What time do you finish here?"

She looked down at the tray, thinking, and then she gave him an up-from-under glance. She seemed amused. "We're not too crowded. Let's get it done with—I'll be out directly."

He left and sat in the car with his elbow out the window. The spot where the dark Volkswagen had been was empty. He hadn't noticed anybody leaving the place except the two lawyers and Kendrick drove a Corvette. So it was Tom Victorio's and that was no real surprise; Victorio had been sweet on Maria and he'd have needed no big excuse to go down to Sunnyslope to visit her while Joe was tucked away in prison.

A surmise; a check on the license number would confirm it. *So it puts Victorio at Maria's house the morning before the breakout. How does that help locate Joe?* It didn't and he put it aside.

She came out of the roadhouse and looked for his car. He flashed the headlights at her and watched her come toward him. Her stride was still lazy but he sensed the tension in her.

She slid in beside him. "We can just sit here if you don't want to waste gas."

"I like the way you sing."

"And I'm far too talented for this dump."

"You could be. If you worked at it."

"I guess I don't want it that much." She gave him a head-on look for the first time since she'd got into the car. "Are you a cop or a talent scout?"

"Come on," he said, "don't get hard-boiled. I'm trying to find your brother, I'm not making a pass."

"Now that's odd," she said, "because I like to think I've learned to tell the difference between the serious customers and the ones that are just looking. Browsing, you know." She was mocking him again. She leaned toward him, her left arm sliding across the back of his bucket seat. "I'm trying to buy my crippled nephew an operation so he can play the trumpet again. Would you care to contribute?"

"It's not your nephew I'm interested in, it's Joe. Let's talk about him."

"I can't tell you anything you don't already know, but I'll go through the motions to save trouble."

"Can't or won't tell?"

"Does it matter? Would you believe me?"

"It's my job never to believe anything too fast."

When she put her back against the passenger door and folded her arms he added, "You're the one who can reach him if anybody can. I'd like you to take him a message. Tell him he's in a lot more trouble if he keeps hiding than he is if he gives himself up."

"Why?"

He hadn't thought that question would have been first on her list. She was not without surprises—or candor.

He said, "Because I have a feeling someone's going to get hurt if he stays loose long enough."

"Maybe that was why he broke loose in the first place. Didn't you think of that?"

"I did, but I don't have any facts."

"You must have some. Otherwise you wouldn't have got that far."

She was giving him the first real break he'd had; there were admissions between the lines of what she was saying —her failure to deny the implications of what he had said. He wasn't sure how to proceed from there; he didn't want to scare her off.

She waited and when he didn't speak she said, "You're kind of new at the job."

"How do you know?"

"I've been questioned a few times." She smiled; it was the same smile as before, it wasn't completed and it left him uneasy. "I break the law a lot, you see. I'm an arch criminal, a menace to society. I smoke grass."

"Gee whiz."

"I wouldn't have told you if I hadn't thought you'd answer like that."

He said, "It's my youthful honesty."

"No. It's just that you're relaxed. The ones that bust you for grass are the ones that twang like guitar strings.

They're upright and pious and I think their parents must all have been drunks."

"It's likely," he said. "Tell me something, what does this mean—*Enju, yutuhu nda?*" He repeated it as accurately as he could remember it. The sounds weren't unlike the Navajo but the words were strange.

She laughed off-key. "Who called you that?"

"A mountain in a satin shirt, driving a '58 Ford pickup."

"Jimmy Oto," she said. "It stands to reason."

So that was Jimmy Oto.

She said, "It means . . . well. *Enju* means anything you want it to mean. Like 'well' or *'alors'* or *'como'* or what do they say in Navajo, *'yatahay'*?"

"That's pretty close."

" *'Yutuhu'* means Navajo and I'm surprised you didn't know that. *'Nda'* means white man.

"That's all?"

"Well the way Jimmy Oto would say it I imagine it would come out meaning something more than just Navajo white man. More like Navajo son-of-a-bitch Uncle Tomahawk selling out to the white man."

"I could go home for that," he said. "Here I thought he was putting the bad eye on me."

"For him it would amount to that. His crowd doesn't believe in the old stuff."

"What about you?"

"I believe in all kinds of things. You'd be surprised."

"I might at that. Some of the folks believe in it. Will Luxan said he'd heard Maria was witched to death."

"Maybe she was," Angelina said.

"Who by? And what for?"

"A lot of people don't like my brother. And some of them maybe wanted him to break out of jail."

He sat and waited for her to continue but she only fished in the pocket of her skirt and found a pack of cigarettes. She hunted around the dashboard and found the lighter and punched it. "This thing work?"

"I don't know, I never use it."

"Oh God. He doesn't smoke. He drinks one beer. I'll bet he eats spinach twice a week."

The lighter popped. She pushed the glowing red end against the cigarette in her mouth and dragged suicidally to get it going. Watchman said, "A second ago you opened a can of worms."

"I did?"

"Joe's enemies. The ones who wanted him to escape. Who and why?"

"Because he didn't kill Ross Calisher," she said.

7.

"Okay. You wrote that letter to the Highway Patrol."

"What letter?" She inhaled smoke, choked, recovered and said, "Quit looking at me like I'm a hundred pounds of poon."

"The worms are starting to crawl out of the can, Angelina, and you're the one who opened it when you sent us that letter. You may as well finish what you started."

"You want a joint?"

"I'll take a rain check."

"I haven't got them on me anyway. Not with a cop in the same car."

He said, "Relax, I'm not going to search you. Now let's talk about that letter. Why anonymous?"

"I'm his sister. If you knew I wrote it you'd ignore it—naturally his sister would think he was innocent."

"That part didn't work. We assumed you sent it."

She made a face. "Well that's not the point. The night Joe was supposedly slaughtering Ross Calisher up at Rand's place I saw him up at Cibecue. He couldn't have been both places at once."

"You didn't tell this to anybody at the time?"

"I told Joe. He told me to keep my mouth shut."

"And you did what he told you, just like that."

"It wasn't like that. What do you take me for?"

"I'm still trying to sort that out," he said.

"Joe said a lot of people would be in a lot of trouble if I said anything. He told me we could both get killed. I believed that."

"Why?"

"Because somebody did get killed. Ross Calisher."

"All right, so you kept your mouth shut then. Why open it now?"

"Because I think all bets are off now."

"Where'd you get your secretarial training?"

"Phoenix," she said. She gave him a surprised look.

"Okay. What do you mean, all bets are off?"

"Joe didn't kill the man. They established the time of death and it was less than an hour after that when I saw Joe and Maria up in Cibecue. They had the baby in the car, they'd gone up to visit our cousin Jesse. But Jesse wasn't home that night. He was sick, that's why we were all worried about him, and Will Luxan was convinced somebody had witched Jesse. So they had Rufus Limita up there for a while throwing spells and they had a big sing. But Jesse wasn't getting any better. Rufus is a pretty hip medicine man, he decided they ought to try the white hospital. That night when I got there they'd taken Jesse away to the hospital. I was leaving when I saw Joe and Maria drive in. They didn't see me. I doubt they stayed any longer than I did, but I know what time it was and Joe couldn't have been killing Ross Calisher because it's a couple of hours' drive from Cibecue to where Calisher lived."

"You're still not telling me what bets are off."

"There must have been some kind of bargain. Don't you get it?"

"Tell me about it."

She was impatient. "Look, Joe confessed. He was, like, *happy* to go to jail for a murder he hadn't committed—it had to be some part of a deal he made, don't you see? Joe goes to jail and then all of a sudden Maria gets rich and moves down to Phoenix and the kid goes into private schools."

"And you think somebody paid Joe to take the rap."

"You know any other way to explain it?"

It fitted together well enough but it was all predicated on the assumption that Joe hadn't killed Calisher and there was only Angelina's word for that.

The cigarette tip dimmed when she took it away from her mouth; she waved it around with abandon. "It couldn't have been any part of the deal for him to escape the way he did. They'd have to know it was going to make the police come up here and start asking a lot of questions. They wouldn't want that."

"All right," he said. "That gets us to the grit. Who's they?"

"If I knew that," Angelina answered, "I think I'd have killed them myself."

8.

Three Apaches emerged from the roadhouse and two of them glanced toward the Volvo. Angelina averted her face and held the glowing cigarette down below the dash. The three men crowded into the cab of a Dodge three-quarter-ton and drove out toward the road. When they made the turn their headlights swept across the Volvo and made Watchman squint.

She said, "I'm a little bit scared if you want to know the truth."

"Then why do you stay around here?"

She had to think about it. "Well I got married once."

"To a white man. I heard it didn't take."

"It wasn't quite like that. I took to it fine. He didn't."

"I was going with a white girl for quite a while." He looked at his dark knuckles on the wheel and wondered why he'd said that.

"And who broke it up? You or her?"

"She did," he said.

"Anglos."

"Dirty rotten savages," he said, and they both smiled.

"I guess I had that coming," she answered. "Well you get stung and then you go home for comforting. I guess that's what happened to me. I never went back to secretarial school. I never wanted to do much after that. I had a big thing for him, you know."

"I know how it is."

"Anyway I never had any real reason to stay here except inertia. But then I never had any reason to feel scared. Not until the other day."

"You could leave now."

"No. For the first time I've got a reason to stay."

"Stubborn," he said.

"That's got nothing to do with it. If I'm pushed I run, that's the way I am. But suppose Joe's around here now and he needs help?"

"So you hang around in case he comes to you."

"Yes."

He said, "In your subtle way you're trying to convince me you don't know where he is."

"I don't give a damn what you believe. In fact as soon as I heard Joe had escaped, I assumed you'd put a tail on me right away."

"I wish we had the manpower for that."

"It's the first thing that occurred to me. It's probably the first thing that occurred to my brother."

"But he could have got a message to you."

"He could have but he didn't. I give you my word."

As a rule Indians weren't liars but Angelina had assimilated a lot; she talked white and behaved white. He had no way of telling if she was playing poker against him.

He said, "Maria had a frequent visitor. We think it was Tom Victorio. Do you think he's involved in the escape?"

"I have no idea. He hates Joe, I can't think why he'd want to help him."

"Hating Joe, is that entirely on accout of Joe marrying Maria?"

"I think so. They liked each other well enough before that."

"If you were Joe where would you be right now?"

She shook her head. The cigarette was out. She dropped it in the ashtray and slid it shut, and he heard the click when she lifted the door handle. "I wish I could help. I really do. If I hear from him I'll let you know, I'll call the Highway Patrol. I think he'd be safer with you than he is now, wherever he is. They want to kill him."

"What makes you so sure of that?"

"They've got to make sure he keeps quiet, don't they? They had Maria before. They had Joe Junior. God he was a hell of a nice little kid, my nephew. But they haven't got any hostages to keep him quiet any more."

Watchman said quickly, "Just one more question. If you're telling me the truth I don't understand why Joe wouldn't have come to us with the story."

"Would anybody have believed him?"

She got out of the car and chunked the door shut. He watched her walk away toward the roadhouse. He saw now what was peculiar about her stride: she was afraid. Uncertain whether she'd get to complete each step.

Halfway to the roadhouse she turned around and came back to the car. Watchman had the engine running; he shifted the stick to neutral.

She said, "Have you got a place to stay?"

"I thought I'd hole up in Showlow."

"Why don't you use my house. It's not much of a place but—look the truth is I'd appreciate the company tonight."

It wasn't a bedroom invitation, it was fear. She saw him thinking it over; she said, "I've got a phone there. If you didn't already know that."

"Why would I know that?"

"I thought maybe you'd tapped it by now. In case Joe tried to call me."

"We're not the FBI," he said. "Where do I find the place?"

"Take a left and head toward the mission."

"Then what?"

"There's a dirt road. . . ." She stopped and threw a glance at the roadhouse. "Never mind, hell. That's my car over there, the Rambler. I'll lead the way. I don't feel like going back in there."

"Won't they miss you?"

"I come and go," she said vaguely. "I don't think I could stand the place any more tonight."

It wasn't far. He followed the red lights of the old Rambler up the road half a mile until she turned off the highway. He steered behind her into a pair of ruts that carried the Volvo uncomfortably up a brushy slope and through a notch between two low hills.

Behind one of the hills stood a cubicle of stucco and wood. A naked light burned above the front door. When the girl stopped the Rambler he saw it had a crumpled front fender.

He was still fifty yards behind her, making a final turn toward the house, when he heard the crack of the rifle.

9.

His hands hit the ignition and headlight switches and extinguished them both and then he let himself fall out of the seat. When he hit belly-flat he kicked the car door shut to cut off the interior dome light. He edged under the side of the car fumbling inside the back of his shirt to get at the automatic.

A long time passed before he got it into his hands and worked the slide to jack a cartridge into the breech. Ahead of him the Rambler squatted motionless; the headlights still burned, lighting up the front of the house and one side of it where the porch light didn't reach. He couldn't see Angelina's head in the car but he saw the slight lurch of the car when the girl inside it moved, probably getting herself down as low as she could.

"Stay put," he called to her, and searched the starlit hillside. The ripping echo of the gunshot hung in his ears and adrenaline pumped a tremor into all his fibers.

He'd been shot at before in his life and knew the sound. It was not a whiz or a zip or a whisper or a fanning sound; it was a sharp loud crack like a small thunderclap and it was caused by the sonic boom of the passing bullet.

This time he was looking in the right quadrant and the side of his vision picked up the wink of the muzzle-flash. Smokeless powder and it wasn't a big lance of flame, just a flicker; but he saw it and two-handed the automatic up with both elbows on the ground and he let go five quick ones in the direction of the visual echo his eyes retained. It left him two in the magazine; he was a cop, he always knew how many he had left in the gun, and he wasn't about to shoot it empty unless it was unavoidable.

His palm stung a little from the recoil and his ears were no good now because they'd been deafened by the noise of his own shooting. But his eyes were all right, adjusting to the darkness. He saw the quick movement maybe two hundred yards up the hill and he aimed at a point well above it and squeezed his hand until the pistol discharged with a petulant bark.

No pocket automatic was going to hit anything at that range but it must have been close enough to unnerve the rifleman; the moving shadow started to zigzag and became lower and thicker because the man was running bent-over now. Watchman saw him disappear over the horizon of the hill, crouched very low against the skyline.

He sprinted to the Rambler. "Angelina?"

"Are you all right?"

"Are you?"

"I'm fine."

He heard her giggle, probably at the inanity of the words. Watchman returned his eyes to the hillside while he refilled the magazine and thrust it into the pistol grip. "Nothing on the other side of that hill except the road, is there? No houses or anything?"

"Nothing that I know of."

The hills weren't altogether barren but it was mainly a studding of piñon and scrub oak and dry brush. The hardpan wouldn't hold footprints, not the kind you could trace in the dark. Still there wasn't much to hide behind. . . .

He got up on one knee and froze. Nothing. Stood up, stood bolt still for the instant it might take a rifleman to take aim, then ran dodging to the base of the hill.

His move drew no fire. He called over his shoulder: "Stay on the floor. I'll be back."

"Where are you going?"

The note was plaintive but he didn't answer her; he went

up the hill fast with his boots scraping and slithering dislodging loose clots and pebbles; careless of the noise he swarmed all the way to the crest and stopped to get his breath while he eased up the last few feet until he could see across to the far side.

The moon was rising, a thin rind not yet in its first quarter. It didn't throw much light and some of the stars in the eastern hemisphere were obscured by clouds left behind by the day's rain squalls. Past the farther hills he caught the glow of lights from Whiteriver. The intervening distance was a wavy rolling of low hills with the narrow highway two-laning across it at an oblique angle. He swept it in a square search-pattern, trying to pick up movement in the edges of his vision. If the man was lying up there'd be no way to spot him in this minimal light but if he was moving there was a chance.

Watchman gave it a full ten minutes but nothing stirred and in the end he carried his pistol back down to the car and said, "We may as well go inside."

10.

At the door he stopped and listened and then asked Angelina for the key. She shook her head and pointed to the latch.

He thumbed it and pushed the door open but he didn't go in; he stood beside the door with the girl behind him. If anybody was waiting inside the silence would shake them up; they'd begin to wonder whether the first thing they'd see would be a human figure or a tear-gas grenade.

It was probably an unnecessary precaution but you stayed alive by avoiding unnecessary risks. After the silence had ticked by for a time Watchman eeled inside and flattened his shoulder blades against the wall to one side of the doorway.

Nothing stirred. He felt along the wall for a light switch, found one where he expected to and flipped it.

The house was a free-standing efficiency apartment with kitchen appliances along the far wall and a bathroom built into one corner. The only living thing he spotted was a house spider.

"Okay," he said. Angelina came in and he shut the door behind her.

There was a narrow bed and not much other furniture: a bedside table with a lamp, a rickety wooden kitchen table with two chairs, a wardrobe that was half closet and half chest-of-drawers. On the walls she had taped up posters from the All-Indian Powwow and the White Mountain Rodeo and Yellow Submarine and a center-creased poster that had come inside a Janis Joplin LP album.

"Sorry it's such a mess," she said. She sat down quickly on the bed as if she had to get off her feet before she fell. "Dear God."

He put his gun away and crossed behind her to draw the burlap drapes.

She turned and lay across the bed in an abandoned sprawl, plucking at the drawer of the nightstand. She took out a couple of joints and offered him one.

"Not now," he said, and went to the other window.

"Well I need one. God my nerves."

"I wouldn't."

"Wouldn't you," she said dully.

"It'd be a good time to keep a clear head."

"Even if it's going to get shot off anyway?"

"He won't shoot your head off. At that range he'd have had you cold. He missed because he wanted to—it was a warning."

"What kind of warning?"

He didn't answer; he thought it out. There was one way it made sense and once he had it sorted out he was pretty sure of it.

She said, "I've got a bedroll. I'll camp on the floor if you want."

"Find out if anything's missing."

"Missing?"

"Just have a look in the cupboards, all right?"

She rolled off the bed and swayed when she was on her feet but she shook off his tentative hand. "I'll be all right. A little dizzy." She crossed to the kitchenette cabinets and opened the bottom one. "The stereo's still here."

It was a cabinet made for cleansers and pails but she had a portable stereo in it and a stack of albums. She closed it and looked in the shelves above the sink. "Wait a minute."

He was watching over her shoulder. She was the kind of girl who'd have at least half a dozen cans of spaghetti and soup and roast-beef hash around because she'd have those days when cooking for herself was a drag. But he didn't see any cans at all.

"He took all the nonperishables, didn't he."

"How did you know that?"

"Think about it a minute and you'll figure it out for yourself."

She turned quickly; surprise and anger and speculation chased one another across her face.

"He stole your things because he knew you wouldn't report it," Watchman said. "At least you know he's not starving to death. Look around, see if he left a message."

"That wasn't Joe," she protested. "Joe wouldn't shoot at me. If you think he'd do that you've got a pretty wild imagination."

"I'll look for it myself if you'd rather."

"I'll look," she said angrily.

He stood in the middle of the room and watched her explore. She went into the refrigerator and all the drawers. He said, "The shooting was for your own protection."

"I haven't needed protecting since I was thirteen." It was flip and automatic and she trailed off at the last word; she stopped and pulled her face around toward him. "What do you mean?"

"He couldn't have known I'd be coming behind you. He was waiting up there to impress you, not me."

"Impress me?"

"He probably figures it's the best way to scare you into getting out of here."

"Well he's right," she said, "but I don't really believe you."

"Of course the whole theory blows up if it happens your brother's a lousy shot."

She went into the bathroom and he heard the squeak of a medicine-cabinet door. She reappeared empty-handed and looked at him. "He grew up hunting. He's a good shot."

"I know he is." He spread his hands, palms out, fingertips down.

"I suppose you could be right."

"Did you look under the phone?"

"Not yet." She went to the instrument and lifted it but there wasn't anything under it. She put it down and smiled a him. It was a bit vindictive. "Thank God. I was starting to think you were *always* right."

"Maybe he figured the rifle shot would be enough of a message. He didn't want you to think he was the one shooting at you. He wanted you to think it was somebody else, somebody really trying to kill you. That would scare you off."

"It would," she agreed, not without irony.

11.

He made a pot of coffee and sat on one of the wooden chairs. It wobbled on an uneven leg. "You might as well try to relax. He won't come back—especially not as long as my car's parked out there."

"You're awfully sure it was Joe, aren't you."

"Had to be. But I'll keep the gun handy if you want."

She turned around and looked up into his face. Her head hardly came up to his shoulder. "You're all right. Have I said thank-you yet?"

"No point trying to keep books on it."

"Well I like you, and that's not just gratitude."

She was offering herself and it made him smile. "I don't think I ought to ask just yet. You might change your mind."

"I'm known for that "

"You might decide to say no."

"I'm not usually known for that." She smiled quickly, and her face straightened equally quickly. "I don't know what made me say that. You get in bad habits, you start talking like that because it's easier than slapping people's hands all the time. I'm not a tramp—why do I keep sounding like one with you?"

"Basic biology. Somebody shoots at you and it makes all the juices run. Why do you think the birthrate goes up in wartime?"

"You're weird," she said. "Weird." She spent a while looking at nothing in particular before she looked at Watchman, his clothes, his bearing.

Her eyes betrayed her nervousness. "You're a long way from your Reservation, aren't you."

"Too far."

"There ain't no such animal."

"Wrong," he said. "It's no good pretending."

"Come off it. I went through that bullshit a long time

ago. When my lily-white husband ditched me I came crawling home and swore I'd never leave the Reservation again as long as I lived. Don't you think I know what it feels like? But you'll get over it. You'd get bored to death if you had to go back to wherever you grew up and live there again. It'd be like going from college back to second grade."

"Maybe."

"It's got nothing to do with race," she said. "The Reservation's a small town and you're a city boy now."

"And you're a city girl?"

"I've been wondering how I've stayed out here this long. When this mess is over I'm moving back to Phoenix."

"Just like that."

"Just like that," she said. "Now tell me the truth, could you go live at home again?"

"Things would be a lot simpler."

"Things are a lot simpler in the grave," she said.

Angelina inspected the clothes closet and left the door open while she wiggled out of her skirt and found a hanger to put it on. She was wearing pink-and-yellow patterned bikini pants. It didn't embarrass her to have him watch and he didn't turn away. She hooked both hands inside the collar of her cowboy shirt and wrenched it apart; all the pearl snaps parted and she let it slide down behind her off her wrists, her movement made sensual by her awareness of his attention.

She grinned suddenly. "One place I worked in Showlow, they asked me if I'd mind going topless. I told the guy I *am* topless. After that they made me keep my clothes on."

He answered her smile in kind.

CHAPTER FIVE

1.

S HE STIRRED against him, thrusting her haunch back; she was curled against his belly, her body in the shape of a Z. She made a little sound in her throat and turned over and kissed him drowsily but with great passion. He was only half awake but it roused him.

She drew back abruptly; a mischievous voice: "Okay. What's my name?"

He laughed at her. "I forget. But it'll be nice to have you around to pick up the soap when I drop it in the shower."

"Sam?"

"Mmmm?"

"That big red body's got a sensational vocabulary."

"I'm glad you speak the language."

"This is a hell of a thing to ask. . . ."

"Go ahead."

"Am I as good as she was?"

He sat up on the edge of the bed. "You're right. It was a hell of a thing to ask."

He glanced at the clock. Getting on for five o'clock. He mixed up a can of frozen orange juice and drank half a quart of it sitting on the edge of the bed with sunlight starting to leak in through the slatted venetian blinds. No point going back to sleep now. He started trying to sort out the facts of the case in his head but within five minutes Angelina was getting up with a bed sheet around her like a toga.

"Sam? I'm sorry."

"Forget it." He managed to smile. Dishevelment suited her, she looked childlike and drowsy and so desirable that he went to her and gathered her against him. Her voice came up, muffled against his chest:

"I really am. It was a rotten thing to say."

"If you still want the answer. . . ."

"I hate to admit it but I do."

"You have a lot more fun than she had," he said. "That means we both have a lot more fun."

"I'm glad." She disengaged herself and palmed the hair back from her temple. "Do you want to come back to bed or should I make us some breakfast?"

"Breakfast. I've got to hit the road."

She went to the kitchen. "What do you like?"

"Fried eggs, piece of toast, a lot of black coffee."

"A man after my own heart."

He looked straight at her. "I may turn out to be exactly that."

She gave him once again her brief unfinished smile. "Let's not talk like that yet."

"Fair enough."

He showered and dressed in yesterday's Levi's and shirt. The coffee made a good smell and he followed his nose to it.

"I'll call Will Luxan and tell him I'll be away from work for a while. He won't ask questions, he never does. He's a good man."

"I expect he is," Watchman said. "I also expect he knows more about Joe than he's willing to tell me."

"He might talk to me. I'll ask him on the phone. Where can I reach you if I find out anything?"

"I'll have to reach you," he said. He got the scratch pad from the phone stand and scribbled on it. "That's my partner. If you need anything that's his home number. During the day you can leave a message for him at Highway Patrol headquarters. I think you'd better stick close to this house until we've got things straightened out up here."

"I get the feeling you're beginning to believe me about Joe," she said. "I hope it isn't just because of—sleeping together."

He shook his head. "It's because I trust you."

She was sitting across the table from him. Her eyes squeezed out tears very abruptly and she reached for his hand. "I think that's the nicest thing anybody's said to me in a hell of a long time," she said and then she began to blubber. "Look at me, I can't stop!"

He laughed at her.

2.

On the phone Wilder said, "God damn it this isn't a homicide investigation. Just find the son of a bitch. Let his lawyer worry about whether he got a raw deal."

Watchman was a little angry. "There are *guns* going off, man. People are going to get hurt."

"Why? Because somebody took a warning shot to scare you off the Reservation? Come off it, they may be tough

‡ 123 ‡

up there but they're not killers. They gave up massacring wagon trains a hundred years ago."

"You don't get this," Watchman said stubbornly. "Joe Threepersons has a rifle. Now why would a man get himself a rifle unless he had it in mind to shoot somebody?"

"You said yourself he's hiding in the hills up there. Living off a few cans of food. He's probably figuring to shoot himself some game. Besides, a lot of those guys would rather go down shooting than get arrested. It doesn't mean he's out to murder somebody."

"I think it does. I think he took the rap for the real killer and for some reason he thinks that real killer murdered his wife and son and now he's up here with a rifle waiting to get his sights on the killer. And I think he's got a pretty good chance of doing it if we don't find the killer first."

"Or find Threepersons first. But that's assuming I buy your story right off the shelf, which I don't. You're basing your whole theory on what the man's own sister tells you. My God, Sam."

"She's telling the truth."

"Why? Because you can't find it in your heart to believe she'd lie to you? Christ the girl must be a hell of a siren."

Watchman let air into the phone booth. "Let's put it this way. I think my best chance of finding Threepersons fast is to reopen the original murder case. Will that satisfy you?"

"Nuts. Even if it's all true the trail's stone cold."

"I doubt it. Those people don't move around much. Whoever it was, he's still there. Otherwise Joe wouldn't be there."

Wilder took a deep breath. "Sam you tracked Leo Hargit through a full-out blizzard. You ought to be able to track one half-witted Indian to his hidey-hole in those hills. You know where he was last night when he took a potshot at you. Follow the sonofabitch's tracks, find him, bring him in. We'll question him and see about the rest of this. Now that's your job and those are your orders and I don't want to see your God damned red face again until you've got handcuffs on him."

3.

Buck Stevens' voice hammered his ear through the telephone. "Well where does this get you, this autopsy business?"

Watchman said, "You don't self-administer a massive dose of barbiturates and then take your kid and get in the car and go out and drive into a truck on the highway."

"People commit suicide on the highway all the time."

"But they don't drug themselves to the gills first."

"I wouldn't swear to that. Who knows what people will do."

Watchman said, "You searched the house, right? You didn't find any barbiturates."

"Maybe she threw the bottle away after she took all the pills."

"Call her doctor. Find out if he ever gave her a prescription for the stuff."

"What'll that prove?"

"It'll prove something if she had no prescription. It'll mean somebody else put the stuff in her grapefruit juice or her coffee."

"Somebody else. You're thinking about that Volkswagen that was at her house that morning."

"Yes."

"And you think somebody tried to murder her with drugs."

"It looks like it to me. And when she started to feel

‡ 125 ‡

herself go under she knew what had happened so she tried to drive to the hospital. The drugs hit her too fast and she didn't make it."

"Why take the kid?"

"Somebody's trying to kill you, you don't leave your kid behind in an empty house."

"But I thought you said this Victorio was in love with her. Would he murder her?"

"I don't have answers to everything, Buck. If I did the case would be solved." Watchman had his notes in front of him on the phone-booth shelf. "Victorio's not the only man in the world who owns a blue Volkswagen."

"Then you're right back to square one."

"Not quite. It just enlarges the circle of suspects."

"It still doesn't make sense to me. You're saying she was murdered. Now if you were the guy who supposedly killed Calisher in the first place—the guy Joe was taking the rap for—presumably you agreed to support Joe's family in style while Joe went to jail for you. You're assuming that was the deal, aren't you?"

"It's one way to explain why Maria and Joe Junior got rich right after Joe went to prison. Somebody was paying the bills and she didn't have a regular boyfriend, not the kind who could pay her bills the way they were paid. Look at it from Joe's point of view. He's always been a loser. He's living out there in a line shack watching his kid grow into a duplicate of himself. He must have decided his own life was pretty well wasted, it was too late for him to make something of himself, but wouldn't it be great if the kid had a crack at a good education and all the frills. Somebody knew him well enough to offer him the deal —his own freedom in exchange for all the things he wanted money to buy for his son."

"But it doesn't explain why anybody would want to screw up the whole thing by killing Maria. They kill

Maria, they've got to expect trouble from Joe. He wouldn't go on keeping his mouth shut and taking the rap."

"That's two questions. I think I can answer both of them," Watchman said. "Question one, why did they kill Maria. What if she got greedy, decided to blackmail them, held out for more money than they'd agreed to? If they felt she was getting too expensive or too risky, they might kill her. But that brings us to question two. As soon as they kill Maria they've got to expect trouble. Joe wouldn't automatically react to the news by breaking out of slam. More likely they'd expect him to go to the police and tell them everything he knew about the case. So it only makes sense one way. If they helped Joe break out of jail, so that they could get at him. To kill him. Wipe him and Maria and the kid off the books, all at the same time."

Stevens said, "Then it's not just that Joe's out gunning for this killer. The killer's also gunning for Joe. Maybe setting a trap and waiting for Joe to walk into it."

"And Joe doesn't know anything about it."

"It's farfetched," Stevens said.

"Most things people do are far fetched."

"Well where do we go from here?"

"I keep hunting around here in Whiteriver. You go down to Florence and find out if Joe had any outside contacts the day Maria died—visitors, phone calls, telegrams, anything. Keep digging until you get us a name."

"That's assuming the name belongs to the guy that helped him break out. That's the theory?"

"I'm taking an option on it. Maybe even a down payment. When we find out more we'll know if we're ready to buy it."

"And you're staying in Whiteriver."

"Aeah," Watchman said. "I think I'll find out if the department's willing to spring for a couple of hounds and a handler. Try and nail Joe before the shooting starts."

‡ 127 ‡

"Dogs. Where's the fun in that?"

"It's not a game," Watchman murmured.

4.

He coaxed the ailing Volvo into Whiteriver at one in the afternoon after a fruitless half-day of scouting and found the dog handler waiting at the trading post with three mournful hounds in his camper-pickup. The handler introduced himself, "Leroy Flagg," and gave Watchman a smile as doleful as a Basset's. "I hate man-trackin', it ain't natural sport."

"It could save somebody's life," Watchman said and saw a kid in a bright crimson shirt wobbling up the road on a bike. The flash of color drew his eyes in that direction and he saw the screened back door of the council house fly open.

Tom Victorio came through the door quickly, his drug-store-cowboy jacket awry; he was waving in Watchman's direction and ran toward him full of excitement.

"He showed up. He was here."

"Joe?"

"Last night." Victorio was a little out of breath. "He busted into Rufus Limita's house."

"Anybody hurt?"

"No—no. But he ripped off Rufus' best rifle. And the Land Cruiser."

Watchman made a face. "What time last night?"

"Two, two-thirty. Pete Porvo said——"

"Hang onto it a minute." Watchman turned to Leroy Flagg and spread his hands. "I'm sorry we wasted your time."

"It's okay, I'll get hourly and mileage for it. Just as soon not have to man-track anyway. Nice meeting you." Flagg shook hands and climbed into the pickup.

Watchman turned back to Victorio. "You want a Coke?" He went up the trading post steps without waiting an answer.

Victorio hurried in after him. "What's the matter with you?"

"If he's been gone eleven hours another five minutes won't make much difference. Maybe you'd like to calm down and tell me what happened. Want a Coke?"

"Root beer."

Watchman bought a couple of cans and they carried them outside. They talked in the car.

"Where's this Limita's place?"

"About six miles. Take the road down toward Fort Apache, hang a left where it says East Fork."

"Anybody home right now?"

"I suppose so."

Watchman got it started and pulled out of the lot. "Okay, what happened?"

"Why'd you send those dogs away?"

"You can't track a car with dogs. You said he stole a car."

"Toyota. One of those four-wheel-drive jobs."

"Well then." The road unwound through the trees and went past the silent rodeo grounds. The pavement was chipping away at the edges from frosts and flash floods. Watchman said, "Anybody actually see Joe to recognize him?"

"Pete Porvo saw him."

"In the Land Cruiser?"

"Naw, it was before. He was on foot, lugging a rifle and a gunnysack. Pete says he was driving up this road here and he saw Joe plain as day going into those trees back there, the ones we just came through."

"But he lost him in the dark."

"Yes. This is where you turn left."

Watchman downshifted for the corner and went hustling

up into the hills on the dirt road. Bits of gravel thumped the undersides of the fenders like buckshot. The road followed the side of the creek, in and out of the line of trees. They passed the occasional wickiup, corrals, here and there a dusty house trailer up on chocks.

"Now that's funny when you think about it," Victorio said.

"What is?"

"If he already had a rifle why'd he steal one of Rufus' guns?"

"Let's find out what kind of rifle it was." Watchman shot a quick sidewise glance at him. "Have you got a prescription for Seconal?"

"Huh?"

"It'd be easy to check," Watchman warned.

"What the hell would I be doing with Seconal?"

"You paid a few visits to Maria while Joe was away, didn't you."

Victorio went silent for a while. There was a bit of pout on his face. Finally he said, "Yeah."

"But you didn't get anywhere with her."

"She was trying to do a brother-and-sister number."

"And you didn't like that."

"It wasn't exactly what I had in mind," Victorio admitted. "But I had to settle for it, it was all she'd go for. The first time I went down there I really wanted to see what I could do to help. But I took one look at that place of hers and I could see she wasn't the one who needed help."

"Who was paying for that, Tom?"

"She wouldn't tell me."

"Somebody was grubstaking her."

"Sure, I could see that. But every time I tried to ask questions she'd turn me off like a faucet."

"You must have made a few guesses."

"I figured she had a boyfriend she wasn't talking about."

"Is that a fact."

Victorio's face swiveled toward him. "What's that supposed to mean?"

"You're not the kind of guy who'd take it quietly if you thought she had some other man. It must have made you a little sore."

"Sure I was sore. Who wouldn't be?"

"You'd have tried to find out who the boyfriend was."

Victorio's lips peeled back from his teeth; it wasn't a smile. "Matter of fact one time I spent a whole God damned two weeks driving down there every night after work and hanging around outside her place like some kind of peeping Tom. But nobody ever showed up."

"So you just gave up?"

"I kept trying to worm it out of her. But it wasn't easy to rattle Maria. She was one of those people, you know, sometimes they're so damned self-confident they make you grit your teeth. There just wasn't any way to shake her up. That was one of the things I guess I loved her for—she wasn't your average hysterical female. This is the place, you drive in the gate here."

Victorio pointed and Watchman turned off the dirt road into a narrow drive with tufts of grass growing on the ridge between the ruts. The suspension clanked once or twice.

It was one of those outfits that accrued structures over the generations. There must have been a half dozen ramshackle buildings—wickiups and shacks—and there were a windmill and two sagging corrals and a profusion of wheeled vehicles in various states of collapse. Chickens and dogs ran loose in the caked hardpan of the yard and five small children played in the trees under the guardianship of two obese women who sat in the shade gossiping.

Getting out of the car Watchman said, "Limita's a medicine man, isn't he?"

"That's right." Victorio turned to look at two of the

shacks alternately and scowled. "I've only been here a couple times, I don't remember which one he lives in."

A butterfly chopped heavily across Watchman's line of sight. A squat figure appeared at the larger shack, the one under the cottonwoods, came out and let the screen door flap shut behind him.

"That's him." Victorio waved and walked around the hood of the car. Watchman went up to the shack with him.

Rufus Limita wore mud-crusted boots and limp khaki pants and an old tee-shirt, its fabric strained by his out-thrust belly. His face was almost a perfect square with a big triangular nose in the middle. He had a wide mouth and amiable eyes overhung by fierce shaggy brows. He was probably in his sixties and couldn't have been much more than five feet tall. His legs were bowed into parenthetical arcs and if the bones had been straight he might have been four inches taller.

Victorio made the introductions with the peculiar respect that elders like Limita commanded. Limita shook his hand and said, "Somebody sure made it bad luck for that boy Joe."

"Did you see him yourself?"

"No, no. That boy is still a pretty good Innun, maybe you don't see him unless he wants you to. But he set the dogs to ruckus, so I know somebody was here, I got up right away and look around. He got my good rifle I guess. Anyhow that time I heard the Land Cruiser start up. I went out but he went away in my Land Cruiser."

Limita held the screen door open and followed them inside. There were good rugs on the floor and the furniture was old but sturdy, some of it handmade of lumber from the tribal sawmill. One wall had a tall gun rack on it and one of its slots was empty; the others were filled with expensive hunting rifles that had been taken care of with knowing attention: their steel gleamed with oil.

Watchman said, "Do you know how much gas was in the tank?"

"I keep them full, all times. Got my own tank pump out there in my yard."

That was a bad break; a full tank would give Joe a hell of a working radius. Watchman approached the gun rack. "This rifle he took."

"That boy sure knows guns. That sure was the best elk rifle I ever had."

"Elk," Watchman said and turned slowly to face him. "Big game rifle, then."

"Sure. Three-seventy-five magnum."

"Jesus," Victorio said. "That's a God damn elephant gun."

Watchman had his notebook. "Weatherby?"

"No," Limita said. "She's a Winchester Model Seventy."

Watchman knew the model. A precision-made bolt-action rifle, high-priced and worth it. "Any telescope?"

"You bet," Limita said. "Eight power Bushnell."

Victorio was standing there with his eyes squeezed shut as if in great pain. "Good God."

If you knew the drill you could reach out and pluck the life from a man half a mile away from you with a rifle like that. And Watchman already had firsthand evidence of the quality of Joe's marksmanship. The shooting last night had sounded like a medium caliber, probably a standard old .30-30 Joe must have swiped somewhere.

Victorio talked quietly out of the side of his mouth. "Man that's an assassin's rifle. He's not out to bag an elk with it."

Watchman said to Limita, "Do you have the license number of the Land Cruiser?" Not that it would likely do any good; of all the cars in Limita's yard Joe had selected the cross-country four-wheel-drive vehicle and that meant he didn't intend to drive too far on the highway.

"I gave it to Pete Porvo that time," Limita said. "But I think it is writ down someplace here." He had an old school desk in the corner; he pried up its lid and pawed through papers, taking a frayed tally-book out and setting it aside. "Maybe Pete took it with him but I think he give it back to me."

Watchman spoke to Victorio in a voice too low to carry across the room to the old man. "You mind waiting outside for me?"

Victorio resented the rebuff but went out. His shoulders were very stiff.

Watchman approached the desk. "Some folks think Maria Threepersons was witched, Mr. Limita. She died last week you know."

"I heard about that." Limita looked up at him and then resumed rummaging in the dog-eared slips of paper.

"Do you think she was witched?"

"Sure, it could happen you know."

"Who would want to witch Maria?"

"I don't know who was doing that to her."

"Do you know anybody who might have had a reason to?"

"Maybe lots of folks don't like that boy Joe. But I don't know who could want to hurt his wife like that. Maybe her own people, those San Carlos kin. I guess they got witches down there too."

"Did Joe know about your rifle collection before he went to prison?"

"Sure. That boy I took him deer hunt two, three times."

"He's a good shot, I hear."

"He is sure a good one. That time I seen him shoot some real long bullets. Good hands on Joe."

Watchman glanced toward the door. "You think maybe Tom there might have had anything against Maria?"

"Maybe so, but that boy's too young for witching. A

‡ 134 ‡

man got to grow up before he get the power." Limita found the car registration. "This is your paper."

Watchman copied down the license number. "Thank you."

"That boy Joe been that way since he was just a boy. Sometimes he drink all the time, even his baby go hungry. Even when folks give him money he spend it on drink. He was crazy to do things like that. You should watch out, I think. He took some cold beer out of my springhouse down there on the creek."

"Thanks for the warning."

"You stay away, then. You get close to that boy he might hurt you."

Watchman smiled; that had been what the old man was leading up to. They all had their own ways of telling him to leave Joe alone.

5.

Victorio was waiting in the Volvo. Watchman shook Rufus Limita's hand and drove out of the yard. The shocks bottomed on the same bumps again. Pretty quick he was going to have to make a big decision: spend a small fortune renovating the old clunker or buy another car.

Victorio said, "Rifle like that, Joe sure as hell doesn't aim to get caught alive."

"That's not why he took that gun."

"No?"

"You said yourself it's an assassin's rifle." Watchman steered onto the dirt road and headed down toward the fork. "He's got it in mind to put somebody away."

"Who?"

"Whoever killed Maria."

"*Killed* Maria?"

"She was murdered."

Victorio stared at him. "Maybe you'd better repeat that for the benefit of the West Coast audience."

"Somebody fed her enough barbiturates to knock out five people."

"I thought she crashed a car."

"She crashed because the Seconals put her to sleep at the wheel."

Either Victorio was a far better actor than he appeared to be or the news did come as a surprise to him.

Watchman said, "You were there that morning, weren't you."

"I was where?"

"Maria's house. A little while before she died."

"The hell I was. Who told you that?"

"Your car was there."

"That's a lie. This was last Tuesday?"

"Monday. Fourth of July. It was a holiday. You weren't in your office."

"Wrong. That's exactly where I was. All morning. I had a brief to finish. And I had my car there and I'm pretty sure I had the keys in my pocket the whole time. You're barking up the wrong tree—I never left Whiteriver that day. We had a rodeo that afternoon and I was there. I was one of the bronc handlers. You ask anybody."

"That was afternoon. You had time to get back from Phoenix by then. Who saw you in the office?"

Victorio thought about it. "Nobody, I guess. Like you said it was a holiday. But somebody might have noticed my car. I always park it there between the council house and the trading post. Everybody knows my car."

"Anybody else around here drive a blue VW?"

"Not that I know of. There's a lot of them around but not right in town."

"Well nobody's arresting you yet," Watchman said. "But somebody killed her. You're right up at the head of the list."

"If I'm such a hot suspect why are you telling me all this?"

"Think about it, you'll figure it out."

He turned the car onto the paved road and picked it up to forty-five heading back up toward the sawmill. Beside him in the bucket seat Victorio sat as tense as a runner in the starting chocks. "It's a frame. A lousy frame. Somebody lied to you. I wasn't anyplace Monday morning, I was in the office. I can show you the brief."

"Sure."

"I think I get it. You figure if I killed Maria then Joe's gunning for *me*. I'm supposed to get scared and confess everything so you'll put me in protective custody."

"Well the idea crossed my mind," Watchman agreed. "How about it?"

"I didn't kill her. For Christ sake I've been in love with Maria since I was in pre-law."

"You told me you were sore at her."

"You murder everybody you get sore at?"

Watchman smiled with one side of his mouth. He saw Victorio's right hand reach the dashboard handgrip and flex around it. Victorio said, "You know what worries me now? Suppose Joe heard the same lie about me and my car? Suppose he thinks it was me? Then he *could* be after me with that damn elephant cannon of Rufus'."

"He sure could."

"Son of a bitch," Victorio breathed.

Watchman drove into town and made the turn at the corner by the council house and pulled into the lot behind it. He parked right beside the blue Volkswagen. Dwight Kendrick's Corvette was farther back in the shade. Over against the trading post wall were parked several cars and one of them was Charles Rand's high silver-grey Rolls Bentley.

Victorio said, distracted, "That's Charlie Rand's."

"I know. Slumming?"

"He was due in today to talk a deal with the council." Victorio sat with his hand tight on the grip even though the car was motionless.

"When's the case due to come up in court?"

"It's already been postponed a dozen times."

"By Rand?"

"Usually. Sometimes we have to ask for a continuance ourselves."

"I thought the tribe wanted to wrap it up as soon as possible."

"Things aren't that simple. It's all juggling and maneuvering. You don't want to go into court at a time that's advantageous to the opposition. Hell a few months ago somebody rifled our files, we lost a lot of papers and practically had to start again from scratch. We've been stalling like mad until we can get the information together again."

"What kind of information was it?"

"Nothing vital. Stuff like references to obscure cases that were tried seventy-five years ago in places like Montana and the Canal Zone. You have to marshal all the precedents. It's boring as hell."

"And somebody stole your notes?"

"Notes, briefs, transcripts, the whole mess."

"Was the theft investigated?"

"Sure. The Agency cops and the County both. Somebody'd pried that window over there. They busted into the filing cabinets and took half a drawer of files."

"Did they steal anything else or just the water-rights materials?"

"Just that stuff. They knew what to look for. It was

Rand's boys of course, but try proving that." Victorio's eyes came around to Watchman. He looked bleak. "I can't help it, I keep thinking about that gamy son of a bitch out there lining up his crosshairs on the back of my neck."

"Tell me something," Watchman said. "How good was your alibi for the night Ross Calisher died?"

"Alibi? Why the hell should I need an alibi?"

"Because somebody killed him. It wasn't Joe."

"It wasn't?"

"I'm pretty sure he was taking the rap for somebody else. Knowingly."

Victorio stared at him, the expression not changing at all; as if his face were frozen. Finally he licked his lips. "So that's how she got that money."

"That's the way I tote it."

"You know that does make a morbid kind of sense."

"Joe was in Cibecue the night Calisher was shot. Does that help?"

"You mean where was I? Hell I was in Tucson. Law school."

"It's only four, five hours' drive from Tucson up to Rand's ranch. Calisher was killed late at night. You could have driven up there, killed him, driven back to Tucson and made your morning classes."

"Why the hell should I kill Calisher?"

"I have no idea," Watchman said.

"Only an amateur tries to make facts fit a theory," Victorio said. "You could be right that Joe didn't kill him, but that doesn't mean I did. Christ I don't think I ever met Ross Calisher more than two or three times in my life, and those times it was only at rodeos up here."

"The way you felt about Maria, you might have been just as jealous as Joe if you found out she was sleeping with Calisher."

"To tell you the truth I never bought that story about

her having an affair with Calisher. She wasn't like that."

"Reverend LaSalle thinks she was just about the fastest thing on wheels."

"LaSalle's got the imagination of a horny old maid. Maria was fast with her lip, she annoyed a lot of people around here because she liked to talk back when she thought it was called for. Sure she had wit, but she didn't sleep around."

Watchman glanced at the Volkswagen beside him. "The truth is I don't think you're guilty of anything except brass. I don't see where you had much reason to want Calisher dead, I don't see how you could have killed Maria, and I don't know where you'd have found the kind of money Maria was living on. But somebody saw a blue VW parked outside her house that morning and I still need an explanation for that."

"I'll damn sure find out what I can, if Joe doesn't bushwhack me first."

"I don't think it's you he's after."

"Jesus I hope you're right."

6.

Watchman got out of the car and heard Victorio shut the other door. Two white-garbed nuns in sailboat hats walked out of the trading post and got into a huge station wagon and drove away. The wagon's place was taken almost immediately by the white Ford of the Indian Agency Police Force. Pete Porvo got out and walked into the trading post and Watchman turned that way; he felt Victorio's presence at his heels.

He hadn't put his boot onto the first step yet when a ruined pickup came staggering down the highway and he stopped and put his eyes on it while it went past. Jimmy

Oto was driving; Oto's hard glance fixed itself onto Watchman and stayed there, the head turning, until the grey truck almost went off the road. Then Oto was gone and Victorio behind him said, "Him you want to stay away from in dark alleys."

"We've met."

"You're lucky you've still got your teeth then."

Watchman pushed into the gloom of the store. He found Porvo at the sandwich counter. The high small eyes whipped across Watchman's face and settled on Victorio.

Watchman said, "Any sign of that Land Cruiser?"

"Nope."

Victorio said, "We just came in from Rufus' place."

"That right?"

Watchman said, "I understand you spotted Joe last night."

"What about it?" Porvo stood phlegmatically rocking heel-to-toe.

"Did you try to stop him?"

Porvo's eyes crinkled to show he knew Watchman was kidding him. "Come on."

"How about it, Pete?"

Porvo's face changed. "What the hell are you trying to pull?"

"I just want to know what you did, Pete. Did you yell out to him? Did you fire a warning shot and tell him to halt?"

"You're crazy. By the time I got the car stopped he was back out of sight in the woods someplace. You think yelling and shooting's going to do any good?"

"Did you take a flashlight and run in there after him?"

"The son of a bitch was toting a rifle. You want me to go in after him with a *flashlight*?"

Victorio was looking on, puzzled. Watchman said, "You had him in sight, you let him go. It was the middle of the night. So if he was close enough for you to recognize him he might have been close enough to stop. That's all I'm asking you."

"If I could've stopped him I would have. That satisfy you?"

"It'll do for right now. I had a shot at him myself, I know how it goes."

Victorio said, "You did?"

"It's a long story."

Porvo finished his sandwich and crumpled the wax paper as if it were Watchman's throat. "Look, porcupine, I don't need Navajos telling me how to do my job."

"Take it easy. My dad was an Agency cop."

"This still ain't Window Rock. This is my bailiwick, Watchman. I wouldn't mind for you to get in some real trouble sticking your Navajo nose in it."

"I didn't come up here to muss up your turf, Pete. All I want is Joe Threepersons."

"Look," Porvo said, "I believe in my job here. It's a lot better to keep house inside the tribe than have outside agitators come in here and stomp law-and-order all over us. Now I told you before—I find Joe, I'll give him to you. In the meantime you can quit pushing your weight around here." He turned on his heel and marched out of the building.

Watchman turned mildly to Victorio. "You want some lunch?"

"You're just a beaming ray of sunshine, aren't you?"

"Deep water is for those who can swim. I think Porvo's making a mistake, taking this too lightly. The next time he comes across Joe he might get shot before he decides whether he should wave hello or pull his gun."

"You're expecting too much. Pete's an Agency cop, his jurisdiction's limited to traffic cases and misdemeanors that don't carry a penalty of more than six months in jail.

The big stuff they leave to the County Sheriff. You can't expect him to know his way around a murder case."

"I can expect him to know his way around this Reservation. If anybody'd know where to look for Joe it would be that cop. I'd like to find a way to reach him."

"You won't do it by insulting him. Pete's kind of proud. He likes that uniform and he likes to think he can fill it."

Watchman considered the selection of sandwiches. "Maybe you're right. But with his kind you don't grovel. I figure he understands authority. It's probably the only way I can break through that Navajo-hate of his."

"Just don't expect too much," Victorio said again. "I mean you *are* a Navajo after all. Try the corn beef, it ain't too bad."

They took the sandwiches out on the porch and ate standing up in the shade beside the phone booth. Watchman said, "This Jimmy Oto. Tell me about him."

"What's he got to do with anything?"

"I don't know yet. Maybe nothing. But he was pretty anxious to scare me off the Reservation last night. He had some anxious-looking friends with him."

"That rat pack of his, I guess. I wouldn't pay him too much mind. He likes to ripple his muscles."

"What do you know about him?"

"He used to be a pal of Joe's. I don't know if he still is. Maria couldn't stand him, wouldn't let Joe hang around with him."

"I understand he hasn't got a job."

"Well he's on welfare, I think, some kind of relief. He's sort of got a job, if you could call it that. You know about Harlan Natagee and that red-power movement of his?"

"Nothing except the name."

"They're kind of extremist. That's a big family, the Natagees. Frank Natagee, he's the chairman of the Tribal Council."

"Then that's where I heard the name."

"Well Harlan is Frank Natagee's brother. They don't speak to each other. Harlan's sort of the black sheep of the family. Some folks say he's a sorcerer."

"A witch."

"Yes. Harlan used to live over in Oklahoma for a while. He made a lot of money, trading oil leases or something like that. Came back here eight or ten years ago with a pile of money and sank a lot of it into stuff like the sawmill and the cattle co-ops. He's helped the tribe a lot but folks walk wide around him. You could call him the local homegrown robber baron. Full of crazy notions how to deal with Anglos. I kind of think he wouldn't mind restoring the good old white institution of scalping."

"How much support does he have?"

"Not a hell of a lot. He's got his pack of kids and a few half-grown toughs like Jimmy Oto—they do what Harlan tells them."

"Like for instance?"

"Well Charlie Rand's had a few troubles up on his ranch —brush fires, busted fences, that kind of harassment. Everybody knows it's Harlan's rat pack doing it."

"Just like everybody knows it was Rand who broke into your offices."

Victorio gave him an amused look. "Yeah."

"Then if Jimmy Oto's trying to warn me off, he's doing it on orders from Harlan Natagee?"

"Maybe. Don't forget Jimmy and Joe Threepersons were buddies. It could be just that." Victorio squinted out toward the mountains; after a moment he said, "I think I get the drift of what you're thinking. A lot of folks keep thinking Maria was witched. Harlan's got that reputation."

"What would he have against Maria?"

"I wouldn't know. Anyhow I don't put much store in that old crap."

‡ 144 ‡

"Sometimes it's real enough."

"You're full of surprises," Victorio told him.

"I didn't grow up white," Watchman answered. He heard the rattle of a woodpecker and looked for it but he couldn't spot it at first and that annoyed him; there had been a time when by auditory evidence alone he'd have known exactly where it was.

Victorio said something but Watchman didn't answer; he was chasing a line of thought. Joe was out there in a Land Cruiser with his .375 looking for somebody to shoot at—that was what it came down to. And Watchman couldn't think of any way to find him until Joe was ready to be found. The combined Apache Reservation covered nearly four million acres and it was all craggy country, beat up into a froth of forests and mountains and badlands. Watchman knew he could spend weeks searching every road for tread-spoor to prove where, and if, the Land Cruiser had left the road. And by that time any tracks would be blown over or washed out anyway. He was on wheels, he could be anywhere.

Watchman had a junk heap of stray pieces whose shapes suggested a design but there weren't enough pieces yet. Joe knew his target and Watchman didn't know. There didn't seem to be any way to get there first.

Watchman surveyed the dry hills. He had an image of Joe in some cottonwood draw sighting in the Bushnell 'scope.

A door squeaked and in a moment four men came walking around the far corner of the council house and turned toward the parking lot. There was a good deal of evident tension among them. Watchman recognized Charles Rand and Dwight Kendrick.

Tom Victorio said, "Charlie Rand's the one with the big hat."

"We've met."

The party reached the Bentley and Charles Rand turned to speak to the fat man at his elbow; Watchman heard about one word in five. Rand stood talking, flicking his trouser thigh with a quirt. His sunglasses reflected points of light. Self-assuredness hung like flags from his back-thrust shoulders and the restively moving square bricks of his hands, and from the quirt that moved like a baton.

"The fat guy's Dwight Kendrick's opposite number."

"Rand's lawyer?"

"Name of Owen Masterman." Victorio rubbed the inner corners of his eyes. "In a minute he'll start sneering and curling the ends of his mustache."

Masterman had no mustache. He had once been a good-looking man and would be again if he lost forty pounds. He wore dark-rim eyeglasses and his reddish hair fluffed out fashionably over the collar of his seersucker suit. There was something shabby about his aspect, as if he were consciously molding his appearance on the image of Clarence Darrow. The face belonged to a man who had seen everything and wished he hadn't. Watchman had a feeling he wasn't as flabby as he seemed. There were secret muscles hidden under the fatty tissues.

Rand said something that made the Indian behind Kendrick step forward and draw himself up like a pigeon. "Frank Natagee," Victorio murmured and Watchman nodded. The chairman of the Tribal Council raised his voice and Watchman heard him clearly:

"Don't talk about taxes and free rides any more to us. The Anglos did not give this land to our tribe. The tribe gave the land to the Anglos. The day we give up our tax exemptions will be the day you give us back the land."

Watchman saw Rand snort but didn't hear his reply; whatever his failings the arrogant industrialist wasn't a loudmouth. Masterman's fat scarlet face, dripping sweat, turned toward Kendrick as if in appeal but Kendrick said harshly, "Haven't you got enough on your plate?" and it made Charles Rand swing toward him lifting the quirt as if to strike him. Kendrick abruptly avoided Rand's eyes and Rand swiveled with an abrupt snap of his meaty shoulders and reached for the door handle of the Bentley. Masterman walked away around the back of the car while Kendrick stood there smiling dispiritedly.

Frank Natagee spoke and Kendrick shrugged without replying. Rand started the car and as soon as Masterman heaved himself into the seat Rand backed up and swung the wheel. The front tires crunched stones as the power steering wrenched them around. Kendrick stepped back just in time; the yawl growled angrily past him throwing dust.

Kendrick and Frank Natagee walked back toward the council house. They stopped by the mesquite tree at the corner and Watchman heard the Indian say, "Want us all to assimilate. What if the Russians took over this country, how long would it take Charles Rand to turn Communist?" A grin streaked the broad grave face and Natagee slapped Kendrick amiably before he strode past the tree and disappeared.

Victorio dropped off the porch and Watchman followed him; he wanted a word with Dwight Kendrick.

The tall lawyer ran fingers through his pale hair. "Hoo boy."

"Told you it'd be a waste of time," Victorio said. "He didn't give an inch, did he."

"He never will until we find a lever to push him with." Kendrick glanced at Watchman. "He can keep buying delays forever. Hell it's a game to him, the money doesn't matter, it's just a way to keep score—chips to play the game with."

"We're buying too many delays ourselves," Victorio said. "We could have had him in court a month ago."

‡ 147 ‡

"Or he could have had us. It would have been on his terms."

"We've got a stronger case than he's got."

"Tom, you've never faced Owen Masterman in a court-room."

"What's that got to do with anything?"

Kendrick said, "I imagine one fine day you'll find that out." Watchman was still standing there and Kendrick addressed him: "Did you want something?"

"I did. I still do. A couple of questions."

Kendrick looked at his watch and shot his cuff; he glanced over his shoulder as if to make sure the council house hadn't gone away somewhere. It was an unsubtle hint. But he said, "Go ahead."

"I understand you're married to Charles Rand's ex-wife."

"Ex-wife by two. What about it?"

"How many wives has he had?"

"I'm sure he's given up counting. Gwen was two wives ago."

"They were still married to each other at the time of the Calisher murder?"

"Yes. I assume you're leading somewhere with this line of questioning? Because otherwise it's in dismal taste."

"I'm just wondering if there was anything between your wife—Rand's wife at the time—and Ross Calisher. It's not a delicate question, I'm sorry: it's not a delicate case."

Kendick said, "There was nothing between Gwen and Ross Calisher. Not to put too fine a point on it, Calisher was beneath Gwen's contempt. He was a rustic, a hillbilly hick with manure on his boots and he didn't have the social graces of a skid-row derelict. He only had two virtues that I can think of, his animal husbandry and his loyalty to Charles Rand. He worshipped Rand. He was far too loyal to entertain even the fantasy of an affair with Charles Rand's wife. She'd have been untouchable, literally. Now

‡ 148 ‡

what's this line of questioning in aid of? Are you still riding that hobbyhorse about Joe's innocence? I thought your job was to track him down, not play detective."

"I'd like to find out who his enemies are," Watchman said. "That could lead us to him."

Kendrick contrived a headshaking laugh. "I don't suppose it's occurred to you that the fact that Joe looks guilty doesn't prove he was innocent."

"I thought he was your client."

"I should think even you would find it hard to get past the fact that he confessed with the murder weapon in his hand. I had a lot of trouble keeping Joe out of the gas chamber—they were still executing Indians here. After all he wasn't psychotic, he wasn't a compulsive confesser."

"Did you talk to Angelina at the time?"

· "Joe's sister? Of course I did."

"She didn't say anything about his innocence?"

"Not that I recall. She kept pleading with me to do everything I could to save him. She seemed more concerned than his wife was."

"But she didn't say anything about an alibi?"

"Alibi?" Kendrick smiled ruefully. "What's she been handing you?"

"It doesn't matter," Watchman said. "Right now the point is Joe seems to think he's got a grievance. He's got his hands on a long-distance magnum rifle with a 'scope sight and I believe he thinks he's got a reason to use it on somebody. I'd like to find out who his target is before it's too late."

"I doubt I can help you."

Watchman studied him. "It's not the kind of thing you can hold back out of professional ethics or statutory privilege. Not any more. If you know anything about this you might save somebody's life by telling me what it is."

Kendrick's mouth twisted a little. He twined his fingers

together and studied the design they made. "I don't know who Joe might have a grudge against. It could be anybody."

Watchman said, "All right. Try another one. Where did Maria Threepersons get the money she was living on?"

Kendrick frowned. "What made you ask me that?"

"What made you freeze?"

Victorio's dark eyes shifted toward Kendrick with new interest. Watchman knew he had something.

Kendrick's long fingers fanned the air by his chest. Finally he said, "The money came from me."

7.

"If this thing blows up it'll come out in the end anyway," Kendrick went on. "You'd find out I signed the checks."

Victorio was watching him with obvious bewilderment. Kendrick waved his sinuous hands at them both. "The money was put in trust for Maria Threepersons. I was the executor of the trust. Now that she's dead I suppose it dissolves and goes back to the original donor."

"I want his name," Watchman said.

"I can't give you that. Under the terms of the trust I'm expressly forbidden to divulge that. I'm sorry."

"Then get in touch with him. Tell him to come forward."

"I doubt that would do any good."

"If Joe knows who it is, he may have a rifle pointed at him right now. Tell him to identify himself—at least we can try to give him some protection."

"I'll try to get in touch with the person who established the trust. I can't promise anything."

"But Joe knows who it is, doesn't he."

"How would I know?"

"Joe was taking the rap for him. He must have know who it was."

"I'm not buying that part of it," Kendrick said.

"Not out loud, anyway. If you'd known about it you could be disbarred or maybe worse."

Kendrick's eyes narrowed. "Watch your mouth now."

"That's the point, isn't it. You can't admit you knew anything about Joe's innocence. If you had evidence that you didn't present at the trial, you could be in a lot of trouble for keeping it to yourself."

"You're out of line, Watchman."

"And you're out on a limb. I want that name."

"I can't give it to you. Look I'll put it out on the table for you, face up. I defended Joe Threepersons the best way I knew how. I did a damned good job. Any other lawyer would have lost him to a life term at best. I got him off with second-degree. It was after Joe went to prison that this person asked me to set up an anonymous trust to support Maria and the little boy. The client didn't explain any motives to me and I didn't ask—I thought it was a generous thing for the client to do. Now you won't find any malfeasance in that so let's just quit throwing raw meat on the floor."

"It must have been a sizable trust."

"What makes you say that?"

"The curio shop. The house. The private school."

Kendrick's eyes flickered. "You could find out anyway, I suppose. I received a capital sum of sixty-five thousand dollars from the client, exclusive of my own fees and commissions. Out of that we made the down payment on her house and paid the first six months of the lease on the Katchina Boutique. The fixtures and inventory were also paid for out of capital. It left something like fifty thousand dollars out of the original sixty-five, and I invested that in ten percent corporate bonds. I paid over the interest every month to Maria—it came to four-hundred-odd a month, and on top of that she had commissions on whatever she sold in the curio shop. The shop

‡ 151 ‡

was self-sustaining after the first few months. She had a good business head, she hired the help herself. The shop wasn't a fantastic success but she made a good living out of it." Kendrick spread his hands out expressively. "It wasn't a big fortune, after all. The fifty thousand dollars' capital was to revert to the client in any case. Maria was only getting the interest on it."

"It's a lot of money any way you want to cut it," Watchman said. "There's one thing you'd better think about. This client of yours could be a killer."

"You're off base a mile. The money doesn't prove Joe didn't murder Ross Calisher. There could be a dozen reasons for it, beginning with honest charity."

"Tell me something. When you come across a case of a gunshot death right after a husband-and-wife dispute, do you believe the story that it was a gun-cleaning accident?"

"What's that got to do with anything?"

"I don't like coincidences," Watchman said. "She gets the money a week after Joe goes to prison."

"Well Joe couldn't support her from prison. Of course there's that connection. It doesn't prove a thing about his innocence or guilt."

"Maybe it doesn't to you. But that client of yours could end up dead within the next few days or maybe the next few hours if you don't give me a name."

"I'll get in touch with the client. That's all I can do. I can't say a word without the client's permission."

"I hope you don't end up explaining that to the client's corpse." Watchman turned on his heel and tramped to the Volvo.

Victorio trotted to catch up. When Watchman looked past him Kendrick was gone. Victorio said, "Man I want to talk to you."

"You've been doing that all day."

"I didn't know anything about that trust fund. It changes

things. Look, why don't we run over to the Arrow, I'll buy us a beer."

8.

The one-armed barkeep sat on a stool at the end of the bar with a fingernail inserted in his nostril. He was very carefully not looking in Watchman's direction.

Victorio appeared from the men's room feeling for the top of his zipper. He called down the length of the bar: "You want another firewater?"

Watchman nodded and inhaled the fumes of his nearly empty beer. It was all surmise. He wanted to believe Angelina but her word was unsupported; she might have seen Joe that night in Cibecue but suppose her watch had been an hour slow? Kendrick was right: there could be any number of explanations for the trust fund, half of them unconnected with Calisher's death. Joe had confessed and produced the murder weapon. Everything else was hearsay and the people who talked to Watchman had attitudes that were colored by their feelings for or against Joe; either way they would naturally tend to make pinks red and greys black.

But he kept coming back to the original proposition because it accounted for the facts, even if it was full of holes. It explained a lot of things that otherwise looked like coincidence. Coincidences offened Watchman's sense of orderliness. If Joe weren't innocent there were too many of them to explain: the coincidence that brought money to Maria when Joe went to prison; the coincidence that sprung Joe efficiently from Florence less than thirty-six hours after Maria's death; the coincidence that connected Joe Threepersons to three murders, at least two of which he could not possibly have committed; the coincidence that placed a .375 magnum in Joe's hands at a time when everything else suggested he had escaped and armed himself in order to avenge the deaths of his wife and son.

There could have been any number of explanations but if you had to put your money on just one of them it had to be Angelina's theory. From that it followed that Joe was not hiding up. He wasn't the quarry, he was the hunter; he wouldn't disappear into a hidden lair, he'd come out. He'd come out shooting.

The incestuousness of the past was disturbing: all the people, ostensibly enemies, who kept crossing paths in the Threepersons case. Kendrick marrying Charlie Rand's ex-wife. Calisher maybe sleeping with Joe's wife. Harlan Natagee, the alleged sorcerer, sending his red-power thugs out to harass Rand while Rand allegedly sent his own thugs to rifle Kendrick's files. Angelina seeing Joe and Maria at Cibecue when Joe insisted he had been shooting Ross Calisher in a place two hours' drive from there. Boundaries and water rights; reds and whites. Maria: level-headed and ambitious, or tart and fast as a doxy? Joe Threepersons: a red man with a white job, and the victim of both worlds. It was taking a long time to accrete an impression of Joe: a young man gone to seed, clinging to the hem of hope and watching the fabric crumble away upon the death of Maria and Joe Junior. A savage killer bent on brutal revenge? Or a confused man hiding in the mountains battling his own conscience?

Victorio sat down and pushed a fresh beer in front of him. "I hate a noisy silence."

Pools of poor light fell into the room from the nicked wall-lamps and the red discs in the ceiling. The place was gloomy and empty with a stale late-afternoon silence.

"It comes down to money," Victorio said. "You see that. The sixty-five thousand."

"You're talking about Charles Rand, aren't you."

"Anybody else around here got that kind of money? Don't you see how it fits together, man?"

Watchman considered the beer. "If your people are anything like my people they don't talk about how much money they've got salted away. Unless they haven't got any, then you hear about it. People like Will Luxan, Harlan Natagee, that medicine man, what's his name?"

"Rufus Limita?"

Watchman nodded. "They've probably got cash socked away somewhere. Not every red man on a Reservation is dirt poor. It's bad form to show it, that's all."

"How come you don't want to believe it's Rand? It's got to be Rand, damn it." Victorio's head moved quickly with his impatient talk; strands of black hair had come loose of his headband and fell over his eye.

Watchman said, "Think about it. If the money man was Charles Rand he'd hardly choose Dwight Kendrick to be his executor."

Victorio's eyes brightened and then shifted away; he scowled. "God knows I'd love to see something pinned on that son of a bitch Rand." Victorio drained his beer and wiped his upper lip. "Maybe he found Calisher in the wrong bed. Gwen slept around."

"Where'd you hear that?"

"God knows. You know how rumors are."

"She was having an affair with Kendrick before she divorced Rand, I gather."

"Maybe. I don't know. The first I knew of it was after she got the divorce. After that Kendrick started dating her, and they got married about a year or a year and a half later. Actually I don't think Rand knew about it at the time. But what's that got to do with this? Gwen could have been sleeping with Calisher too."

"A little while ago you were just as eager to see Joe's head in that basket."

Victorio grinned. "Yeah, I guess I was."

"How far would you go to help?"

"Help what? Find Joe or clear him?"

"One may lead to the other."

Victorio shook his head. "I don't know any more about it than you do but I guess I'd be willing to try. I keep remembering that yarn you heard about my car being down there that morning in front of Maria's house. If Joe heard the same yarn you heard it still could be me he's gunning for." He felt the knot of his necktie and poked his jaw forward to stretch his throat against his collar.

Watchman pushed his chair back and stood. "Let's go talk to Jimmy Oto."

"Me?"

"He knows you."

"I doubt that means much. You ever see a bulldozer shoving rocks over military graves in the movies? That's Jimmy."

"I'm not asking you to hold my hand. But he might say something to you that he wouldn't say to me."

"I doubt it. But if you say so."

9.

Watchman filled the Volvo at Will Luxan's pumps and Victorio told him where to drive: back into Whiteriver and then left up a dirt-road fork. "You may not believe it when you see where he lives. It's where the local derelicts go when they go slumming."

"Things weren't all that rich where I grew up, either."

Victorio went on as if he hadn't heard. "Babies dying with sores on their mouths. You know eight Apaches have starved to death on this Reservation in the past ten years and five of them lived up here in Cuncon. They get in hock to the trading post, up to their asses, and once they get too far in the hole the store won't let them buy anything except for cash. It used to be you could always count on your relatives but that was before welfare. And the old ones that haven't got any family left and can't read the welfare forms to fill them out—they're the ones you find by the smell. Man it breaks your heart. The Indian Bureau gets that damned appropriation from Congress every year, a thousand dollars for every Indian in the country, and it all ends up in some white crook's pocket and these people starve to death. You know the life expectancy down here? Forty-six years."

"That's some better than the Navajos."

"Cuncon," Victorio said. "You know what Cuncon means?"

"No."

"Big shit." Victorio laughed out of the side of his mouth. "No shit. It means big shit. Except in the anthropology books, they call it large feces."

"Sure."

"In the old days the people up there shat big turds because they had plenty to eat. The soil was damned good, they had all kinds of corn and pumpkins and stuff. But that was because they didn't farm it full time. Right now you can't even grow cactus up there, it's right down to sand and bedrock. But those *Twagaidn* clans never moved away from there." Victorio was talking from the gut and his speech was beginning to lose its veneer of law-school polish; the cadences were older, he sounded more like an Apache.

He seemed to realize it; he twisted the side of his mouth defensively. "Anyhow you want to look out when we get out of the car. It's the kind of dump where you can end up in a garbage can with a pleat in your skull."

The road narrowed and deteriorated. Past the last valley

farms it climbed into dry hills. It went north for a mile, the car's elongated shadow racing alongside, and then turned past the back of a hogback ridge until the Volvo lost the race and the shadow was out ahead. "Jesus," Victorio said, "you think this heap's going to hold together?"

"I pray a lot about that. It's beginning to sound like a busted shock absorber to me."

The road went through a roller-coaster dip and climbed between the shoulders of eroded hills; half a mile farther it entered a narrow climbing canyon, clinging to a shelf against one steep wall.

"Next bend's a killer, you might want to tap your horn."

The road curled slowly along the side of the cliff and swung abruptly out of sight three hundred yards ahead. Watchman shifted down into second. Victorio pointed past him to the left. "You can see Cuncon down there now."

Beyond the bend the opposite ridge had crumbled away in prehistoric time, leaving a wide cut through which could be seen a tilted dusty table of earth. Maybe a dozen wickiups were scattered around; their condition looked wretched. It seemed ten degrees hotter up here but that was probably visual, the reflex association of heat with barren dust: nothing bigger than weeds grew among the rocks anywhere in sight.

Coming up on the bend Watchman hooted twice and listened for an answer; there was none and he put the car dead-slow into the bend, lugging it in second. Hairpin was hardly a word for it; the road virtually doubled back on itself along a steep downward tilt.

He glanced to his right through the windshield, halfway through the turn. Something glittered at him from the tumble of rocks four hundred feet below.

He braked, stopped, set the emergency, got out and walked to the lip of the bend.

The tracks showed where it had gone over. For a moment he had lost sight of it but he found it again by taking two slow side steps; the sun winked off the broken glass and that drew his eyes.

The battered steel had crumpled a great deal and was not very different in color from the drab rocks around it. What had made him stop the car was the square-cornered shape of the tailgate, sticking up at an odd angle. The cab had been crushed almost flat and one wheel, complete with tire, lay twenty feet away on a flat rock.

It had come to rest more or less right side up but it had tumbled several times getting there. Various impacts had squashed the whole thing and twisted it into the proportions of a wrecked buckboard wagon.

Victorio walked up to his shoulder and made sounds in this throat.

Watchman glanced back at the tracks where the wreck had crumbled two pieces of the edge going over. There was no guardrail.

Victorio said, "Shit. He sure as hell didn't get out of that alive."

"Let's go down and have a look."

"I wouldn't leave my car right there. Next guy comes around the bend'll push you right over to join the pickup down there."

Watchman moved the Volvo fifty feet farther down the road and then they started looking for a way to get down into the gorge on foot.

10.

He'd seen them worse. The head-ons on the limited access highways, like the one that had wiped out Maria Three-persons. But the pickup was bad, bad enough.

The door had come off halfway down the mountain and

got stuck between boulders. Evidently Jimmy Oto had flung himself out of the opening in a desperate plunge but the pickup had toppled over on him and then slid on down to the bottom. Oto's body was barely recognizable.

"Dear sweet God," Victorio muttered. Watchman looked away. Victorio swung violently away and soon Watchman heard him retching in the rocks.

He peered into the crushed cab. All the glass had burst; shards of its glittered everywhere. The roof had squashed the steering wheel. The column stick seemed to be in the second-gear position, which was where it would be, going around that bend.

Victorio came slowly over. "Sweet sweet God . . . what are you looking for?"

"How long did he live up here?"

"I don't know. Most of his life."

"He knew that bend, he could have cornered it blindfolded," Watchman murmured.

"What do you mean?"

"I'm looking for evidence that it wasn't an accident."

11.

Somebody might have been waiting in a car. Heard the pickup coming and lunged forward from the concealed side of the bend, and shoved the pickup right over the edge. It could have happened like that. If it had there would be traces of car paint somewhere. He examined every exposed surface but there was nothing but rust and raw broken steel and the mottled grey paint. The nonfunctioning tail-light was still intact, improbably. The rear bumper and fenders hadn't taken too much punishment.

Victorio said, "Why would somebody want to do that on purpose?"

"I don't know. But it's too much of a coincidence."

"Hell he was always a reckless son of a bitch."

"He never got this reckless before. Why today?"

"Why not today? Everybody dies." Victorio buried his face in the crook of his elbow and wiggled his head, rubbing his eyes on the cloth. When his arm dropped away he looked stunned.

"Have they got a phone up here?"

Victorio didn't respond. Watchman stood up and spoke louder. "Any phones up here?"

Victorio shook himself. "No. No phones, no electricity. Hell they've only got one well for the whole village."

Watchman looked up across the canyon bottom but Cuncon wasn't in sight from here. There was a mound of pocked massive boulders and it was a hundred feet or more up to the bottom of the earth-cut through which he'd had his glimpse of the settlement from the high road. Here there was nothing but rocks and weeds and the twisted remains of Jimmy Oto and his old pickup truck.

Victorio said, "He won't tell us much now, will he."

"That's why he's dead."

"What?"

Watchman knew it in his guts but there was no way to explain how.

Victorio took two paces toward him. He looked baffled. "You trying to say Joe wiped him out to keep him quiet?"

"How would I know?" Watchman almost snapped it. He turned away and got down on his back and slithered underneath the rear corner of the pickup; it was the only corner that still left enough clearance to crawl under, and that was only because it was propped up on a two-foot boulder.

The drive shaft had telescoped against itself and burst.

The two halves of the front axle had jabbed themselves into the ground at odd angles and the engine had fallen through the frame to lie on the rocks. There was no sign of the tail pipe or muffler; they had to be somewhere up on the cliff. The shattered oil pan had made a viscous puddle behind the engine and Watchman could see the socket of one headlight where it lay on the ground like a severed eyeball. The fuel tank was bent and dented but it hadn't burst and there had been no fire; there must have been a slow leak somewhere because he could smell the fumes. They weren't strong enough to alarm him.

The cable that ran from the emergency-brake handle to the rear wheels had frayed and burst; one end of it lay curled near Watchman's nose. That was mechanical; he was looking for the hydraulics and he found them and traced the hoses up along the base of the cab, crawling an inch at a time through a space that barely accommodated his shoulders. He was acutely conscious of the possibility of the wreck slipping off its uncertain moorings and pinning him beneath; he moved with great care.

It was not inspiration; the logic was that if the truck hadn't been pushed it must have been disabled, either by accident or by design, and when a vehicle was going to have to negotiate mountain roads the best and easiest shot was at the brakes or the steering. He expected to find a cut brake hose.

"What the hell do you think you're doing under there? This thing's perched like a golf ball sittin' on a wobbly tee."

He pulled himself back with elbows and toes and slid out from under. When he sat up Victorio was making exaggerated brow-mopping and mouth-whooshing gestures of relief. "Man I've had enough coronaries for one day. Don't *do* that."

Watchman moved his feet under him, got up and went

around to the front of the wreck. Victorio trailed along. "You didn't find anything, did you?"

"Not what I expected to, no."

"That mean anything?"

"Find me something to pry this up with." He was trying to lift the hood but it was wedged fast.

"Uh—shouldn't we report this to the police?"

"I am the police. See if there's a jack handle or something back there."

Victorio went around back. Watchman got down on his knees and bent low with his cheek along the ground, trying to look up past the end of the broken axle under the fender. He couldn't see much and what he could see was twisted beyond belief.

The brake hoses were pretty mangled under the frame but there were no indications that they had been tampered with. A knife would have left a neat cut and the only breaks he'd seen had been jagged, traceable to the crushing and ripping the truck had suffered during its long end-for-end tumble.

He heard Victorio crunching toward him. "I couldn't find the handle. This do?"

It was the thin rectangular steel jack post, perforated where the bumper-jack device was supposed to ride up and down on its ratchet. Watchman hefted it. It was about the size of a crowbar and only a little lighter. "If I can squeeze it in. Lend a hand."

They jammed the bar under the crumpled edge of the hood and heaved down on it. The metal gave but didn't pop open. Watchman moved the bar farther to the back and they tried again. He heard Victorio grunt with effort. They both had their full weight on the bar when it gave; it sent Victorio asprawl.

"Are you all right?"

"I guess so." Victorio scrambled to his feet. There was

a small rip near the shoulder of his suit jacket. He limbered his joints as if to test them for cracks and contusions. "I'm okay."

The hood had popped partway open and Watchman pushed it up as far as it would go. He propped the bent jack-bar under it and looked down into the tangle of rusty metal where the engine had once squatted on its mountings.

The battery had squirted acid everywhere. Spark-plug wires dangled from the twisted distributor and the broken blades of the fan had imbedded themselves in the surrealistic mess of radiator grille.

It had to be there and he spotted it, down past where the frontmost engine-mount had been.

"You found something?"

"Have a look."

Victorio peered in past his shoulder.

"So?"

"Tie rod."

"I'm no auto mechanic. What's that mean?"

"The tie rods are the gizmos that keep both your front wheels pointed in the same direction. When you break a tie rod it leaves you with no steering control at all. Both front wheels toe out in opposite directions. Sometimes a front wheel falls off. That's what happened here."

"Okay, so he broke a tie rod. What of it?"

"It didn't break," Watchman said. "It was cut. You can see the way it sheered off. Somebody took a hacksaw and cut three-quarters of the way through it. The first time he put enough stress on it, it broke."

The broken end of the twisted steel rod glimmered faintly. The broken surface was smooth except for a thin section shaped like a first-quarter moon; that bit was jagged where it had broken of its own accord. It wasn't more than an eighth of an inch thick.

"We'll need experts to confirm it," Watchman said, "but it was a hacksaw."

Victorio looked at him with evident awe. "You knew," he said.

"It had to be something like that."

"But you knew what to look for."

"Like I said," Watchman answered, "I don't believe in coincidences."

12.

He got the keys out of his pocket. "Take my car and get to a phone. We'll want the County Sheriff's people."

"What about you?"

"I'd just as soon not give anybody a chance to monkey with the evidence. I'll wait here."

"It'll be dark in an hour."

"Then you'd better quit standing here jawing and get yourself to a phone."

"Shouldn't I tell Pete Porvo?"

"Tell him if you want. It's a murder case, it's out of his jurisdiction. But we might be able to use an extra hand. You'd better tell the county people to send plenty of flashlights and a long cable with the wrecker."

"You think they'll be able to haul it out from way up there?" Victorio looked up at the shelf of the road far above them; it was a good four hundred feet and most of it sheer.

"They'll want the cable to get the corpse out of here. It'd be pretty hard trying to manhandle him up that cliff."

"Okay." Victorio turned away but then he hesitated. "You gonna be all right?"

Watchman could feel the automatic against his spine. He nodded and waved Victorio on his way.

He had another look at the tie rod and it was still hacksaw-shiny, he hadn't been mistaken about it. He walked a complete circle around the wreck, not sure what he was looking for; in the end it occurred to him and he put the back of his hand against the block of the engine underneath the truck. It wasn't cold but neither was it tactably hot; the sun had only moved across the hilltop within the past half hour and that might account for the residual warmth in the metal. He turned and made his way up the steep incline, using his hands, until he came to the body. The face had been battered but it was still visibly Jimmy Oto's face. He lifted Oto's left arm and it moved without too much stiffness; he heard the ends of broken bones grate together and he dropped the arm back to its original position.

No rigor mortis yet so it hadn't been more than a few hours. Sometime today, probably sometime since noon.

Time-of-death was no reliable indicator in this case; the tie rod could have been cut any time in the past few days. It was brutal enough to chill Watchman, the idea of it; Oto often carried a whole truckload of friends around with him and whoever had done this must have known that. Known it but not cared.

13.

Ten minutes later a car stopped on the bend above him and a man in a big black hat walked to the rim to look down. The man studied the scene and turned to speak to someone in the car; then he walked back to the car and it started down the steep slant of the road.

The sun no longer reached into the hollow. Shadows

blended the boulders and the high air had a little chill. Watchman went through Jimmy Oto's pockets but there were only the usual licenses and identification cards in the creased old wallet which also contained seven dollars and a pair of condoms that had worn circular welts into the leather.

In the open glove compartment of the wreck he found half a pack of dry forgotten Camels and a flashlight that didn't work, and the registration for the truck, and an untidily refolded map.

He spread the map on the ground. It was a Topographical Survey drawn to a scale of 1:5,000 and it showed every footpath and every building that had existed in 1966, the year of its preparation.

There were no pencil marks on it but just the same the reason for Jimmy Oto's death now became somewhat less baffling. The map showed the northeast quadrant of the Florence district and it included part of the State Prison at the right-hand side.

There was no consciously audible warning but Watchman knew the man was behind him, knew what direction and how far.

He rose like a corkscrew, turning the half-circle in smooth synchronization with the rise to his feet.

His senses had misled him in one respect: it wasn't one man. There were two of them.

They were coming at him without sound from the rocks below. The larger one in the hat looked vaguely familiar; he was the one who'd stopped the car and got out for a look fifteen minutes ago but Watchman had seen him somewhere before that.

It was the small one who brought it back. The toothpick rolling from one side of the mouth to the other.

They swarmed in too fast for him to try for the automatic under his shirt. As soon as he had begun to rise they had abandoned stealth and rushed. The little one came first and Watchman parried the knife-wrist with his left hand and brought the heel of his right hand up under the man's nose. The toothpick lanced his palm but he heard the crush of cartilage, felt the spurt of blood on his palm. Watchman got a grasp on the knife-wrist and flung the man back into the path of his partner.

The two Apaches went down in a tangle and Watchman kicked the knife out of the little one's hand; the man was bleeding at nose and mouth and didn't care much about the knife any more.

Watchman backpedaled quickly while they got loose of each other; he yanked the automatic out from under the back of his shirt and leveled it.

The little one rocked back on his haunches with both hands over his face. The one in the big hat got to his feet and scowled. He wasn't armed. He said, "Man that ain't fair."

"I didn't know we were playing a game," Watchman said. "Turn around and hit the truck. Hands on the roof."

He made a mistake; he got one pace too close and the Apache swung on him, going for the automatic. It spun out of Watchman's grasp and then the Apache was turning against him with the effortless fluid movements of a man whose musculature was in perfect tune. The fist rammed the angle of Watchman's jaw and his head rocked back in sudden agony; he wheeled to one side shaking his head to clear his vision.

The Apache trusted that punch too much: he attempted it again and Watchman was ready. He went under it, pulled his head aside to let it slide over his shoulder.

Slugging the Apache was like hitting a padded rock. It had no visible effect. Watchman threw his foot between the Apache's ankles and heaved.

‡ 168 ‡

The Apache was trying for a clinch but Watchman's foot tripped him and Watchman's rigid hand bladed him across the back of the neck. The big hat fell off and the Apache stumbled to his knees.

Watchman crossed the six feet of earth with two strides and snatched up the pistol. He jacked the slide and fired. The bullet screamed off a rock two feet from the Apache's boot; it left a white smear and the ricochet echoed up the canyon in pulsing waves of sound.

It had the sobering effect Watchman had intended. The Apache got up slowly and lumbered to the truck and laid his arms out across the roof, palms down.

The little one was sitting on the ground swaying slowly, moaning.

Watchman frisked the big one and took a folding knife out of his pocket. He stepped back and glanced at the little one, walked over to the discarded pigsticker and put it in his own pocket for safekeeping. "Come over here and sit down with him."

The Apache lumbered through the rocks to his bleeding partner and hunkered down. "Christ you smashed his face all to hell, man."

"You could get ten years apiece for this little ballet."

"Hell we got carried away."

"You could get carried away in a box if you pull something like this again." Watchman stood with the sweat drying on him. "What's your name?"

"Sanada."

"Full name."

"What the hell. Danny Sanada."

"What about him?"

"Name of Nelson Oto."

"Oto." Watchman glanced at the dead body up in the rocks above the truck. "His brother?"

"Yeah, yeah. You do that to him?"

"No."

"Well Nels thought you did."

"Next time you might try asking first."

"Ask a cop?" Danny Sanada took out a pocket comb and slicked back his hair. "Yeah."

"Who sent you up here?"

"Sent us? What you talking about, man? We live up here, Cuncon. Right over the hill there. We seen the wreck, we walked in from the bottom of the road. Seen you picking over him that way, Nels figured you was up to something."

The weapon in Watchman's hand was getting heavy. He picked up Sanada's hat and tossed it to him. Sanada put it on and turned his brooding stare toward Jimmy Oto's brother who was beginning to whimper. "We ought to do something for him."

"It'll stop bleeding," Watchman said. "When did you two see Jimmy last?"

"What's it to you?"

Watchman sat down with his back to a rock and let the pistol hang from both hands between his upraised knees. He spoke without heat. "If I push charges they'll toss you away in jail like a squeezed lemon. Now that would be a waste of everybody's time. Somebody's hanging Jimmy's scalp on a door right now and you could help find out who did that."

"So we was right. It wasn't no accident."

"No accident. His tie rod was sawed through."

"Aw son of a bitch," Sanada said. "You hear that Nels?"

"I hear." Nelson Oto's voice had a stuffy twang; his nose was plugged with wreckage.

Sanada said, "I didn't see him since last night down to the Arrow. I don't know about Nels. We was both working all day down to the sawmill, day labor."

Nelson Oto lay back slowly until his head touched the earth; then he twisted his face to one side so the blood wouldn't run back into his throat. He had trouble getting his breath. "I saw him this morning."

"Where?"

"Home, man. Before I went to work."

"What time was that?"

"I don't own no watch. Breakfast time. Man I don't know—maybe six, six-thirty, seven o'clock. He said he had some money, he was going down to the post sometime today and get his bill paid up."

"Where'd the money come from?"

"I don't know. That's the truth."

"Was it from Harlan Natagee?"

He couldn't see Nelson Oto's face very well. Sanada reacted to it sharply but it was more surprise than secretiveness. Nelson said, "Could be. I don't know."

"How big was his bill at the store?"

"Not much. He paid the whole thing off a week ago maybe. He just had the one week's stuff to pay for."

"Where'd he get the money a week ago?"

"I don't know that neither. He had some private things working, you know."

"Like what?"

"If I knowed that, they wouldn't be private, now would they."

"Who was he hanging out with besides you boys?"

"I got no idea. He had his own truck, he was out by himself a lot of the time."

"How many of you were in on the jailbreak?" Watchman asked.

Sanada looked genuinely puzzled. Nelson Oto said, "What jailbreak?"

"Joe Threepersons."

"Man you think we done that?"

"I'm asking."

"Didn't know a damn thing about that," Nelson Oto said.

"Then why was there a map of Florence in Jimmy's truck?"

"I didn't see no map. You see a map there, Nels?"

"I never seen no map of Florence anyplace."

"There you go," Sanada said. "Fuckin' A well told."

The way they both talked they hadn't been out of the Army very long. Watchman got his handkerchief out and inspected it for cleanliness. It wasn't too bad. He took it across to Nelson Oto. "Here, clean your face off."

14.

Under portable searchlights it was nearly midnight by the time the Apache County officials and technicians had finished in the canyon. They cordoned off the wreck and put two deputies on guard; Watchman heard the Undersheriff promise to relieve them by eight in the morning.

There was a rustic unhurried manner to the operations of the Sheriff's deputies, the County Coroner and Attorney's men, the ambulance crew and the wrecker-crane operators; but they were professionals and did their jobs carefully. Fingerprint men dusted every inch of the wreck and afterward the entire steering assembly was dismantled and wrapped in manila paper and carried uphill through the rocks to the county station wagon.

When the gathering broke up, Tom Victorio said, "I'm afraid I still need a ride. You want me to hitch a lift with one of those guys?"

"You can ride with me." Watchman eased the Volvo along between the ranks of parked official vehicles until he cleared the tight bend. Light from the quarter-moon glimmered on the rocks. Watchman said, "You handled those two punks like a pro."

"I'm an ambulance-chaser at heart. I can use a few clients."

"Those two haven't got a dime to rub together. You won't get rich on the fee."

"But the word will get around. I stood up for Nels and Danny. Next time some Apache wants himself a lawyer in a hurry maybe he'll think about calling Tom Victorio instead of Legal Aid."

The road ran close under the lee of the foothills and the Volvo's tires slithered on the corners. Victorio added, "Besides I don't think those two had anything to do with it. Nels' own brother?"

"He only wanted to take them in for questioning."

"Then let him get a warrant."

They emerged from the notch in the hills and Watchman picked up a few late-burning lights of Whiteriver down the valley. "Where can I drop you?"

"My car's still in town."

"You live around here?"

"Live with my folks, fifteen miles down toward Cibecue."

"Where does Kendrick hang his hat?"

"He keeps an apartment in Showlow. He doesn't live around here full time—matter of fact he's a partner in a firm in Phoenix. They all specialize in Indian work."

"But Kendrick's been concentrating mostly on this area for several years, hasn't he?"

"Yeah. I imagine if we ever get this water-rights mess straightened out he'll move on to some other tribe."

"Leaving you to pick up the baton here."

"I'm kind of hoping it'll turn out that way." Victorio cleared his throat. "Jimmy Oto was nobody's favorite character but I'd dearly love to find out who killed him. I'd like to find out quick, before everybody in the tribe starts suspecting his neighbor. We've never had a sneak murderer in this tribe that I know of and that's one ancient tradition I'd just as soon keep. I want to find out who did it and I want it not to be an Apache."

"You could help find out the answer."

"How?"

Watchman braked at the fork and turned onto the macadam. The headlights swung across poor houses and a windmill tower. "Find out who Kendrick's client is. The one who laid out the money for Maria."

"Find out how?"

"You work in the same office. You've got keys."

Victorio didn't reply right away. Watchman steered into the lot between the trading post and the council house. A night-light burned in the store but the only car on the lot was Victorio's beetle.

Victorio's face was tipped toward his knees. "You're asking me to rifle Dwight's files."

"We need that name."

"I'm no sneak thief. Anyhow if you obtain evidence unlawfully you can't use it."

"You can't use it in court. I don't give a damn about court. I'm trying to find Joe before we start finding more corpses."

"I still don't understand what Jimmy Oto had to do with it."

"He had a detail map of Florence in the truck."

After a silence Victorio said, "Yeah, okay."

"Of course it still could be that Joe killed him."

"Why should he?'

"Maybe Oto knew where Joe was hiding out. Maybe Joe killed him to keep him quiet."

"No. That wouldn't be Joe's style. Sawing through the steering gear? Never, man. Joe'd use his fists or maybe a gun. A gun's farfetched enough. He's not what you'd call a subtle thinker."

"Then let's find him before somebody outthinks him and Joe ends up out in the bushes with birds picking over him."

Victorio bit a knuckle. "I don't know. I just don't operate that way. I'm getting the shakes just thinking about it. Suppose I get caught?"

"It's your own office. You're not doing anything illegal."

"They're not my files, they're Dwight's."

"You're splitting hairs. It's the same law office." Watchman got out of the car. "I've got a few calls to make. If you find something I'll be over in the phone booth."

15.

He dialed the local number first and Angelina answered on the first ring.

"Did I wake you up?"

"No, I was waiting for you. Where the hell are you?"

"Whiteriver," he said. "Everything all right?"

"It's boring out," she said. "I've had more fun watching test patterns."

"Well you'd better stay where you are for a while yet."

"Why? Has something happened?"

"Jimmy Oto was killed."

There was static on the line while she absorbed it. "It wasn't Joe. . . ."

"I doubt Joe had anything to do with it. But it looks like Jimmy Oto died because he knew something."

"Killed," she said. "You mean really dead. It's a little hard to believe, just like that."

"Anything happened there?"

"Not much. I talked to Will Luxan on the phone. He said it would be all right, any time I wanted to come back to work."

"Did he say anything about Joe?"

"He's a cagey old man. He didn't say anything you could pin down. But I do have a feeling. I think he knows something. Maybe he knows where Joe is."

"Any special reason to think that?"

"I don't know. You have to know Uncle Will. It's nothing he said. Except maybe that he told me I shouldn't worry my head too much about Joe. The way he said it, I took it to mean he knows Joe is all right. How would he know that if he hadn't seen Joe or something?"

"You could have a point there."

She said, "It's awful late. Are you coming back tonight?"

"Maybe in a little while."

"Be careful who shoots at you this time." But her voice wasn't as light as she meant it to be.

"Take care," he said.

"Yes. You too."

He held the cradle down with his finger and glanced across the way. Only the front of the council house was visible and he didn't see Victorio anywhere. He rang Buck Stevens' home number, collect.

Stevens' groggy voice was half an octave lower than usual. "The hell time's it?"

"About one. I couldn't get to a phone before."

"Uh."

"Get a notebook."

"Okay, wait a minute. . . . All right. Pencil and all. Speak."

"We had a murder up here," Watchman said and kept talking over Stevens' interjections. "Young fellow name of Jimmy Oto."

"Otto?"

"Oto. One tee. He's got a surviving brother named Nelson Oto and there's a friend name of Danny Sanada. Got the names?"

"Spell Sanada."

Watchman recalled the spelling from Sanada's driver's license. "Now one of them's dead and the other two are here on the Reservation but I'd like to run R-and-I checks on all three of them, see if they've got records. I think Jimmy Oto helped engineer that jailbreak."

"Not according to what I got," Stevens said. He sounded a little pleased with himself. "I went down to Florence today. Joe Threepersons had a visitor. Twice. The day before the escape and the day *of* the escape. Fellow signed in under the name of William Jojolla."

"Late twenties, big as a house, driving an old grey Ford pickup?"

"They didn't say anything about what he was driving. But they remembered him because he was big. A big big guy."

"I don't suppose they keep fingerprints or mug shots on visitors down there."

"No. But they'd have a couple of samples of his handwriting from where he signed in both times."

"I'll get a handwriting sample," Watchman said. "Now the next thing, try to find out if the Pinal County Engineer had any customers lately for one-to-five-thousand scale maps of the northeast quadrant of Florence. Oto had one in his truck—maybe somebody bought it for him. They couldn't have had that many inquiries about that particular quad."

"This guy got killed just today? How do you know it wasn't Joe Threepersons that did it?"

"It wasn't Joe's modus-O. Somebody hacksawed Oto's tie rod, it broke on a mountain bend."

"Christ."

"Joe stole a three-seven-five magnum last night, 'scope sight. He's got somebody to kill but it wasn't Oto." He glanced up as a car rattled by. It didn't stop. He said, "Another item. Put out an all-points on a stolen 'Seventy-one Toyota Land Cruiser, color forest green, noncommercial plates Arthur Bravo Seven Five Niner Seven X-ray. The Agency police had it this morning so it's probably on the stolen car list already but I'm not much interested in the hot sheet. I'd like an APB, Joe Threepersons appears to be driving it."

"Yeah? Then he could be in Wyoming by now."

"I doubt it. It's a four-wheel-drive, he's probably back in these mountains right around here. First thing in the morning I'd like you to get an audience with Lieutenant Wilder and see if the department's willing to spring for a couple of days' helicopter coverage up here. It probably won't spot the Land Cruiser but it might caution Joe into keeping his head down a little while until I can get at him. Will you try that?"

"Sure. He might get Captain Custer to go for it, if people are getting murdered right and left up there."

"Put it to him that way," Watchman told him. "Now what's happening at your end?"

"Bits and pieces. I tracked down Maria Threepersons' doctor. He never prescribed Seconal for her. Never gave her any kind of barbiturates. He said she never went in for that kind of stuff. She hated the idea of drugs. He says she was the type who liked to be at the controls herself. So that confirms one thing, she didn't have a prescription and it doesn't look like she'd have drugged herself."

Stevens went on: "Then I went on down to Florence and asked around about Joe's visitors. The screws remembered that big guy. He was there twice—I guess I told you that. The second time was two o'clock on the fifth, which is about three hours before they busted out."

"And he had a map of the area in the truck," Watchman said. "That's not a coincidence."

"Nothing is. Or so you keep telling me. Anyhow then I

‡ 178 ‡

took a flyer, I drove on back up here and went to see Dwight Kendrick's wife. You know, the one Charlie Rand was married to before. You were talking about her and I thought maybe she could tell me something."

"Did she?"

"I don't know."

"How'd you find her?"

"Police radar," Stevens drawled. "I looked it up in the phone book."

Watchman grinned. "What did she say?"

"She's not exactly demure." Stevens' voice was thin along the wires; there was interference in the circuit. "She looks like she's run some pretty fast tracks. I told her about the case a little, got her talking about the old days. She sat there on a lawn chair, she kept snapping her thumbnail against her front teeth. I got vibrations from her. She kind of liked Joe Threepersons and she hates old Charlie Rand's guts. I asked her about Ross Calisher. She said he was kind of a blowhard, always making muscles at girls. Big rodeo hero, all that stuff. She said she wasn't impressed."

"She said it. Did you believe it?"

"Yes. I did. Why should she lie about it? It's all dead and over. She went to some pains to insist Calisher never touched her. He was too loyal to her husband, she said, and she said it with a kind of sneer if you know what I mean—as if anybody that loyal to Charlie Rand had to be too stupid for words. Having an affair with Calisher would have been bad taste, to her. He wasn't on her level. That was the idea she put across."

Watchman gnawed on it. "What did she say about her husband?"

"Which one?"

"Both, I suppose."

"Well she hates Rand. She said he courts them like

a royal prince and then as soon as he marries them he files them away someplace and forgets they exist. She got tired of being ignored, and looking at her you can understand that. She's one of those hearty types, you know, probably drinks more than she needs to, kind of bawdy, I guess she's a natural blonde. By the time Kendrick came along she was looking around for ways to get even with Charlie Rand. She said she thought about Calisher but he was just too big and stupid and crude to be believed. All he ever knew about was rodeoing and bossing crews. She met Kendrick on account of that water-rights case they were starting and she says she took up with him to spite her husband but after a while it got sticky because they both got serious about each other. Finally she divorced Rand and a little while after that Kendrick married her."

Stevens paused. "I'm looking at my notes." Then he resumed. "I asked her about the murder. She didn't seem to know much about it. She sort of liked Joe Threepersons but he was just a hired hand. She hadn't liked Calisher anyway, she thought it was good riddance and she's not too bashful to say so."

"She have any opinion? On Joe's guilt?"

"I asked her. She said she just didn't know much about it."

"Rand never talked to her about the case?"

"Rand never talked to her about much of anything."

"What about Kendrick?"

"I don't know. She's a little murky on that subject. She didn't want to talk to me about him. Maybe she thinks it would be disloyal."

"Did you get the feeling she thought she had something to hide?"

"Maybe. I don't know, Sam. She didn't say it in so many words but she left the possibility open. But hell she left any possibility open. She just didn't say anything."

"So the significant thing isn't what she said, it's what she didn't say."

"Could be. I'm new at this game, maybe I didn't ask the right questions. She's polite but she's holding a lot back. I don't know if that means she knows anything about the case. It could just be she doesn't want anybody prying into her private affairs. You can't blame her for that."

"Okay," Watchman said. "Have you got anything else?"

Stevens didn't. Watchman reminded him about the helicopter in the morning. Stevens said, "First thing. Listen, shouldn't we report on that Oto murder to Lieutenant Wilder?"

"Tell him in the morning. It's a county case, we haven't got any official business mixing into it."

"But that map you found in his truck, on top of that description of him down at Florence—it ties him right in."

"We're not supposed to investigate murders," Watchman said, very dry. "The assignment is Joe Threepersons. That's what we're doing. That's *all* we're doing."

"Okay, I've got it."

"When you get done talking to Wilder in the morning, drive on up here. I'll meet you at the trading post around noon."

"Fine. You got a place to stay?"

"Yes. See you." Watchman hung up and opened the booth door. He went across to the front corner of the porch and tipped his shoulder against the post. Victorio was still inside the law offices at the back of the council house; he saw light in the high window and shadows moving across it.

The moon was way over west, it was well after one o'clock and he'd been up since five. He was a little hungry and very tired. The pale silver earth stretched away past the trees of the settlement, breaking up against the foothills; the mountains were vague heavier masses against the stars. He stepped off the porch and walked fretfully up the shoulder of the road, unable to keep still, disquieted by the uncertainty of this case and his place in it. He was deliberately trying to keep Wilder and Captain Custis at arm's length, not reporting directly to them and it was largely because he was doing everything intuitively. There was no science to it, only innuendoes, and in Phoenix they wouldn't buy any of it. The moment Watchman had begun to believe it possible that Joe Threepersons was innocent he became one Indian trying to protect another Indian and there was no way to expect support from Phoenix; at the same time he was a Navajo hunting an Apache and the Apaches weren't helping, except for Victorio and it was hard to get a clear impression of Victorio's motives in the scheme of things.

The frustration was in the way they were all protecting Joe, each in his own way: the department by refusing to reopen the old case officially, the tribe by preventing Watchman from getting near Joe. If he could reach Joe he might reason with him: if it could be proved that Joe hadn't murdered Calisher in the first place then Joe was home free—but not if he proceeded to kill someone for real.

There were so many vulnerable parties; why hadn't any of them cracked? Or if they had why hadn't Watchman spotted it? It had to be his own identity: they couldn't talk to him, they couldn't be sure if he was red or white, they had no way of knowing whose side he was really on. So all of them from Luxan down to Danny Sanada and Pete Porvo presented faces as hostile and protective as the face of a dog guarding a bone.

He turned and began to retrace the route to the center of town. A big jack bounded across the road, ears erect. He heard a toilet flush nearby; a light went off in a small window across a weedy lot and a moment later he heard water pipes bang. He crossed the apron of the filling station and kept walking toward the intersection but a car came up the south road and made a right turn past him and he recognized the two men inside it. He changed course with an abrupt jerk and ran across the parking lot probing his pocket for car keys.

The Volvo gnashed and whined before the engine caught. He spun a little gravel getting out of the lot; turned right to follow the other car and didn't turn his headlights on until the red taillights of the car ahead of him had disappeared over a rise in the road.

It was Will Luxan driving that car and the passenger with him was old Rufus Limita, bare-chested with something glittery hanging around his neck. It had to be ceremonial gear and it could mean there was going to be a curing ceremony. Anything that would draw those two men out together at this hour of the night implied either urgency or a need for secrecy. It could be some old woman who'd had a sudden seizure. It could be something else. Angelina had said she thought Luxan knew where Joe was.

They were hustling northeast along the main road at a steady fifty-mile clip in Luxan's Pontiac. Watchman closed the distance to a few hundred yards and hung there. They knew he was there but Luxan wouldn't make anything of it unless he turned off the road and found he still had a tail.

The night air had a distinct bite to it but he kept the windows wide open; it helped keep him awake. He hit a little bounce in the road and the suspension banged ominously.

Victorio would be coming out and wondering what had happened to him but it couldn't be helped, there hadn't been time. Whatever Victorio found could wait.

The Pontiac led him almost due north along State Highway 73 until after ten miles or so Watchman saw the brake-lights flash. He took his foot off the gas. The Pontiac made a right turn onto some sort of dirt track and crawled off through the brush, jouncing.

Watchman drove past. He stayed on the highway until he'd gone over the next hill, switched off his headlights, made a U-turn in the road and slowly drove back over the hill with his eyes slowly adjusting to the night. The moon would be down in twenty minutes or half an hour but the stars provided a fair illumination in blacks and greys.

The Pontiac had gone not more than a quarter of a mile; it wasn't built for rough travel. He saw the taillights heaving up and down and the frequent angry blare of the brakes. Watchman parked off the side of the highway, concealing the Volvo as well as he could in the bushes.

He took the flashlight and got out of the car, not switching the torch on. He tested the thumb-strap over the pistol in his small-of-the-back holster; he didn't want it falling out.

Then he went after the Pontiac, on foot, jogging it.

Using the car would have been too risky. He had no idea how far they had to go but once they stopped they'd be able to hear the telltale clank of that busted shock absorber. He didn't think they'd have used the Pontiac if they had far to go along this rutted track and he knew there were no other paved roads back in here. The only real risk was that they were being clever, doing a loop that would take them back to the main highway, to evade pursuit; but it wasn't too likely.

He was out of shape from too much sitting and he settled in to a pace somewhat slower than he would have chosen five years ago, or ten. Cross-country running was a sport of every young Navajo. He had frequently run the length of Canyon de Chelly but that had been fifteen years ago and while his mind remembered the discipline his muscles weren't ready for it. The ache started at the fronts of his thighs and worked down into his ankles. He had the flashlight in his left hand but he didn't use it; there was enough light. He stayed on the tufted hump between the ruts because there was less chance of turning an ankle over an exposed stone. Bunches of piñon and scrub oak went by, close enough to scrape the sides of a car; it was a Jeep trail and it probably led back to an old-fashioned farm cluster, the kind of wickiups where you'd still find horses and a buckboard wagon. Some isolated clan still living in the old way.

The thing to concentrate on was the breathing; you had to keep the engines fueled with oxygen. Once you allowed yourself to start panting you were finished. Let everything out of the lungs and then whoosh in a deep long breath, as much as the chest could contain without bursting; hold it in long enough for the oxygen to get into the lung-linings and then shove it all out and collapse the lungs and start over, long and deep and slow, four footsteps to the breath. Elbows bent, fists up at chest level. A good arm swing from shoulder to elbow. Pick up the feet because you couldn't afford to stumble or trip, you'd lose the rhythm. Saw it in, saw it out. Count miles, not feet.

The moon was down. He couldn't see the old Pontiac any more but he could see the reflected glow of its head-lights moving across the hill crests. Going up the slope he cut his pace by a third and finally a hundred yards below the top he walked it. His legs were wobbly; he'd run about seven miles.

At the top of the hill the rutted track divided. The left fork was the one still in use but the Pontiac was below him to his right, crawling across a little valley at a pedestrian's pace. The ruts were overgrown and washed out; Watchman crossed the skyline quickly and low and skittered down the back of the hill on his bootheels. At the point where the old wagon track leveled out he began running again but he didn't try to keep up the speed he'd set earlier. The Pontiac had something better than a mile jump on him but the valley sloped evenly away from him and he didn't lose sight of it for a full ten minutes; then the lights disappeared so quickly that he knew they had been switched off. So the car had reached its destination.

It was all a thin hunch. It could turn out to be a child with whooping cough or an old lady with the miseries. But Will Luxan was in that car. . . .

He touched the pistol at his spine and jogged on.

CHAPTER SIX

1.

DAWN BROUGHT him awake. He eased out from behind the juniper and had his look downhill.

The smell of burning piñon drifted up at him. He could hear the chant of the medicine song, Rufus Limita's voice. Two or three other male voices mumbled along with him.

He had slept three hours, confident that any sudden change in the Sing would have awakened him.

He couldn't see any of them, they were inside the wickiup. The Pontiac was parked up on top of the ridge; they had taken a narrow foot track down to the place from there. There was a Jeep station wagon beside it and that was why he had not moved in during the night; he had no way of knowing how many there were or whether they had posted sentries.

He saw no one but that didn't mean much; in country like this it was just like the old days, the only time you saw an Indian was when he moved. Watchman studied the scene with care as light flooded across the valley, scattering the shadows.

The place had been a farm but it had gone dry with erosion. There were three wickiups in various stages of decay and behind the corral was a broken latticework which once had been the base of a windmill tower; it looked like something that had been bombed.

The wickiups faced various directions; the Navajo always built his hogan with the doorway to the east but this was not so among the Apaches. One of the wickiups was very large but part of its thatch had caved in; there was the glint of light on metal through the broken roof of this big wickiup. He had a feeling that was the Land Cruiser, concealed inside.

Watchman moved around a little, working his legs and shoulders, flexing the ache from them.

The light gained strength; shades of violet and lilac suffused the distant peaks. He was still studying the hillsides and finally he decided to take the chance that they trusted their safety to isolation and hadn't posted a watch. On his elbows he sculled across the slope to a lower point from which he could command a clear 180-degree field of view.

There could be as many as six or seven from the Jeep and he didn't want to tackle them all; but most of the people would have to go to work in an hour or two. Watchman planned to wait for their departure.

The way he had it worked out, Joe had got sick and somehow passed the word to Luxan. Maybe it was some ordinary bug and maybe it was nerves, and maybe it was the sorcery they thought it was. It usually amounted to the same thing in the end; whether the curative power was in the sick man's mind or in the Mountain Spirits, the chant-songs of the Singers had as much chance of success as the pills of medical science. The best remedy for most ailments was tincture of time; some were cured faster by pills and some by faith and some by the spirits.

There was sorcery in the case from the beginning. If Luxan believed the deaths of Maria and Joe Junior had been caused by a witch then he would certainly call upon the medicine man at the first sign of malady in Joe.

You acquired supernatural power by dreaming about the animals and mountains in which those powers began; you bought from some wise elder the songs and rituals by which you activated the powers. It was easier to witch a man than to cure him because evil was the less difficult state of being. It was easy for a sorcerer to cast a spell which would cause sudden illness: dizziness, fainting, stomach pains, nausea, general weakness. The poison entered through the victim's ears. The medicine man could counteract the spell by summoning the Spirits of the mountains, and of White Painted Woman who was Mother Earth, and of Child of the Water, her child, and of the remote supreme Life Giver. But the ceremonial rituals that were required for this were complex and precise and very expensive and took a great deal of time. Even this little ceremony was probably costing Luxan a hundred dollars and if it ended before noon Watchman would be surprised.

2.

At seven they filed out of the wickiup, three of them carrying dancers' masks and one toting a drum. He hadn't heard any drumming; that probably meant Rufus Limita had ascertained that Joe's illness was not too severe.

There were five of them; Watchman recognized Danny Sanada. Limita and Luxan came as far as the door and watched the five Indians walk up the hill to the Jeep wagon. Limita wore an amulet and a medicine pouch on a string around his neck.

Watchman stayed put without moving while the Jeep backed up and turned and went away.

Limita and Luxan stooped to go back into the wickiup and as soon as they were out of sight Watchman brought out the pistol and walked down the hill without sound. His knees were a little watery.

Limita's hoarse singing started up again. Watchman crouched just outside the wickiup and closed his right eye tight and stayed that way for several minutes until he judged his right eye would be able to see in the dimness within. Then he curled inside, opening the eye, going in like a seed squeezed from an orange.

Luxan heard something and reached for the .30-30 but Watchman had the pistol on him and Luxan dropped the rifle.

Limita sat cross-legged, dripping colored sand onto the edges of his sand painting. He looked up and the song stopped.

Joe Threepersons sat drooping in the middle of the sand painting on the floor. His clothes were very dusty and there was a sweat-shine of fever on his face. The cauliflowered ear picked up a little light from the fire hole and Joe's eyes regarded Watchman bleakly, without surprise.

Watchman said, "Hello Joe."

3.

He nudged the .30-30 with his foot, brought it over and grasped it. It was a Winchester '94 saddle gun, lever action, and Watchman jacked all the cartridges out of it.

"Where's the magnum?"

Three pairs of eyes stared boldly at him and finally it was Luxan's that drifted off to a point behind Watchman. Luxan nodded dispiritedly and Watchman found the big rifle in back of him propped against the wall. He emptied it with care and laid the two rifles behind him and made a little heap of the cartridges.

Years and weather's incursion had turned the walls driftwood-grey. The floor was rammed-earth and the ashes of the night's piñon fire lay smoking to one side of the sand painting on which Joe sat but the residue of smoke didn't quite mask the rancid smell of sickness.

Rufus Limita's hand grasped the medicine pouch at his chest as thought it were a bludgeon. "I didn't finish this time."

"I'm sorry I had to interrupt." Watchman was a little dry.

The old Singer brooded at him. Will Luxan played with the imitation-briar pipe in his fingers, and slid it away in a pocket of his shirt. Joe Threepersons coughed and stared, emanating hatred.

Watchman said, "I'm Highway Patrol." He showed his badge.

"Good for you."

"How're you feeling?"

"Rotten. I think I got Montezuma's Revenge."

Dysentery. Joe Threepersons looked it. As if an elephant had kicked him between the eyes. His breathing was thin and rapid. Watchman said, "You think somebody witched you?"

"Maybe." Joe's round face was closed up, bitterly aloof. Watchman caught a sour whiff of sweat. Joe had nerved his stomach into knots; it wasn't surprising he was sick.

Will Luxan was the key. Watchman addressed him gently. "Somebody wants to kill Joe. I need help to stop it."

Joe said, "Man you got it backwards."

"Who's the rifle for, Joe?"

"I guess that's my binness."

"You didn't kill Ross Calisher, did you."

Joe showed his grudging surprise.

Watchman said, "Listen to me, Joe. Maybe I can get you off the hook. If you can help prove you never killed Calisher you can be a free man."

"You turn around and walk out of here, I'm a free man."

"It won't happen that way. You know that."

Joe closed his eyes. Watchman could see the eyeballs roll under the clenched lids. Joe's jaw muscles worked and his fingertips quivered. Watchman said, "Right now it's open season on you. You understand that?"

"Man these are my friends."

"Somebody wants you dead. They killed Jimmy Oto."

"What's that got to do with me?"

"Jimmy broke you out of the joint. He knew too much. Now if Jimmy knew too much, where does that put you? You know a lot more than he did."

"Well they got to find me first."

"That's not too hard," Watchman said and saw Joe think on it and not like the conclusions: Watchman was a stranger up here and if he could find Joe then how much trouble would a local have? Watchman said, "How'd you manage to hide out in Florence and beat the roadblocks?" He said it conversationally.

"I don't remember."

"You'd make a hell of a witness." Watchman smiled at him.

"Shit. I crawled up in the loft, one of them buildings up at the old, what used to be the Federal slam. Jimmy drove me there so there wasn't no scent for the dogs to get at on the ground. He let me know when you pulled down the roadblocks. What difference it make now?"

"I was just curious. I've got to take you back, Joe, but as long as they want to kill you they can reach you whether you're up here or down there. You can't stop it, neither can I."

"I can stop it. I can get to them first."

"Joe you haven't got that choice anymore."

Joe eyed the two unloaded rifles and his face crumpled. He stared at the corner of the sand-painting. It was as if he was beyond caring any more.

Watchman turned toward Luxan. "Who witched him, *Tio* Will?"

Luxan's square face was troubled. "I can't say a name, you know. It would be up to Joe."

"Tell him to tell me, then. Tell him it's all right. Tell him I want to help him stay alive."

Joe's head lifted sharply. "Why the hell should we trust you?"

"Because I'm an outsider. I haven't got an axe to grind. They're all strangers to me."

"Then what's that make me, man? I never seen your face before. And you're a cop. You said you was a cop."

"Don't blame the cops for your troubles, Joe. You confessed to that murder."

"Yeah and I served my time like a good boy but it never stopped those motherin' screws from pushing me around. You go in slam, you learn about cops."

"I'm not a screw," Watchman said, and went on even though it was a cheap shot: "I'm an Indian just like you."

"*Yutuhu*," Will Luxan murmured. It wasn't contemptuous, merely informative; Joe nodded to show he understood.

"Navajo," he said. "Man that don't cut no ice. They had a Navajo down in slam tried to rape me once. I busted the son of a bitch all to hell."

"Well that wasn't me, was it." Watchman tried another foothold: "The night Calisher was killed you were up in Cibecue. I *know* you didn't kill him."

"So you talked to Angelina." Joe's eyes shifted quickly

to Luxan and his face changed "What you done to my sister, man?"

"She's all right."

"You mean I don't play ball with you, something happens to Angelina. It's like that, hey?"

"No," Watchman said, "it's not like that. Nothing's going to happen to her. I don't play that way. I'm just trying to keep her out of the line of fire. The people that want you dead, maybe they want her dead too. You thought of that?"

It was clear by Joe's expression that he hadn't.

It had always been Watchman's ace but he hadn't wanted to play it.

Will Luxan said, "Maybe this time you tell him, Joe."

Joe rubbed at the sweat on his face. "Man you know what you're saying?"

Luxan said, "It is for you to say. But maybe this one could be right."

Rufus Limita watched from the far side of the wickiup, his eyes dull and guarded. He didn't stir at all. He was humming a little but so softly it was hardly audible; continuing the ritual song inside his throat.

Joe studied his hands. The muscles ridged at his throat, as if something physical were straining to burst out of him.

"Harlan Natagee," he said, half choking it.

4.

"You figure Harlan witched you? Why?"

"It's sort of been an enemy clan for a long time, you know? And everybody knows the son of a bitch is got all kinds of *diyi kedn*. He's been witching people for years, everybody knows. He witched my woman and my kid. He's trying to get at me but I think we got Rufus here in time." It came out in a rush from wherever Joe had been holding it pent up.

"What's Harlan got to do with you and Maria?"

"It ain't that." Joe was impatient with Watchman's stupidity. "It ain't me, it ain't Maria. They put Harlan up to it."

"Who did?"

"I guess it must have been Mr. Rand."

"How could Rand put Harlan up to anything?"

"I heard tell they had a deal together, Harlan Natagee and Mr. Rand. Like under the table, you know?"

"You mean all that tough Indian nationalism is a smoke screen."

"Man you don't get as rich as Harlan by kicking white people in the teeth all the time. He's got to be making deals all over the place. You heard about how they bust into that lawyer's place, Kendrick, and they stole his papers?"

"Yes."

"Well that wasn't Rand's people did that. Ain't no gang of Rand's going to bust into Whiteriver without everybody seeing them. The people would be watching them too close for them to get away with busting in anyplace, you follow me? No, man, that wasn't Rand, that was Harlan's boys did that."

"You were in prison then. Who told you about it?"

Joe shrugged. "Jimmy. He was one of them, he helped bust in there and get those papers. It was Harlan told him to do that."

"Why did Harlan want the papers?"

"Man I don't know that, except I'll bet you Harlan turned around and gave them right over to Mr. Rand."

"But he couldn't have used that excuse with Jimmy Oto, could he? He must have given Jimmy some reason."

‡ 195 ‡

"I don't know what that was."

Will Luxan said, "Harlan is always against the man Kendrick because these lawyers and their paper, they take years, they delay everything, Harlan wants to stop all this lawyer business and get all the people to go over and dump rocks down those wells of Rand."

"Sure," Joe said. "If the white guys ever caught a bunch of Innuns trying to wreck Mr. Rand's wells they'd throw the tribe's whole case out of court. That wouldn't be no good for the tribe. But it'd be fine for Mr. Rand."

Joe stirred and it disturbed the pattern of the sand-painting. Watchman said, "Can you prove Harlan Natagee's working with Rand?"

"No. But it's got to be, man."

"Did Jimmy Oto tell you they had a deal between them?"

"Jimmy didn't know nothing about that. He never stopped to think much. Me, I worked it out like I'm telling you. Harlan didn't have no cause to steal those papers. It was Mr. Rand had the cause. You check it out, I bet you find out Harlan turned them right over to him."

"You think Harlan witched you all because Rand put him up to it?"

"Maybe—maybe."

"All right, now you can tell me why."

"Why what?"

"Why did Rand want all of you dead?"

"I guess he got tired of footin' the bill," Joe said.

5.

The pistol was a loose weight in Watchman's hand. It was past time to pile Joe into Luxan's car and take him out of here in handcuffs but there were questions that still needed exposure. Confine Joe inside anything other than this wickiup and there was an excellent chance he would go silent.

Watchman said, "You kept your mouth shut all these years for your wife's sake, for your little boy's sake. There's no reason to, now."

Joe's eyes sought help from Will Luxan but the old Mescalero only brooded upon his own fantasies and finally Joe rocked his face forward and back. "Well he was going to pay Joey's way right through college."

"That was your deal with Rand."

"Yeah."

"Did Rand kill Calisher?"

"I wouldn't know. I wasn't there. I come home that night, I got a call from Mr. Rand on the phone out to my line shack, he said he wanted to see me right away. It was the middle of the night, man, but he said it had to be right now. I drove over there and he walked me down to the foreman house, old Calisher was down on the floor there and this gun was on the chair. You could smell the powder smoke, you know? I guess he got shot a couple hours before that but you could still smell it. All Mr. Rand said to me, what he said was he had this dead body on his hands and I could help him out of this little problem, and he said he'd pay Joey right through college. So I listened to him, you know, I mean I wasn't never gettin' rich out in that line shack. He said all I had to do was take that gun off the chair and take it home and tell the cops I killed old Calisher because I found him trying to rape my wife. He said he'd make sure I didn't spend more than a few years in the slam."

"Was the whole thing a lie? There was nothing between Calisher and your wife?"

Rage stiffened Joe. 'She was always straight with me."

"But Calisher was hot for the ladies, wasn't he?"

"She never give him the time of day, I'll swear it on a Bible. She liked him but it wasn't nothing like that."

"Who hired Kendrick to defend you?"

"I guess the tribe did. I never saw the bill. Mr. Kendrick didn't know about Mr. Rand, my deal with Mr. Rand. I told Mr. Kendrick I done it, I killed Calisher. He said he thought they'd throw the book at me and I'd get life, but I think maybe Mr. Rand made a deal with the prosecutor up there. I'm just guessing, I don't know about that, you know, but Mr. Rand told me I'd be out in seven or eight and that's the way it would've turned out except I bust out first. I pulled fifteen but you always get parole."

"Nobody ever did a paraffin test on your hands?"

"A what?"

"It doesn't matter," Watchman said. "Kendrick paid out that money to your wife. Why Kendrick?"

Joe puzzled it out. "Well what Mr. Rand told me, you know, he said he couldn't afford to get his own name mixed up in that. He said he had to fix it so we got the money through somebody that couldn't be, like, connected with him, you know? That was why he picked Mr. Kendrick to do that for him, he said nobody was ever going to believe they had anything to do with each other."

"But why did Kendrick go along with it?"

"Well I guess Mr. Rand paid him, didn't he?"

"What about Harlan Natagee? Where'd he fit in all this?"

"I don't know nothing about that." Joe's ingenuous frown slipped into place.

Watchman switched back. "How did Rand explain to Kendrick the money he was paying you?"

"I don't know that neither. I wasn't there."

"Didn't Kendrick ever say anything to you about it?"

"No, man. That money didn't start until I went in."

"Then you don't have any real way to prove the money came from Rand, do you."

"Well look, he told me I'd get the money and then I got the money. You put that together for yourself." Watchman reached behind him and picked up the magnum rifle. It was heavy with a great carved wooden buttstock. The thick telescope had black caps over both lenses. There was a little dust on the piece, clinging to the oil. Watchman said, "Who was this for, then? Rand or Harlan?"

Joe looked up and his eyes changed just a little. In that instant Watchman sensed weight behind him; the reflexes turned him around and Danny Sanada was crouched just outside the oval doorway with a double shotgun aimed at his face.

The hammers were cocked.

6.

It was a range at which two loads of 12-gauge buck would tear the head off your shoulders. Watchman froze.

Danny Sanada said, "Yeah. It figured." He moved the barrels an inch, a warning gesture.

Watchman slowly laid the automatic pistol on the ground and pushed it away from him with his foot. Sanada said, "Drop that magnum too, man."

Joe Threepersons said, "It ain't loaded. He took the shells out of it."

"Put it down anyway," Sanada said and Watchman obeyed. Sanada came inside. "You shouldn't leave that Volvo around like that where folks can spot it. I knowed you was here."

Joe bent over. He stretched his hand to the rifle and dragged it to him and started picking up the cartridges. His movements destroyed most of the patterns of the sandpainting and Watchman became aware that Rufus Limita had stopped humming.

"We got him," Sanada said. "Now what do we do with him?"

"Maybe just hang onto him while I get clear," Joe said.

"Yeah. Then he goes and gets a warrant on all of us for obstructing justice and kidnapping a police officer. Sometimes you don't think too straight, Joe."

"What do you want to do then? Kill him? Man he ain't done nothing to get killed for." Joe glanced at Will Luxan and the old man said something in Apache and after that all of them talked in their own tongue. The sounds were familiar but the words meant nothing to Watchman. It was like a bad dream in which everything looked real and natural but nothing was comprehensible.

Watchman glanced at the pistol but Sanada's shotgun never wavered. He couldn't fight that kind of drop.

His mind worked quickly and clearly but his thoughts seemed to focus on irrelevant abstractions. Sanada had spotted the Volvo along the roadside. Had he got out of the Jeep wagon and sent the others on their way? Or were the others out there on the hillside watching? More likely they had gone on to work. But Sanada didn't need any help, the shotgun was all the authority he needed.

The talk paused and Watchman cleared his throat. "Think about it, Joe. You could turn yourself in now and clear yourself. You'll be a free man soon enough. Cut loose now and you'll be a fugitive for whatever's left of your life."

The side of Sanada's mouth curled up; no one made any other response but Will Luxan launched into a passionate speech in Apache; he addressed himself mainly to Rufus Limita but he kept glancing at Joe while he spoke.

Joe began to shake his head with resolute negation and before Luxan stopped talking Joe picked up the loaded magnum rifle and got his feet under him. Sweat broke out like gel on hot dynamite across his face; he stumbled but kept his feet and when Luxan stopped in mid-sentence Joe said something brief and decisive. Luxan did not speak again. Joe carried the rifle around behind Danny Sanada and paused, bent-over, in the doorway. "You go back to Phoenix, you tell them you never found Joe Threepersons."

"No," Watchman said. "I'll find you again. It's only a question of whether that happens before or after you get killed."

"Ain't nobody getting a chance to kill me," Joe said. "But if they did it wouldn't be no great loss to anybody." Then he went out.

7.

No one spoke; no one moved. Watchman heard Joe's feet crunch across the weedy yard and there was some crashing around, things being flung aside. Then there was the grind of a starter and the chug of a low-geared engine that could only be the Land Cruiser. Its tires crushed the ground for a while and diminished and finally the sound was absorbed by distance.

Watchman said, "How long do we sit here?"

"A while," Danny Sanada said.

"You were right about one thing. All three of you are up against pretty serious charges."

"I guess sometimes you can't go by that," Sanada said ruefully. After that no one talked for quite a while.

Watchman looked at Rufus Limita's granulated features and the medicine man returned his scrutiny without guile. The three of them sat cross-legged in a loose circle around Watchman; none of them seemed especially perturbed but that was the role they were playing—patience was one of the oldest traditions.

The time ticked by.

8.

They held him more than three hours. At the end of it
Danny Sanada nodded and Will Luxan picked up the .30-30
and Watchman's pistol and they all got in the Pontiac
with Sanada beside Watchman in the back seat holding
the shotgun cocked across his lap.

They dropped Watchman at the roadside by his Volvo.
Sanada unloaded the pistol and gave it back to him. "You
gonna be coming after us?"

"Maybe."

"Well when it comes to these two here, I'd kind of like
for you to remember it wasn't neither of them that held no
gun on you."

"I'll keep it in mind."

"You do that," Sanada said. His gaze was intent but
there was no heat in it. Luxan and Rufus Limita hadn't
got out of the car; they sat in the front seat watching
through the windshield. Sanada eased the two shotgun
hammers down to safety-cock and slid the gun into the
car through the open back window. "I guess you'll know
where to find me. I ain't going nowhere."

He watched Sanada get into the car. It went away
toward Whiteriver and he walked over to the Volvo.

The left rear tire was flat. There didn't seem to be any
puncture. They had opened the valve with a toothpick
and let the air out of it. The spare in the trunk hadn't
been fooled with. This time they hadn't meant to set him
afoot, just delay him a little more. That other time he was
pretty sure now that it had been Jimmy Oto who'd shot
out the four tires of his HP cruiser. Jimmy had been sitting
on the tailgate of his old grey pickup at the horse ranch,
swigging beer, and Jimmy must have followed Watchman
up to where Watchman cut the sign of Joe's horses. That

had been Jimmy's style. Sanada was a little less crude than that.

He changed the tire and his clothes were drenched by the time he finished; July was getting vicious, even up here in the high hills.

He got the box of shells out of the glove compartment and filled the magazine of the pistol and snugged it back into the Myers holster; he had a look under the hood, even examined the tie-rods and brake hoses underneath but nothing had been tampered with. The shock absorber was broken at its upper end and that was why it set up such an infernal banging against the resonating metal of the car's body.

When he tried the key it started up right away and he went bashing up the road at sixty-five, which was a little too fast for the curves. But the Volvo held it in spite of the broken suspension and he kept the pedal down hard.

The wind sawed across his face, so hot that it did not cool him once the sweat had evaporated. He went north on State 73 into the piney woods until the high dark forest crowded close against both sides of the road. Along here the shade gave relief. He was headed away from Whiteriver, away from Sanada and all the rest of them because the nearest telephone was at Indian Pine on the northern border of the Reservation.

9.

There was no number listed for Tom Victorio; he called Kendrick's office and the secretary put him through to Victorio.

"Where the hell were you last night?"

"It's a long story," Watchman said. "Is my partner in town, do you know?"

‡ 203 ‡

"He's sitting right here in the office with me. We were thinking about calling out the United States Cavalry."

"What did you find last night?"

"Nothing." Victorio continued quickly: "I'd rather not talk about it right now but the answer's nothing. Pure nothing."

"Maybe he keeps the stuff at home."

"Let's just drop it," Victorio said and Watchman knew it was because he had no way of being sure who might be listening on the line: Kendrick, the secretary.

Watchman said, "Did Danny Sanada drive into town a little while ago?"

"I wouldn't know. I'm not a traffic cop."

"Put Buck Stevens on, will you?"

Stevens came on the line. "Jesus we were worried about you."

"Things are breaking," Watchman told him. "We've got to move in a little bit of a hurry."

"You want to fill me in?"

"I will when I get the time. Right now find out where you can locate a man named Harlan Natagee. Ask Victorio about him. When you find Harlan tell him we think Joe may be gunning for him. Don't let him get near any open windows—Joe's still got that magnum rifle."

"Do I put him under arrest? Protective custody?"

"You put him under arrest for suspicion of conspiracy to commit murder."

"Jesus."

"Suspicion of conspiracy, remember it. We don't want a false-arrest suit later. We may end up with no proof he's done a thing. But I want him under wraps."

"Who's he supposed to have conspired to kill?"

"Don't tell him anything. Recite him his rights. Tell him it's mainly for his own protection."

"Sam, have we got a warrant?"

‡ 204 ‡

"No. I have grounds for presumption that a crime's in progress."

"What crime?"

"Joe's out there with a loaded big-game rifle. Isn't that enough? Let's worry about the formalities later. Now listen, this is important. When you arrest Harlan it's got to be public, very public. When you put him in your car I want everybody to know you're taking him with you up to Charles Rand's ranch. Got that? Victorio can tell you where it is. I'll meet you there."

"You want the whole town to know about it?"

"I want the whole damn Reservation to know about it. Now have you got it straight?"

"Yeah. I find him, I arrest him real loud and we go to Rand's place and meet you there."

"Bring Victorio if he wants to come."

"I'll ask him."

"Harlan's got a right to legal counsel."

"Yeah."

"See you," Watchman said.

There was no listing for Charles Rand but he found Rand Enterprises and dialed and listened to it ring.

A woman chirped at him. "Rand Enterprises, may I help you?"

"I'd like to talk to Rand, please."

"I'm sorry, Mr. Rand is on a long-distance call at the moment. Could I take a message?"

"You'll have to bust in on him."

"Well it's a very important call, really. I'm sure he wouldn't like it if I——"

"It's an emergency," Watchman said. His teeth were beginning to grind. "Get him on the phone, will you?"

She chilled. "Very well, I'll try. Hold on please."

Finally a baritone twanged at him. "Charles Rand. What's all this about an emergency?"

"This is Trooper Watchman, Mr. Rand. I'm in Indian Pine right now. I'd like to come over and——"

"I'm pretty busy right now, Trooper. Can't we make an appointment?"

"There's a man gunning for you with a three-seventy-five magnum rifle right now, Mr. Rand. He might be focusing his crosshairs on your window while we're talking. I'd like to come over there and make some arrangements to prevent you from getting your head blown off. I'll be there in half an hour."

He hung up, maliciously pleased with himself: he'd planted the seed of terror in Rand and broken the connection before Rand could think of the right questions to ask. It was going to be a bad half hour for Charlie Rand.

CHAPTER SEVEN

1.

WATCHMAN had a plan now but it was distinguished less by artfulness than by desperation and he didn't hold out great hope for its success.

In the pines, in the pines, where the sun never shines ... The tires whimpered on the curves, the white line dash-dash-dashed under the left fender, the treetops stood aslant in marching ranks, all bent the same way by the prevailing hard winds.

He drove through a series of sharp turns toward the rim. Below him the water of a lake looked like blue cellophane and reflected the dark bellies of clouds coming in from the west. Not far beyond it a ditch skewered the road and then at the junction of the county highway with a blacktopped side road there was a mailbox for Rand Enterprises.

A Ford Pinto was coming out of Rand's drive; there

was a young woman at the wheel. She looked like someone's secretary: she even had the white collar on her dress. She nodded to Watchman as she drove away past him.

The Volvo rattled loudly across the grated rails of the cattle-guard in the fence and Watchman put the car up the blacktop looking for signs of the ranch buildings. This was timber country but a great deal of it had been cleared; the alfalfa was growing, very deep green, and the road went up a steady slope along a dead-straight line between the fields.

The buildings had to be beyond the ridge crest ahead of him and that was a good three miles' climb. It had cost a fortune to blacktop a private road this long.

Gusts made deep shining ripples across the fields and when he reached the top there was a wind sock standing out swollen from its pole. The plateau stretched away a mile or more in all directions and the road made a turn along the crest; the bend took him along to the west with a smooth dusty airstrip just beyond the barbwire fence that ran parallel with his route. Across the airstrip stood a big fuel tank and an open-sided hangar shading a pair of single-engine airplanes, one of which had its cowling off. A man on a stepladder was doing something with the exposed engine.

They were small old planes, both of them; the kind modern ranches use for herding and rocksalting and crop-spraying. There was probably a corporate Lear Jet for Rand's personal use; that would be why the airstrip went on for the better part of a mile. Beyond that stood a variety of wooden corrals and a little home-rodeo arena with highschool-style bleachers along the south side where spectators wouldn't get the sun in their faces.

There were stables and barns and the road passed between them. Watchman picked up the strong stink of horses and cattle and old straw. A row of trees screened the main buildings and then he made a last turn and the ranch was spread out in front of the Volvo and he had his look at it while he drove up to the main house.

The place had a ski-lodge flavor to it because there were four large buildings all constructed of unsplit logs. From the architecture it was evident the buildings had been here longer than Rand had but the sixty-foot swimming pool and the tennis court, green asphalt, were probably of Rand's devising. There was an open-fronted six-car garage and the blacktop drive made an elegant circle from there past the front of the house. In the center of that circle stood a strange fountain in the guise of a somewhat misshapen nineteen-fortyish airplane standing on its tail. It was probably a sculptor's rendition of the fighter-plane design that had begun Rand's fortune.

A galleried wooden verandah ran the length of the front of the house. There were double doors made of hand-hewn planks four inches thick. Watchman found a push button and pressed it; within the house a bell rang.

2.

"The stupid fool needs a bib," Charles Rand said in his muted Texas twang.

"Maybe you don't understand what I'm trying to tell you, Mr. Rand. Maybe you want me to spell it out in blood."

"I understand all right. The bastard's chucked a hell of a big rock into the pond."

"Maybe that's because the water's getting up over his head. Joe Threepersons got taken. Like a hick in a whorehouse. He wants his money back."

His face rigid with suppressed feelings, Rand presented

his back to Watchman and looked out the window, indicating he didn't want further disputations. The window looked out into the trees and not much light filtered through. The room was big, dark-paneled, rendered gloomier by its somber velvet drapes; massive furniture was strewn around with masculine carelessness and there were antlers over the mantel.

Finally Rand said, "Don't shit a shitter." He turned and fixed Watchman with baggy eyes. "Legally, Trooper, you can't even ask me if the sun's shining. You've got no proof of any of these allegations."

"We're not in court, Mr. Rand." Watchman tucked his chin in toward his Adam's apple. "I'm not slinging accusations. I'm telling you what Joe believes. Whether it's true or not, he believes you had his wife and boy killed."

"Maybe instead of barging in here you ought to be out there stopping him before he does take a shot at somebody."

"That's what I'm trying to do. I need your help."

Rand inhaled to argue but then abruptly stalked toward the door. "Wait here." He left the room and Watchman went over to the window and examined the woods outside. A dead-easy place to creep up on the house; Joe could be out there right now not more than twenty-five feet from him, unseen.

When Rand returned something was dragging down the pocket of his leather jacket. Probably a handgun. His breath was touched with whiskey. The heat wasn't intense up here but it seemed to be getting to him; chest-hair showed through his white shirt between the lapels of the jacket and sweat pimpled his forehead. He didn't look as urbane as he wanted to; when his eyes flicked Watchman's they were as bright as the eyes of a nocturnal animal pinned by the beams of headlights.

"He's a stinking ingrate," Rand said. "It's a tissue of

lies, you can see that for yourself. Why should I kill his wife and boy?"

"He thinks you got tired of paying for their support."

"I never paid for their support. Who told you that?" It was a question but Rand didn't await the answer. "Threepersons, of course. I never thought he had that much imagination. But it's pretty flimsy. You'll never prove I paid anything for their support, because I didn't. My records of cash flow are wide open, God knows—the Internal Revenue boys see to that."

"Fight me tomorrow, Mr. Rand. Help me today. Help yourself, you're the one he's gunning for.

Rand's indignation seemed ready to soar to its peak but he kept a flimsy rein on himself; Watchman couldn't tell how long it would hold. "This is getting out of hand. Way out of hand."

He went over to his desk. Picked up a letter-opener and turned it in his hands while he spoke. It was Turkish in appearance, a brass weapon with a carved handle. His voice was measured, every word dropping like a separate brick:

"All right. This goes no farther than this room. I'll deny it if you bring it up afterward. Understood?"

"I don't sign that kind of blank check, Mr. Rand."

"You're an Indian. I state it as a plain fact, I'm not trying to insult you. Your word wouldn't stand up against mine in court. You understand?"

"I'm listening." Watchman did understand. It didn't matter that Watchman was a state police officer and a non-Apache; in court a good lawyer would make him out a biased witness because of his skin and Rand was right, they'd discount his testimony.

"It's not that I don't sympathize with that poor stupid fool," Rand said. "I've got a little company doing biological experiments. I've watched a time or two when they put a laboratory rat into a no-exit maze. That kind of vexation, that's where Joe is right now. He's no thinker, he lives from crisis to crisis, he grabs at straws and I'm the only straw he can think of. All right, I understand that, but I'm not ready to get killed on that account. I didn't kill his wife. I've never killed anybody. I guess I could but I've never had to."

Rand circled the desk and sat; he kept his concentration on the letter-opener, twirling it so that it shot fragments of reflected light off its blade.

"Nearly six years ago somebody walked into my foreman's house. Took a pistol off the wall and shot him to death. You saw the house outside there, it's the small one just this side of the fork in the driveway—over there on the far side of the fountain. I was the only one here that night. I heard the shot. By the time I got outside there was a car going away and the lights were still burning in the windows over there. I went over to see what the trouble was. I didn't recognize anything about the car, all I could see was the taillights going away. I went in and found him dead. I have no idea to this day who killed him.

"But it put me in a bad spot. Calisher had been having an affair with my wife, the woman who was my wife then. She's married to Dwight Kendrick now but that's neither here nor there. The point is I believe several people knew about this affair. I'd only found out about it a day or two previously. Now my own story was damned flimsy when you come right down to it. I was the only one there that night besides Calisher himself. I had the opportunity. I had the motive—it could have been demonstrated in court that I had just learned about him screwing my wife. I probably wouldn't have been convicted, there was no direct evidence to prove that I'd killed him—how could there be if I didn't kill him? But I was involved at the time in several very sensitive pending mergers and take-over bids and I simply couldn't afford to have my name linked, even remotely, with a sordid crime like that. It would have been one of those tedious cases where a rich man bought himself off in spite of his guilt, you see what I mean? Nobody would have believed in my innocence and every damn one of those deals could have fallen through, not to mention the damage those rumors would have done to all my future dealings.

"I persuaded Joe Threepersons to get me off the spot. In the privacy of this room I'm ready to admit to you that I was guilty of suborning Joe to perjury and tampering with evidence and maybe half a dozen other crimes on that level. But I didn't force Joe to do it, there was no extortion. I offered him a deal and he took it. I knew he would; I make it a point to know the character of the people who work for me.

"Now it may well be that whoever killed Ross Calisher decided he had a reason to kill Joe's wife and boy but I wouldn't know anything about that. All I'm sure of is that if he's gunning for me he's gunning for the wrong man."

3.

Watchman said, "A few minutes ago you told me in no uncertain terms that you weren't the one who was paying his family off."

"Well I'm not exactly retracting that. Let's just say I plead *nolo contendere*. Suppose we drop that. It's just a sideshow anyway."

"There's another item doesn't ring true. You're telling me your wife was having an affair with your foreman. That's not the way I've heard it."

"Then you've heard it wrong. If I wasn't in a position to know, who was?"

"Your ex-wife," Watchman murmured. "Kendrick's wife."

He watched for the effect and was rewarded. Rand didn't move at all but somehow his look became the look of a man who was holding his arm before his face.

"So it just isn't quite good enough," Watchman told him.

"She's a liar," Rand murmured, but it was without conviction. "Naturally she'd try to slander me. She hates me. I think that was what attracted her to that slime of a lawyer in the first place. It was the thing they had in common, their hate for me."

"When did she start seeing Kendrick?"

"When?"

Watchman just waited and finally Rand shrugged as if it didn't matter. "I suppose it was around that same time."

"Before or after the murder?"

"I didn't find out about it until some time after the night I found Ross dead. It may have been going on for some time before that."

"You've been divorced three or four times, haven't you?"

"What of it?"

"How can you afford it? This is a community property state."

"I learned, after the first one. They all signed quit-claims against any properties of mine. Before I married them they had to sign. Gwen came to me without much more than the clothes on her back and she left the same way. I sent her to Nevada to get the divorce. There's no community property law up there."

"That kind of quit-claim wouldn't hold up in an Arizona court, would it?"

"What's this supposed to be leading up to, Trooper?"

"I'm just wondering if maybe you weren't alone here that night. Maybe your wife was here to."

"She wasn't. She was in Phoenix overnight, I believe. Or at least she said she was. She may have been, well, visiting some friend of hers."

"Like Kendrick?"

"I doubt it but it's possible."

"I understand she's not exactly a shrinking violet. She'd make a pretty tough antagonist in a fight, wouldn't she?"

"What are you aiming at?"

"Maybe she wasn't having an affair with Calisher. Maybe he wanted her to but she didn't want any part of him. Maybe he tried something with her and she defended herself by shooting him. Then maybe you told her you'd cover up for it if she'd be a good girl and go away quietly and get the divorce without demanding half your belongings."

Rand's head tipped over a bit to one side. He smiled a little. 'That's pretty good. There's no truth in it, but it's pretty good. You want to try that one on the judge, see how he likes it?"

It was the wrong tack then. Somewhere back there Watchman had taken the right tack but he'd got away from it; he could see that in the way Rand had relaxed. It wasn't a pose. Rand was almost anxious for him to continue along that line of reasoning and so Watchman dropped it. If push came to shove he'd find that Gwen Rand had a perfect alibi for the night of Calisher's murder. Nothing short of that kind of insurance could make Rand this confident, not in the strained state of fear he was in right now.

He said, "Joe tells me you've got Harlan Natagee working for you."

"Does he." Rand contrived to maintain his attitude of amusement. "Now that's pretty far out."

"Since we're in the privacy of this room, the way you keep pointing out, what about it?"

"What can I say? The only way Harlan Natagee would like to look at me is over the sights of a gun. He's a red-necked tin pisspot agitator, he likes to blow things up just to hear the noise. I wouldn't have dealings with that bastard if he was the last Indian alive. How could you trust an idiot like him? He's most likely a little bit psychotic, you know."

"I understand it was Harlan Natagee's men who broke into Kendrick's office and stole the files on the water-rights case."

"It may well have been."

"You're the only one who could have benefited from the theft."

"If that's what you think then you don't understand the workings of minds like Harlan Natagee's. He'd do anything he could to discredit a lawyer, particularly a white lawyer. He wants to take it all back to the days of tomahawks and scalping knives."

"What do you think of Kendrick? Personally."

"I hate his guts."

"Because he stole your own wife from under your nose?"

"No, not really. Kendrick's the jealous type, I'm not. He was more jealous of her than I was, even back in those days when she was still my wife. I didn't care if she wanted to amuse herself with trash but I think it bothered Kendrick that she still had to put up the front of being my wife. He couldn't stand that. He talked her into getting the divorce even though she'd have been a lot better off financially if she'd stayed married to me. They could have gone on having their tawdry little fling in motel rooms."

"And that didn't bother you?"

"I've got better things to do than work myself into a

‡ 216 ‡

fury over things like that. She hadn't been much of a wife to me and I wasn't sorry to get rid of her but I'd have let it ride if she'd been willing. She made a pretty good hostess, she always knew which fork to use and she kept a good eye on the house staff here."

"And you'd have settled for that?"

"Why not? Hell, a man can always hire sex by the hour. I didn't need her for that."

Watchman felt uncomfortable; he knew there were men like that but in his gut he didn't understand them. What was the point in marriage if there wasn't something more to it?

"If it wasn't on account of your wife, why did you start hating Kendrick?"

"He's slime."

"You said that before."

Rand had dropped the letter-opener. Now he picked it up again and abruptly stabbed it down into the desk top. When he removed his hand the letter-opener stood erect by itself, impaled in the wood.

Rand said almost musingly, "The son of a bitch is color-blind, did you know that? When he gets a little upset he runs red lights because he can't remember whether it's red on top and green on the bottom or the other way around. I saw him run over a dog in the road once and the damn dog was right in the middle of the crosswalk on the green light. You imagine how tough it must have been for that dog to learn about crosswalks and green lights? And Kendrick wiped it right out like that because the bastard couldn't be bothered to think about whether the red light was on the top or the bottom."

"And that's why you hate him? On account of a dog?"

"No. But it's a symptom. I look pretty ruthless to most people, don't I, but it's mainly because I'm a successful man. I've never treated another man like dirt. I just pick

‡ 217 ‡

the best people for the jobs, that's my secret. I picked Joe Threepersons for that lineshack because I knew he was pretty thickheaded, he wouldn't get bored with the job and he had a sense of responsibility to his hire that you don't find much in men any more, especially when you've got to stick them out in the woods somewhere on a job where nobody's going to supervise them. I took one look at that wife of his and I knew she'd make sure he did his work. She had the puritan work-ethic right up her spine, that girl. Funny, considering the background she came from. Her father was a drunk."

"Maybe that's what made her the way she was."

"Maybe. Who knows. But Kendrick, he's the kind of man who'll pull the rug out from under anybody at all if he sees an advantage to it. He'd stick a knife in his own mother's back and twist it if he could get a good price for her blood. The day's going to come when he finds a better lay than Gwen, and when it does he'll throw her out like an old shoe. I never threw her out, I just didn't stand in the way when she elected to walk out. That's the difference between Kendrick and me."

Now Watchman began to see it. Rand wasn't as callous as he wanted to think he was. He still had something for Gwen and wanted to think himself a better man than the one she'd left him for. Rand was never going to admit it but he had been hurt by Gwen's decision. Badly hurt, and that was why he hated Kendrick.

There were gaps. The identity of Maria's benefactor went unexplained; Rand first denied it and then hedged on the denial and why would he be vague about it if he had simply kept his word to Joe and put up the money for Maria and Joe Junior?

Watchman said, "There's a lot you're holding out. Right now I've got no leverage to pry it out of you but sooner or later I'll get it. You could save us the time."

"I've told you everything I know that's relevant to the

case. I've told you a whole lot that isn't. I don't think you're entitled to any more than that, and besides I can't think of anything else that would help. I've wondered myself, all these past six years, who it was that killed Ross. I even thought of hiring a private agency to look into it but I decided against it; the case was officially solved and if people started asking questions it could stir up trouble. From my point of view it was better to let Ross's killer go free than ruin my own position."

"Didn't you make any guesses?"

"Of course. It could have been some irate husband. It could have been somebody with a grudge from Ross' past. He had a pretty checkered life on the rodeo circuit. Maybe it was some woman he'd left at the altar somewhere, who knows. It could have been anybody."

"But it wasn't," Watchman said. "Anybody like that, they'd have had no reason to kill Maria Threepersons."

"I can't answer that one, I'm afraid. I'm as mystified as you are."

The telephone rang.

Through the first three rings Rand didn't react to it; he was following some private line of thought. Then he jerked his head back. "Hell I forgot Wilma left for the day." And reached for the phone. "Hello?" Then he waved the receiver at Watchman. "For you."

Watchman crossed the room. "Hello?"

"How, red brother." That was Buck Stevens. "Listen, I'm still in Whiteriver."

"Didn't you find Harlan Natagee?"

"Seems he's in Oklahoma this week, something about an intertribal powwow, some Indian nationalism outfit he's tied up with. They don't expect him back for three, four days."

"I guess that's just as well. Keep him out of the line of fire."

"What you want me to do now?"

"I think maybe——"

"Hey," Stevens interrupted, "I'm in that phone booth at the trading post here? I've got Tom Victorio tugging on my sleeve, he wants to talk to you."

"Put him on."

Victorio came on the line. "Listen, I couldn't talk before, I was on the office phone. I got to talk to you."

"Go ahead and talk then."

"It's what I found and what I didn't find last night. Dwight's got two file cabinets there. They're both locked. I've got a key to one of them, but I know he keeps the key to the other one in his desk so I got into both of them last night. You know those files on the water-rights case, the ones that were stolen?"

"What about them?"

"I found part of them. In the dead files, man. A whole bunch of my notes on precedent cases, they were in the case-closed file right down at the back of the bottom drawer. That's part of the stuff that was stolen. If I'd known that stuff was there it would have saved three months of work."

"Any idea how it got there?"

"You bet your ass. You know Lisa Natagee, the girl on the front desk in the council house? She's the one who usually locks up the place at night."

"She's Harlan Natagee's daughter?"

"She's Frank's daughter, he's the chief. But she's Harlan's niece."

"Would she have a key to Kendrick's files?"

"She might know where he hides the keys in his desk. She does have keys to the offices, all the rooms in the building."

"Is she the only one?"

"No, there's a lot of people with keys but it looks fishy to me. I mean she could have slipped in there one night and just moved that stuff from the active file into the closed files and nobody'd ever think of looking down there."

"I thought you said there were jimmy marks on the window."

"There were. And some of the missing stuff's still missing. But I still want to know how that stuff got there."

"What about the trust fund?"

"There isn't any trust fund," Victorio said. "At least no records. I even looked under Maria's maiden name. No file. The only file under Threepersons was the murder case. Now that ain't like Dwight, he's methodical, he keeps everything in triplicate just the way the Army does. I think he's got every letter he ever wrote or received."

"What about the checks?"

"Nothing in the check stubs, man. Nothing at all. No deposits, no checks."

"Couldn't they be in his personal checking account at home?"

"Sure. But this is a case, right? He's a lawyer representing a client. There ought to be records where he billed the client, collected his fees, all that stuff. I didn't find a thing. I mean if somebody hands you sixty-five thousand dollars to establish a trust fund you've got to show where the money came from and where it went. Otherwise the tax people climb all over you. But there's no sixty-five-thousand-dollar figure recorded anywhere on the books."

"It was a sensitive arrangement," Watchman said. "He probably didn't want it to show on the firm's books. He could have done it privately with any bank."

"I know that. But at least you'd think he'd show receipts for his fees. Unless he never charged a fee. And that ain't like him, he never does anything without charging for it. Hell even the paper clips come off the clients."

"All right," Watchman said. "Then what do you make of it?"

"I don't know. It just doesn't make any sense at all. This whole case is screwy as hell if you ask me."

"Did you tell Kendrick about the files in the dead drawer?"

"No. You want me to tell him I've been burglarizing his office?" Victorio drew an audible breath. "What you figure to do now, Navajo?"

"Think a little, first. Put Buck Stevens on again, will you?"

In a moment Stevens took the phone and Watchman said, "I'm coming down there, Buck. Stay where you are."

"What's up?"

"Maybe we got ourselves a killer. Meet you at the trading post."

When he hung up Charles Rand was staring at him through the specks of dust that twirled in the shafts of light slanting in through the window.

"What killer?"

"I don't like to talk about guesses." The new thought had grenaded into his mind while Victorio was speaking but he wanted to reason it out and see if it worked in all the right places.

"You came in here convinced I'd killed Ross Calisher. What changed your mind?"

"Did I say I'd changed my mind?"

"Come off it, Trooper, you know I'm not guilty."

"You're guilty of stupidity, Mr. Rand, and from that there's no appeal. Now if I were you I'd get over to the bunkhouse and put a crowd around you for a while. Joe Threepersons is probably coming this way. It'll take him a while to get here and he'll take his time working up to the house but he'll be here—tonight, tomorrow maybe. He was gunning for Harlan Natagee first but somebody'll

‡ 222 ‡

tell him Harlan's out of the state and it's a good bet Joe will figure you for a first-rate substitute on his target list. He still thinks you hired Harlan to do the dirty work."

Watchman walked toward the door but he stopped with his hand on the latch. "Joe can't use the open roads getting here. It'll take him a while. I've got business in Whiteriver but I'll try to get back here before sundown. You keep your head down, hear?"

"Wait a minute. You said you'd got the killer." Rand came around the desk. "I'm going down there with you."

Watchman didn't like it but it would be safer all around. "All right."

"We'll take my car."

That was all right too. Watchman didn't trust the Volvo more than ten miles at a time any more.

He got into the high leather seat of the Bentley and put his head back, thinking.

4.

It worked in his head. Joe was gunning for Rand and that was what had confused the issue—that and the vagaries of circumstantial evidence. But nothing proved Joe was necessarily after the right man.

It could just as well mean that a third party had carefully arranged the evidence against Rand in order to convince Joe that Rand was responsible for the deaths of Maria and the boy. Now if Joe carried his vendetta to its obvious conclusion it would result in Rand's death but that didn't prove Rand was the right man.

If Rand died it would benefit a large number of people. It would be a feather in the cap of Harlan's red-power movement, especially if an Indian's finger was on the trigger. Rand's elimination would ease the pressures on the tribe's leaders, who needed successes in their war against Rand's destruction of the Reservation's lakes and pastures.

Rand's death would make the job easier too for Kendrick and Tom Victorio because Rand might have successors but they would be corporate and few dictatorships outlasted the lifetimes of their founding dynasties. As far as Watchman knew, Rand had no children to carry on the leadership of his feudal empire. The corporate heirs in their eastern boardrooms would never marshal the same single-minded fervor that Rand could summon when he went into a fight. They would lose interest, they would consider the public face they had to maintain, they would give way before liberal pressures from both the tribe and the Establishment.

It meant there could be a dozen men with reasons to want Rand dead.

Joe Threepersons had been loaded, cocked and aimed at Charlie Rand. But Joe was somebody's tool, and Watchman had too much invested in the case to leave it go at arresting Joe.

As far as that went he had his plan and he expected Joe would walk into it.

But it just wasn't enough.

5.

Rand was a sure driver, he kept his big fists at a steady ten-minutes-to-two configuration on the wheel and the big Rolls chewed up miles in air-conditioned silence. Halfway to Whiteriver they spent ten minutes in a thunderstorm and batted through it with the wipers slapping the heavy rain aside.

Rand spoke very little and Watchman spent most of the

ride with his eyes shut, working it out. In the middle of the afternoon the big car crunched down the highway past the filling station and pulled into the lot between the trading post and the council house. Rand switched off the ignition and pocketed the key. "Your move."

Buck Stevens must have been inside the trading post. He came around the corner in uniform, giving a half-wave of lazy greeting. Watchman made the introductions and Stevens showed his admiration for Rand's automobile.

"Where's Victorio?"

"I guess he went back to his office."

"Kendrick in there too?"

"I suppose so. That's his car, isn't it?"

Watchman glanced at the Corvette and nodded. He said, "Joe Threepersons has been used, Buck. The man who broke him out of prison wanted him to kill Rand for him."

"You talking about Harlan Natagee?"

"No."

"Then you're not making too much sense."

"I've got a theory. We'll see how it works out. Just follow my lead and try to look wise."

"Easier done than said." Stevens grinned at him.

Charles Rand said, "Where do I fit in?"

"You keep your mouth shut until you're asked to comment. Fair enough? Otherwise you can sit in your car and wait for all I care."

"It's your ball game. You call the rules."

"Keep it in mind," Watchman said and walked away across the parking lot with the two men at his heels.

He went right past the fat girl at the reception desk and strode the length of the corridor to the law offices. Pushed the door open and went straight through to Dwight Kendrick's office.

Kendrick looked up from his desk with raised eyebrows.

Watchman waited for Stevens and Rand to come into the room behind him. Then he said to Kendrick, "You're under arrest."

Kendrick's face remained fixed in its expression. "On what charge?"

"First degree murder. Four counts."

6.

Kendrick leaned back in his chair. "Haw. Haw."

Rand's eyes had gone hooded, concealing his emotions. "Four counts?"

The question revealed something but Watchman let it pass momentarily. He ticked them off on his fingers. "Ross Calisher. Maria Threepersons. Joe Threepersons Junior. Jimmy Oto."

Kendrick said in a mild way, "Where's your warrant, Trooper?"

"I'll get one. In the meantime I'm in my rights holding onto you."

"You'll end up looking like a prize ass. You know that."

"What, no indignant denials?"

"Would there be much point to that?" Kendrick laced his hands behind his head. "It doesn't matter what I deny. I don't know how you managed to jump to these ridiculous conclusions but if I were you I'd——"

"Button it up a minute," Watchman said. He made a gesture to Stevens and Stevens moved reluctantly toward Kendrick, motioning him to stand up. While Kendrick decided to adopt an air of unamused disgust Stevens looked at Watchman, got a sharp nod and took out his handcuffs.

"Now that's ridiculous," Kendrick said. "Put those damn things away."

"Put them on him," Watchman said. "And frisk him."

"I'm not armed."

"Make sure, Buck."

Stevens went over Kendrick professionally and snapped the manacles on his wrists. Charles Rand brooded at all this without stirring until Watchman swung toward him with intentional abruptness. "Kendrick killed your foreman. Joe never knew the truth—Kendrick was just his defense lawyer, that's all he ever knew. But you knew it. You *knew.*"

"I'd watch my mouth if I were you, Trooper."

Watchman shook his head. "Buck."

"Yeah?"

"Ask Mr. Kendrick for his car keys. Go out and have a look in the trunk of that Corvette. If you find a hacksaw put an identification label on it and impound it. Don't get your prints on it or wipe his off."

Kendrick sat back down in his chair and shook his head. "You search nothing without a warrant. Nothing."

"All right then we'll wait here until I get a warrant." Watchman went to the phone but paused before he picked it up. "Understand, you don't move out of my sight until your car's been searched. And your home—I expect we'll find the Seconal there if it's not in the car too."

Kendrick said, "You get yourself a warrant and then we'll see what you find."

"You know damn well what we'll find," Watchman said. "We'll also have a look at your personal checkbook."

That one seemed to surprise Kendrick more. "What the devil for?"

"To show the payments you made to Maria Threepersons."

"I already told you I made those payments."

"Out of your personal account? With no corresponding deposits from your nonexistent trust fund?"

Rand said, "What the hell are you talking about?"

"It wasn't you who paid that money to Maria," Watchman said to Rand. "It was Kendrick—his own money. That's why there's no record of any trust fund in this office."

Kendrick sat bolt upright. "How do you know what records we've got in this office?"

Buck Stevens said, "Didn't he tell you? He's got X-ray vision."

Kendrick ignored it and Rand went to one of the visitor's chairs and lowered himself into it as if he had just aged fifteen years.

Kendrick reached for his desk intercom; it was an awkward movement with manacled hands. "Tom. Get in here."

Rand just sat and watched: clearly he had decided not to say anything more until he found out how much Watchman had pieced together. He adapted well to changing realities; you had to give him that. But nevertheless a kind of bleakness covered his face like a film, a dismal overlay that made his eyes dull.

Watchman said to him, "We still need the motive. Why did Kendrick kill your foreman?"

"I told you I never saw the killer."

"You told me a lot of things. You set it up for Kendrick —you made the deal with Joe, you gave Joe to Kendrick to be the patsy who'd take the rap for him. There's no way for you to slide out of it. You're an accessory."

Kendrick said, "He's only an accessory if you can prove anything against me, and you can't."

It was a shrewd remark: it reminded Rand that to speak now would be to dig his own grave. What Watchman had to do was find a way to shatter that silence.

Watchman spoke not to Kendrick but to Rand; it was Rand, of the two, who had less to lose. "The tribe had a stronger case than yours. If you went into court over those water rights you were bound to lose. Hell every water-rights lawyer with a shingle to hang out knows the Winters-versus-U.S. case, it's broken all these private water deals down and it'll break yours down just as fast if you ever get hauled into court. You didn't want to go into court. You didn't want your wells closed down. So you did a deal with Kendrick. You kept him out of prison and he kept you out of court."

Victorio walked in during Watchman's speech and when Watchman paused he caught Victorio's eye. Victorio said, "What the hell is this?"

Kendrick said, "They pretend they've got some reason to arrest me for murder. Four murders, the man says."

"*What?*"

Kendrick leaned forward and stared at him. "Did you rifle my files, Tom?"

Watchman spoke quickly. "Don't give him the satisfaction, Tom."

Victorio said, "What files?"

Kendrick half-shuttered his eyes and sat back again.

Victorio made an interrogatory throat-clearing sound but Watchman waved him back. He turned to Kendrick. "It's been six years since you killed Calisher. The water case still hasn't come to court. You must have pulled every delaying tactic in the book. Not Rand's lawyers—you. And when you ran out of legal delays you stole your own files to set the case back another year."

Victorio's head rocked back. "Ah," he breathed. "Yeah. Of course. Jesus Christ. Him!"

Watchman glanced at him. "You can confirm that part of it—the unnecessary delays Kendrick kept making."

"You bet your ass I can."

Kendrick said, "Tom, you're jumping in before you find out if there's any water in the pool. You're in a lot of trouble with me as of right now."

Watchman got the ball back. "You ran out of delays

and you couldn't afford to take the Indians' case into court—because you knew you'd win."

Rand made a sound. He was thinking about inveighing. Watchman's angry eyes pinned him back. "He couldn't afford to win it, could he Mr. Rand. Because if you lost it you'd throw him out in the cold to stand trial for murder."

"You're talking yourself into the goddamnedest slander suit that's ever been brought in the state of Arizona," Kendrick said. "Go right ahead, Trooper—finish digging your grave."

"Not my grave. Yours." Watchman went back to Rand: "It had to be like that. You forced him to keep the case out of court. And that's why I know you've got the evidence to prove he killed Calisher."

7.

Kendrick attempted to laugh but he didn't bring it off. And the false smile slid from his face when Rand suddenly stood up.

Rand said, "Let's go outside. I want to talk to you." He was talking to Watchman and Watchman nodded and turned to go with him but Kendrick bounced to his feet and bellowed. "Where the hell do you think you're going?"

Rand sounded weary. "Shut up, Dwight. Come on"—the last to Watchman.

Victorio said, "Use my office."

Watchman followed Rand into it. The cluttered cubicle was hardly big enough for the two of them.

Rand didn't sit down. He leaned his shoulder against a bookshelf. His face was not readable. "I want to know how much you've got."

"That's better. You don't——"

"I'm not admitting a damn thing, Trooper. Not now. Put your cards on the table face up and we'll see how good your hand is. Then I'll decide."

"Fair enough." It was as good as Watchman was going to get; it was a little better, in fact, than he had expected. It could save a lot of time.

He said, "Here's what happened. Kendrick got desperate, he didn't have any delays left in his pocket. He knew the tribal beliefs about witchcraft and he set it up to look as if Maria Threepersons had been witched. Last Monday morning he borrowed Victorio's Volkswagen—Victorio knew it but at the moment he's not admitting it. He will. Kendrick drove down to Maria's house in Phoenix, in Victorio's car. A witness saw that car drive away from her house. It ran the red light at the corner. You told me yourself that he's color-blind, he tends to run red lights when he's upset. You telling me about that dog he killed —that's what made me see how it was."

"You're saying he killed the woman in cold blood."

"Maybe he didn't mean to kill her. He probably took the powder out of some capsules and dropped it in her coffee. It wasn't supposed to be enough to kill her—just enough to make her damned sick. He didn't count on her getting in the car and passing out at the wheel and driving head-on into a truck. How could he? He didn't intend that, he only meant for her to get sick. Then he planned to send Jimmy Oto down to the prison to convince Joe that somebody was witching Maria. Then Jimmy was supposed to help Joe break out. Kendrick planted an idea in Joe's head that Harlan Natagee had witched her and Harlan was working for you. The whole idea was to get Joe mad enough to kill you."

"Nobody's that devious," Rand said. "I don't believe it."

"It's not far-fetched. Kendrick wanted Joe to kill you

because it would solve all his problems at once. It would get you off his back and he'd be free to go ahead into court and win the water case. And it would destroy whatever credibility Joe had left as a witness against him Look at it—if Joe kills you, who's going to believe him when he says he never killed Calisher?"

"I guess that makes a kind of sense," Rand said, bemused. "I mean it's one way to look at things, isn't it. But all this sly business about dragging Harlan Natagee's name into it and persuading the kid that Harlan was working for me—that just doesn't follow."

"It does. Because Kendrick had to cover his own tracks in case anything went wrong. He couldn't afford to have you find out that he was trying to have you killed. You'd have thrown the Calisher case wide open and had him arrested. He had to be roundabout—he had to keep Joe in the dark. There was always the chance we'd catch Joe before Joe got to you and if that happened Kendrick had to be in the clear. So he arranged to put the suspicion on Harlan."

"But what about Maria?"

"I told you I don't think he meant her to die. But it worked to his advantage. It gave Joe more reason than ever to kill you. And it got a big financial load off Kendrick's back. You don't have to pay dead people.

"Victorio's car puts Kendrick at the scene of the crime," Watchman went on. "And I expect after we get a warrant we'll find the Seconal and a hacksaw that matches the marks on Jimmy's tie rod."

Rand's face was pale yellow against the somber books. "If that's all the evidence you've got you won't convict him on a jaywalking rap, let alone murder."

"I think the hacksaw will turn up. It'll connect him to the Oto murder. We may never prove in court that he was responsible for the deaths of Maria and little Joe but we'll prove he killed Calisher. We'll nail him cold on that one."

"With what?"

"The evidence you give me."

"Out of the goodness of my magnanimous heart?"

"Out of the Anglo-Saxon businessman's enlightened self-interest, Mr. Rand. You're wide open to prosecution. Extortion. Bribery. Withholding evidence in a felony case."

"Prove that."

"Do you think I can't?" Watchman demanded.

Rand met his gaze. That he was not sure of his ground was clear enough; he knew the extent of Watchman's knowledge but he wasn't sure how much evidence Watchman could produce.

Watchman had to play the last cards.

He said, "You'll still have some of your hide left intact if you use your head. Look: whatever happens to Kendrick, the tribe won't go on using him to represent them. There'll be another lawyer. It may be Tom Victorio. You won't have a lever against him. He'll drag you into court and you'll lose every drop of water you've got up here."

"That remains to be seen."

"Come off it, Rand."

Rand's eyes flicked at him irritably.

Watchman said, "The tribe's got an axe to grind too. It would be pretty good if they could nail down proof that all these sneak murders had been committed by a white man. That kind of thing's damned important to them. I imagine you'd find a more sympathetic ear in Whiteriver if you went partway down that road with them."

Rand stared at him, half in disbelief. "I didn't take you for a cheap politician, Trooper."

"I'm not talking about a frame. If an Indian had been guilty of any of this we wouldn't be here talking about it. I'm giving you an incentive for telling the truth."

Rand watched him through half-lidded eyes that failed to convey the indifference he was trying to display.

Watchman said, "A few years ago the Tribal Council offered you a compromise, didn't they?"

"One acre-foot in ten," Rand grated. "It wasn't enough. Not near enough."

"There's a few thousand Indians down here, Mr. Rand. How many mouths have you got to feed on your ranch? I imagine the tribe thought it was a damned generous offer."

"They thought so. I didn't."

"Maybe it'll look a little better to you now, since it's going to be a choice of one-tenth or nothing at all."

Rand just watched him.

"You'd have to quit irrigating some fields. But your cows wouldn't go thirsty. I don't know how your white mind works but if it was me I'd rather have one-tenth of that water than none of it."

"Assuming what you say is true, why should the tribe offer to renew the compromise if they think they can win a hundred percent of it in court?"

"I think they'd go along with it. Provided they had your help convicting Kendrick."

"Convicting him hell. You haven't got a scrap of evidence."

"That's why we're still here talking, Mr. Rand, and not on our way to the nearest county jail." Watchman decided there had been enough of this; he changed his tone. "When he goes down you'll go with him unless you do something to prevent it right now. Later's too late. You follow me? If you don't get off Kendrick's ship right now you sink with it. The last lifeboat's being lowered right here in this room. Right now. Nobody's going to be able to keep your name out of it, nobody's going to protect your public image. It's too late for that. But you can avoid prosecution."

"Go on. I'm listening."

"You know damn well I'll get enough on him to send him up for the Jimmy Oto murder. Somebody must have seen him drive out of town in the direction of Cuncon the day he sawed through Jimmy's axle rod. He wouldn't have snapped his mouth shut and started bleating about a search warrant *if* that hacksaw was out of sight and *if* he didn't have a Seconal prescription that'll match the contents of the dead woman's stomach, and *if* he didn't have those payments recorded in his private check stubs. And I'll tell you one other thing. As soon as all this leaks out of this building and the word gets around the Reservation it won't be just Joe Threepersons who's out there gunning for your hide. It'll be every Apache in these mountains. Now you think that one over, Mr. Rand."

"You bastard. Whether you had any proof or not you'd throw me to the wolves just the same."

"Because you and I both know I wouldn't be throwing an innocent man to the wolves. My conscience would get along just fine."

"You're a class-A son of a bitch. You're supposed to operate according to certain rules, Trooper."

"Oh I learned all about rules when I was a Navajo kid in a mission school, Mr. Rand. I learned exactly what you can do with the rules."

"You're a strange bastard to be a cop, that's sure as God made little green apples, ain't it." Rand took a deep breath into his chest and held it there momentarily and let it out noisily. His attention bobbed around the cluttered cell and came back to rest against Watchman. Finally he spoke again. "Let's put it in the form of a hypothesis. No admissions of fact."

"Put it any way you want to," Watchman said. "Just point me to the evidence."

"Kendrick was having an affair with my wife. All right. Hypothesis. Suppose Ross Calisher stumbles across the two of them one night. He's ignorant of this affair. He threatens to tell me what he knows—unless Gwen bestows the same favors on him that she's been bestowing on Kendrick. You follow?"

"Go on."

"Kendrick's got a jealous streak a mile wide. It's a funny story, Trooper, it's a Goddamned comedy. Kendrick doesn't want Calisher screwing *my* wife."

"There's more than that."

Rand nodded. "Hypothesis. Kendrick doesn't know I'm already fully aware of his affair with Gwen. He knows if she goes to Nevada, say, and files for divorce, she won't get much of a financial settlement out of me if I can file a countersuit and charge her with adultery and prove it. In a state that doesn't recognize community property, adultery is grounds for getting cut off without a penny. Now Kendrick's just as greedy as anybody else. He not only wants my wife, he wants my money.

"Here's the next part of the comedy routine: he doesn't know about the quit-claim Gwen signed, the deal she made when she married me. So Kendrick thinks he can't afford to have Calisher be a witness to my wife's adultery. He thinks it would cost him a lot of money if I had a witness like that. It's damned funny. I laughed a lot at the time. He kills a man for profit and then it turns out he's bought a pig in a poke. This is all hypothetical, you understand."

"Sure it is."

"But now we get into a little trouble," Rand said. His voice was getting smoother all the time. "I'd like to help you out but here's the rub. Let's finish the hypothesis. Let's assume I caught Kendrick red-handed when he shot Calisher. Let's assume I brought him up to the office and got the whole thing on tape. A conversation between Kendrick and me in which Kendrick admitted his crime. Now the problem is, I can't allow that tape out of my hands, can I? It's got my voice on it as well as Kendrick's.

If it goes into court there's no way I come out of it with a clean record."

"Lying," Watchman said, "is getting to be a habit with you. You just don't know when to quit." He had no patience left for this. "If that was your evidence it wouldn't have been any use to you. Kendrick would know you could never afford to give it to the police—it would take you right down with him as an accessory after the fact. Now let's have the truth. You're stalling and there's nothing left to stall for. You've got evidence on him and it's leakproof or you wouldn't have kept him in your pocket all these years."

Rand made a fist and opened it, empty. "All right. What the hell. I've got two things. One's a paraffin test. I had a private lab do an analysis on Kendrick's hand the morning after the shooting. It's dated, bonded and notarized. It shows he'd fired a gun within the past twenty-four hours. The second thing's his own signed confession. Holograph, all in his own handwriting. Dated the day after the murder. He put in every detail. Every single detail except the fact that I'd seen the shooting through the window. My name never appears in it except as Ross's employer and Gwen's husband. It's in the form of a suicide note. If I ever decided to produce the thing I could always say I just found it and he must have written the note and gone out somewhere to kill himself but then changed his mind."

"And where was the confession supposed to be hiding between then and now?"

"What difference does that make? I'll produce it."

"No good. It's not admissible evidence unless we can show how we got it.'

"That's your problem," Rand said. "You asked for the evidence, I'm producing it. How you use it is your problem."

"Maria," Watchman said. "She could have had it."

"What?"

"My hypothesis this time. Suppose somebody was to plant the confession among Maria's effects where some eager-beaver County Attorney could find it. She was using it to blackmail Kendrick, see, and that'll also explain why Kendrick paid her all that money."

"Kind of irregular, Trooper."

"You got a better idea?"

"Not a one."

"All right, where is it?"

"Not here. It's in a safe deposit box in Phoenix. I'll get it to you."

"Get it to Victorio. I don't want to lay eyes on it until it's been discovered legally."

"All right, I'll do that. And I'll get to Masterman first thing in the morning and tell him to start writing up the papers for an out-of-court settlement on a nine-to-one basis. If the tribe accepts it I'll deliver Kendrick's confession to Victorio."

"There's one other thing," Watchman said. He was very tired now and it amazed him the sun was still shining in the window. It was only half-past three.

"Such as?"

"Joe Threepersons."

"He's your problem."

"You're the one he's gunning for. You can help us with him."

"How?"

"Bait, Mr. Rand."

Rand thought it over. "I don't like that much."

"You owe him a lot more than that."

"Let the son of a bitch sue me."

"Come on," Watchman whispered. "Come on."

"Shit," Rand said.

"Let's go."

In the office Kendrick sat as if a spring were coiled beneath him. Watchman said to Buck Stevens, "Locate Pete Porvo—he's the local cop. Tell him to put Kendrick on ice until we come back for him."

Kendrick said, "Wait a minute, you can't—"

"Can it, Dwight," Rand said, and the tone of his voice told Kendrick all he needed to know. Kendrick sagged but his eyes lay against Rand with an incredible force of hatred.

Victorio said, "I'd like to ask him some more questions."

"I don't need his answers," Watchman said. "He's sewed up. Come on, Tom. We've still got to catch Joe Threepersons before somebody gets killed."

CHAPTER EIGHT

T HEY WENT up to Rand's ranch in two cars, the Bentley and Victorio's Volkswagen; Watchman didn't want Stevens' cruiser to be seen there.

They parked in the driveway. Rand got out and looked past the house into the trees. In his consternation he turned a full circle, searching; the pressure of possibilities sucked sweat onto his forehead. He stood there for a moment like a floor lamp and then abruptly said, "Let's go inside."

Watchman trailed Stevens and Victorio inside after him. Rand closed the door and led the way into the back room. It was getting gloomy outside; the storm clouds were moving in—they'd just driven through it a few miles back. Rand reached for the desk lamp but then withdrew his hand from the switch and went to the drapes; he drew them shut and only then turned on the lights.

"All right. I'm supposed to be bait."

"You," Watchman said, "or somebody to double for you."

"You mean somebody to play the part of the duck in Threepersons' shooting gallery."

"Yeah. He'll come here with that magnum rifle. Maybe tonight, maybe tomorrow, maybe next week. But he'll be here."

"And I'm supposed to wait around and get shot so you can arrest him afterward. That's a hell of a brand of law enforcement you boys practice. I wouldn't—"

"Nobody's asking you to be the bait. Just give us the trap, we'll provide the bait. Let us use some of your clothes."

Rand's square fingers were at war.

Watchman said, "Just keep away from windows. Now I could use one of those tailored jackets of yours and a pair of your sunglasses."

Buck Stevens murmured, "You'd never pass, Sam. I'm about his build, better let me do it."

Tom Victorio chewed his lip; Rand stared at Stevens and then withered a little, as if the reality of it were slowly reaching him.

"Sam, you know it's got to be me," Stevens said. "I won't be a sitting duck for him. I'll show myself but I'll keep moving. It's the only way to do it."

The silence was such that Watchman heard Rand's lips pull apart with a sticky gumming sound.

Watchman gave him a reluctant nod. "All right. Better bring the artillery from the car, and let's get both cars out of sight." He handed the Volvo keys to Stevens and turned to Rand. "We've got one rifle. I could use the loan of another one."

Rand pivoted toward the door. "Rig him for a crossfire. Sounds good to me. I've got a pretty good 'Ought-Six, that do?" He left the room without waiting a reply.

2.

There was rain.

It came with a slow heavy beat against the roof. It was only just past five o'clock but the daylight had drained out of the sky and the house was dismal in gloom. Wearing one of Rand's tailored rodeo jackets and a pair of Rand's tinted glasses Buck Stevens went around the house switching on lights, taking risks but moving fast enough to discourage a chance gunshot from any window.

Rand had explained the emptiness of the house. His current wife was a film actress currently on location in Spain; in her absence Rand had wanted solitude and dispatched the house staff for a long weekend in Las Vegas. None of the ranch crew was likely to come up to the main house; Rand's privacy was respected by those who worked for him.

Rand restricted his movements to those rooms in which they had drawn the drapes tight. Stevens played Rand in the rest of the house. Victorio raided the kitchen for cold roast beef and lettuce and went around distributing sandwiches and beer; Watchman wolfed down two sandwiches and wondered when he was ever going to put his belly around a decent meal.

He phoned Angelina. "I had him but he got away from me. He's got a little dysentery but he's all right. So far."

"What's going to happen, Sam?"

"I can't tell you anything happy," he said. "We'll try to take him alive, that goes without saying. It's mainly up to him."

"My dumb brother." There was a depth of concern and affection in her voice. "Isn't there anything at all we can do to clear him?"

"He's already cleared. We arrested Dwight Kendrick

for the murders. But Joe's got a poison in him, he wants to kill."

The line crackled; it was a broken interval of time, not susceptible to measurement. At the end of it she said, "Try to keep anybody from getting hurt, Sam. Joe or anybody else."

He pictured her face, the hair falling around it. He sketched for her what had happened. She asked a few questions but he cut her short. "I'll call you later. Maybe have some good news."

"I hope so. I haven't prayed in a long time, Sam. But I don't want anybody hurt. Anybody."

"Then praying can't hurt. I'll see you."

When the connection broke he stood with his hand on the receiver and felt the sweat of it.

3.

The rain beat at the window. Watchman checked the time. Nearly five-thirty. Buck Stevens walked past the window, past the ten-inch gap between half-drawn drapes; he sat down at the side of the window, out of the line of fire. "What if he doesn't come?"

"The little hairs on the back of my neck tell me he's around here right now."

"Come on. There's a limit to that stuff, Sam."

"Well it's not just instinct. Joe knows things today that he didn't know yesterday. He talked to me this morning, he knows I know he's going after Rand. It stands to reason he'd either abandon the whole thing or try to get here before I could get Rand out of his way. So if he's coming at all he'll come now. And he's coming because if he wasn't he wouldn't have walked away from me this morning."

It took great effort of will to maintain the patient waiting. Finally he put down the beer can and slid along the wall to pull the drawstring and close the drapes. "I'd like to speed this up. Let's take a little chance."

"I'm just as tired of this as you are," Stevens said. "Name it."

"Let me have that jacket you're wearing."

"Hold on a minute. You know he'll never buy that. You're too thin, you're too dark. You don't look anything like Rand."

"Outside in the rain he'll never spot the difference." Watchman took one of Rand's white cowboy hats off the rack and settled it above his ears. "Come on." He beckoned and Stevens reluctantly shrugged out of the jacket and handed it over. It hung a little loose on Watchman's shoulders. There was a transparent plastic rain-slicker hanging on the peg and he put that on. "Get Victorio in here."

"You sure about this, Sam?"

"It'll smoke him out if he's around here, I'm sure about that."

Stevens left the room with a brooding face. Watchman checked the loads in the .30-'06 and worked the bolt to slide the top cartridge into the chamber. He left the safety off.

When Victorio followed Stevens into the room Watchman handed the rifle to the lawyer. "It's ready to go, the safety's off. Can you handle it?"

"I'm fair, that's all. Just fair."

"Don't kill him if you can help it."

Stevens said, "What's the script?"

"You take the window on the porch at the corner out in the front room there. Tom takes the window on the side of the house, same corner. No lights in the room behind you. Between you you'll cover that whole quarter from the house. Keep your eyes on the trees between here and the bunkhouse because that's where he'll show himself."

"He will?" Victorio said. "Why should he?"

"It's a rotten light for shooting. That 'scope won't be any good to him. He'll have to get in close to make sure he doesn't miss."

"And you're just going to stand out there and wait for him to pick you off?"

"I don't know about you no-account Apaches," Watchman drawled, "but up where I come from we don't believe in suicide. No, I'm not going to stand there and let him pot me."

There was a *Western Horseman* magazine on the table by the office door. He picked it up and folded it open. "This'll do. Some papers in my hand, that's what I want him to see."

He led them forward through the house. At the end of the hall he reached around through the doorway and hit the wall switch inside the front room. It plunged the room into near blackness.

Rand's voice came out of the dark television room. "How the hell long do I sit in here?"

"It won't be long now," Watchman said. "Just stay put ten minutes."

He went into the front room with Stevens and Victorio and posted them at the corner windows. Slowly they raised the sashes. Rain sprayed in, bouncing on the sills.

Watchman said, "I'm going to make a run for the bunkhouse with this paper in my hand. I'll go inside and pass the time of day with whoever I find in there. That should give Joe time enough to work his way down in the trees here. Right now he's probably up behind the house someplace, looking for a way in, but he'll see me run across and he'll come down and wait for me to come out of the bunkhouse and back to the house here. That's when he'll make his play."

Stevens said, "Jesus. He'll nail you cold."

"I won't give him the chance."

"Shouldn't one of us be out there in the trees, wait for him to come down and get in behind him when he shows up?"

"He won't show himself. He's careful. And if anybody leaves the house right now he'll spot it. This'll have to do."

"You better zig and zag like a son of a bitch."

"Bet your bottom."

4.

Moving as if he had lead in his shoes he dropped off the porch and jogged toward the fountain, the plastic oilskin flapping around him. With the hat pulled low over his face it was hard to see much of the trees but there wasn't much chance Joe was anywhere near here yet.

He skirted the grass by the fountain and made an abrupt turn; just in case. Ran on toward the bunkhouse, then stopped suddenly as if he had forgotten something; shook his head in exasperation and ran on. The performance was designed merely to destroy Joe's timing if in fact Joe was close enough to be aiming at him.

The rain seemed to be letting up a little but the light hadn't improved yet. He kept his shoulders back the way Rand always did; he had the automatic pistol clenched in his right hand out of sight and the open magazine in his left, visible but covered by the transparent plastic poncho. Twice as he trotted up to the bunkhouse porch he swept the line of trees than ran from the side of the bunkhouse along to the back of the house but nothing moved in the rain except the wind-tousled treetops. He crossed the last corner of lawn and went up the steps two at a time, fumbled for the door latch and almost dropped the magazine; and twisted inside.

He slammed the door behind him with his foot. Two card players bounced to their feet like soldiers and showed their surprise when Watchman took his hat off and wasn't Charlie Rand.

He said, "Highway Patrol." His eyes picked out the locations of the windows and he stepped into the corner where the only visible windows were on the far side of the building, the far front corner; Joe wouldn't expose himself outside by going around to those windows.

He flashed the badge in his wallet. The two men just stared: at Watchman and at each other.

He said, "There may be a man out there with a rifle. Be a little safer if you two went in the back of the place for a while."

He dropped the magazine on the seat of the chair behind him. One of the cowhands said, "Who's got a rifle?"

"Just a fugitive. We think he's around here. Best to keep your heads down until we've arrested him."

"Mr. Rand know about this?"

"He's cooperating."

The second cowhand said, "You need a hand maybe? I got a rifle in my kit."

"Thanks for the offer. But we'll handle him." He didn't want trigger-happy cowboys killing Joe. "Go on now," he said, making it gentle.

They went.

The air, even inside, was sticky and close. Rain battered the bunkhouse and suddenly a white flare winked in through the windows; three seconds and then the thunder exploded like racks of billiard balls. He placed it somewhere to the northeast and that meant the center of the rainstorm had passed. The room had the steamy odor of damp-swelled wood. Watchman had to guess how long it would take Joe to get down here from the higher slopes; probably Joe would hurry it because he couldn't know how much time Rand planned to spend inside the bunkhouse.

It would be best to give Joe time to come close but not time enough to get settled in too well; but there was no way to guess where the dividing line was and so Watchman just waited until fear began to pump the sweat out of him. Then he made his move.

5.

The edge of the timber made an arc from the side of the bunkhouse to the back corner of the main house; it left a curved patch of open lawn clear as a field of fire.

Two-foot piñons and junipers squatted here and there along the crescent of grass, haphazardly spotted. They weren't much protection but they would conceal a prone man well enough in this poor light; he was counting on that for safety but if Joe was there it was still a matter of avoiding the impact of Joe's first shot.

It would take a certain fraction of time for Joe to see him come out of the building and another fraction for him to react and steady his aim. Then Joe would have to judge the speed at which Watchman was moving, and the range, which would tell the hunter how much of a lead to give his moving target. There would be hesitation because things were hard to see in the dark shimmer of slanted rain and that would be countered by urgency because Watchman was only going to be in the open for a short time.

So Joe would have to take his first shot before Watchman reached the midway point between the two buildings. If the shot missed he would still have time to work the bolt of the .375 and squeeze off another shot before Watchman could reach the house. There might even be time for three tries. That was the way Joe had to figure it.

So Watchman had a set of limits, beginning and end, and had to work within them: he knew Joe wouldn't shoot earlier than a given moment, nor would he delay past a certain moment. Between those two moments lay the uncertainty and that was where intuition had to sustain his judgment. And if his intuition was wrong it would be too bad because a mere graze from a .375 magnum would knock him twenty feet across the earth and a solid hit anywhere in the torso would kill.

It was no comfort knowing how likely it was that Joe wasn't there at all. He had to assume he was there; odds didn't enter into it.

. . . . Coming out the bunkhouse door he had the pistol in his fist across his chest, the muzzle under the jacket lapel so it wouldn't throw a telltale flicker. He paused fractionally on the top step, still under the porch roof, and lifted his head as if to look at the weather; actually he was scanning the ring of trees. He didn't expect to see anything and he didn't. He waited long enough to be spotted but not long enough to be shot; he turned past the supporting pillar and went down the steps, taking the top two deliberately and then abruptly jumping the rest when the rain hit him. He broke into a slow lumbering run along the outside curve of the driveway, took four measured running strides and then doubled the pace without warning. Three strides that way and he dropped back to a dogtrot and the sudden noise of the exploding cartridge ripped a gash through the fabric of the rain.

He heard the bullet rip up ten inches of the airplane fountain but he was already reacting then, diving straight toward the trees and skidding across the grass on his belly.

He slid up against the tiny bole of a juniper and tried to see through the branches. Buck Stevens spoke loudly through the open window to his right. "You're surrounded, Joe. Unload and come out."

Watchman had the pistol up but he didn't want to use it. Stevens said, "You all right Sam?"

"Come on out, Joe," Watchman said. "Nobody wants to shoot you."

Then he heard the snap of brush and he took the chance: gathered his legs and ran half the distance to the trees and flopped down before Joe could tag him. But Joe didn't shoot at all and Watchman wasted a little time before the crawled off to his right and got around the far side of the clump and ran straight into the woods.

In the lofty pine cathedrals the light was murky and rain splattered the puddles, confusing the ear; but Joe was on the run and Watchman heard him—ahead of him and up to the left. There was a dim reflection of lightning somewhere far behind Watchman. He moved toward the sound, going from tree to tree. Thunder crashed back there in the mountains to the north. Watchman had been waiting for it and when it began to roll he broke into a run, knowing that Joe's hearing wasn't going to be very acute right now after that magnum charge had gone off right next to his ear.

He stopped forty yards into the woods and listened.

There was the drip of rain and he heard a door slam behind him. His eyes burned through the grey light, seeking corner-of-the-eye movement but when something drew his attention and he stared it turned out to be a squirrel leaping from branch to branch.

Then a little grey bird made a brief racket and spun up into the rain and Watchman swung that way, moving with more care, smothering his sound.

‡ 250 ‡

Something had scared that bird. He reached the spot and froze and turned his head slowly to pick up what he could on his retinas and the flats of his eardrums. There was a faint murmur of distant thunder; he hadn't seen any lightning this time. The rainfall was distinctly thinner than it had been five minutes ago; the edge of the storm was nearby. But no sign of Joe.

He kept moving. His clothes clung and grew heavy inside the slicker and his feet squelched as he walked. The diminishing rain made a spongy hiss. He began to picture Joe squatting in the cool dripping shadows like a malignant mushroom waiting for Watchman with the big rifle lifted; he stopped in his tracks, afraid.

Which way now? He couldn't get this close and then lose Joe again; it was too much to ask.

Uphill. That would be the instinct: uphill, west, back toward the Reservation. Get off Rand's property, get back to the sanctuary of the White Mountains.

He went up, angling left because that was west. The curve of the ground took him over a little hump and he keened the dripping forest all the way, looking for sign that Joe had passed this way. But the matted floor of needles retained nearly nothing by way of impressions.

The music of water ahead. He crossed the slope and it became a little louder and he kept moving west, drawn by the sound.

The water came down from the higher reaches; it plunged along like a thick dark tongue, probing its way into cracks and gullies, dividing around tree-trunks and cascading through the creases in the land. As Watchman moved toward it the earth became treacherous with slime because all the run off was sliding down beneath his boots to join the rain-swollen stream.

There was a distinct line of twigs and debris that ran along parallel to the torrent two or three feet higher than the surface of the water and this meant the level had dropped significantly in the past several minutes. Half an hour ago this had been a flash flood. Now it was subsiding but there was still power in it, a tremendous volume of water cascading down onto the plains somewhere out in the middle of Rand's acres.

It meant something important: it meant Joe hadn't crossed, couldn't have crossed. Joe was still somewhere on this side of the river.

And he wouldn't have gone downstream. Not back into Rand property.

He was above here. Either running or standing to fight; but he was above here.

Watchman clawed his way up from the flooding, up to the spine of the razorback, up the slope of the spine through the lodgepole forest. He heard himself wheezing as if he needed oiling: but Joe was in bad shape too, worse shape probably. Watchman pumped the air in and out and ran on up into the rain, not blinking as drops splashed his face.

He wanted to get to Joe before Joe got beyond the trees because here in the confinement of the pines the range of the big rifle was meaningless; out in the open there'd be no way to get near him.

He ran past the edge of the storm and then it wasn't raining any more; an aftermist hung in the air and the smell was thick and strong, the pine resin carrying on the mist.

A scar of rocks ran across the slope from north to south, clear of trees in a belt a hundred feet wide. It was boulders and loose broken shale and Joe could be staked out behind any rock. Watchman looked both ways but it went on forever, he couldn't go around it.

He moved along the fringe of the trees. The water pelted down through the rocks to his left; he moved to the right.

And found Joe's spoor: the heel of Joe's boot had left its impression in the earth.

It was an indentation that had been made after the rain because its lips weren't washed in. Within the past fifteen minutes Joe had come this way and the heel-print pointed straight into the rocks, or across them.

He took it slow and listened to the beat of his pulse. Boulder to boulder; lie up, run, lie up again. Here the shale had been disturbed, the pale dry sides of chips had been overturned. Here the groundwater was still seeping into a depression which therefore couldn't have been made long ago. Here the side of a boulder had been scraped white, perhaps by the inadvertent scratch of a rifle's steel buttplate or the buckle of a belt.

The trail of little signs led him straight across the belt of rocks and into the stunted timber above it. Watchman discarded the rain-slicker and Rand's hat and jacket. He glanced at the sky: an hour's light left, and things were clearing up ahead of him, ribbons of blue beginning to show through as the clouds broke apart. Sundown soon.

The thin high air chilled him through his soaked shirt. He winced now when the trees dislodged moisture onto him; he moved along quickly, watching the ground, watching the forest shadows ahead of him. Joe had passed here, and here, and again here: his track was becoming easier to read because the trees were thinning out and the ground was softer and there was rain to wash away the spoor.

It kept turning from side to side. Once Joe's knees had made dents in the earth at the crest of a rise where he had paused to survey his own back trail. How long ago? Had he seen Watchman coming?

Angling farther to the right the trail went briefly into thicker scrub pine and then the trees became clumps with wide slopes of mud separating them; he could have followed Joe's track here on a moonless midnight. He had discarded caution; the trail led uphill at an angle across the slope on an almost steadily exact course, west-northwest; these weren't the splashed out prints of a man in panic. Joe was making the best time he could and that meant he now had a specific destination in mind.

Pulse thundered in Watchman's eyes and breathing was painful. The shirt lay matted against his back and the wet Levi's rubbed his thighs. The climb got steadily more sheer. At the end he was using his hands as well as his feet and when he reached the top at last he squatted on elbows and knees, just puffing.

The plateau ran west away from him, spotted here and there with growth. Up here the wind blasted the flats constantly and allowed no forests to take root.

The figure was out ahead of him, small, maybe a mile ahead, bobbing along at a steady run. When Watchman's eyes cleared of pressure he could make out the rifle strapped diagonally across the running man's back, the easy rise and fall of arms and legs.

Watchman gathered himself and climbed onto the table and put himself into the agony of the run.

6.

A Hereford steer was half-decomposed and the passage of the running man disturbed the buzzards from it. Watchman's passage eight minutes later disturbed them again and they flapped around, talking, circling the eyeless corpse.

His muscles worked only in spasms. He was running into the setting sun and he missed it when Joe Three-persons stopped.

By the time the angle widened enough for him to see

Joe he had gained a quarter of a mile, which put him something like nine hundred yards away.

Joe was down on one knee, sighting through the Bushnell 'scope.

Watchman kept going. Nine hundred yards was a possible shot with that rifle from a benchrest but the wind was gusty and Joe was out of breath and weak and that one-knee position wasn't the steadiest.

Half the sun burned, perched on top of the horizon. Joe's silhouette crouched to the right of it, shimmering against the red-banded sky. Watchman began to tack. Eight strides on a northerly quarter, six on a westerly quarter, seven to the right again. He counted them because he wanted a random pattern to the changes and if he didn't count he'd fall into a regular rhythm; the body always chose symmetry and you had to reject it consciously.

Eight hundred yards. He was angling across the line now to put Joe farther to the right of the sun. At this angle of incidence he could almost see the sun's movement; another fifty strides and it would be down.

Seven hundred and fifty. He began to zigzag more violently but he didn't drop the pace. His shoulders were lifted to give him more lung space and sharp pains laced across the collar muscles. He hadn't much feeling left below the hips. He didn't credit Joe with a decent shot at more than six hundred yards under Joe's present circumstances; at that point he'd start ducking from scrub to scrub but in the meantime Joe was giving him a good chance to close up some of the distance and Watchman was taking it.

Seven hundred. Joe fired.

Watchman heard the crack. It was startlingly loud for the distance but the wind was at Joe's back and carried the sound. It was all Watchman heard of the bullet—there

was no nearby sonic bang; either the slug had rammed
into the earth ahead of him or it had gone far wide of
him. He suspected the latter: Joe had fired a warning
shot.

Tack right, tack left. Six hundred and fifty. Joe fired
another.

It was still the amiable warning shot because by now
he could have made it come pretty close if he'd wanted to.
With luck he could have made a hit.

Watchman saw why Joe had chosen that spot to stop.
The rim of the plateau was just behind Joe.

Did that mean he was trapped with his back against
an open precipice?

No. Joe's run had been too purposeful for that. He had
a destination in mind: probably the Land Cruiser, parked
below the rim somewhere.

Six hundred, judged by a hunter's eye. Watchman made
an abrupt quarter turn to the left and dodged among the
little scattered trees. With the blood slamming in his
ears he pounded from clump to clump, zigzagging sharply.

The magnum roared again and this one came closer.
He didn't hear the bullet but he saw it crash through a
juniper maybe fifteen feet ahead. Pieces and twigs fell
off the plant where the big leaden projectile had severed
them.

Joe's shot was a five-hundred-yard one now but the
target was moving erratically and the field of fire was
interrupted by all the clumped junipers and scrub oaks;
they dotted the plain like tufts on a bedspread. It made
for unlikely shooter's luck and no hunter would try that
shot on a running deer at that range in this terrain.

Still there was the possibility of luck and if Joe fired
enough bullets he'd hit Watchman.

But Joe wasn't blazing away. He was taking his time
and after a while Watchman began to realize that Joe

was not shooting to kill. Joe was still trying to scare him away or at least force him to keep his distance. An earnest kill-try would have come a lot closer than any of Joe's bullets had.

Watchman made the circle a little wider because he didn't want to corner Joe against a panic. For a little while he was actually running away from Joe on a tangent; but the darting vectors of his route were taking him closer to the rim all the time and that was what he wanted, a chance to spot the Land Cruiser and beat Joe to it.

He was still a quarter of a mile from Joe, making a ragged quarter-circle; he had the sunset spectacle ahead of him.

A bullet made a spout in the earth ahead of him. He jazzed to the left.

The ankles were wobbling now and he wasn't sure how much he had left in him but he wasn't going to give it up before the legs did. He was fighting for oxygen; the altitude was probably seven thousand feet. The earth began to buckle as it approached the top of the escarpment and he watched for pitfalls. Off to his right Joe's rifle was stirring; Watchman dodged to the side. He heard the shot but not the bullet. Possibly it had gone behind him.

Joe had fired seven. Watchman had handled that rifle, he had unloaded it himself, but he couldn't remember how many the tube-magazine held and that irritated him. Right now it didn't matter because Joe had had plenty of time to reload between shots but the time might come when that was important.

His left ankle tipped and he stumbled but he got his footing and went on. Only a hundred yards to the rim now, the length of a football field; he was going to make it that far at least.

Joe discerned the same thing and when Watchman glanced that way he saw Joe on his feet, turning. Watchman instantly abandoned his tacking and made a straight run for the nearest point on the rim but Joe was already going over, dropping from sight; he'd seen he wasn't going to dissuade his pursuer so he was taking advantage of what lead he had left.

Watchman's legs weren't going to handle an abrupt stop. He slowed down like a train approaching the yards and when he walked the last two paces to the rim his legs felt absolutely boneless under him.

He swayed drunkenly and gulped like a landed trout. Blood-haze made a red film over his eyes that turned the sunset colors into a blinding crimson that suffused the world of his vision.

He willed his eyes to clear: he looked down from the rim into the Reservation.

7.

It was nothing like a sheer cliff but it was steep enough to deter a casual stroller. It dropped away to a whorled contour of ridges and hills three miles below.

He was surprised to see a habitation there, and a dirt road.

The road was a switchbacking shelf that zigzagged up from the ridge-canyons like a cartoon illustration of a lightning bolt with the hillside dropping away on the open side.

The earth was mostly grass and the dark spots on it were whiteface cattle grazing. The road came up at least two thirds the height of the escarpment and ended in the yard of a wickiup cluster. Several horses were penned in the corral and a rider in a high-domed black hat was trotting across the hillside toward the wickiups, chousing a calf ahead of him, swinging a rope at his side.

Joe Threepersons was scrabbling his way down the slope a quarter of a mile to Watchman's right, angling toward the wickiups.

The Land Cruiser was parked next to the pickup truck just beside the nearest corral fence.

The triangle of approach made the distance shorter for Watchman than for Joe. Watchman went over the rim and skittered down the slippery grass on his bootheels.

He had the better part of a mile to cover and his legs were troublesome and he still didn't have his wind but Joe was in no better condition and he was lugging twelve pounds of big-game rifle.

Watchman kept a steady eye on him and when Joe decided to stop and snap a shot at him, Watchman sprawled belly-flat in the grass and Joe lost his target.

He watched until Joe gave it up. It gave him a chance to catch his breath. As soon as Joe moved, Watchman moved.

There was a crease of ground that would give some cover. Once inside it there was no more of him than his bobbing head for Joe to see. The crease ran down, fanning wider and getting shallower until it bled itself flat into the slope but it afforded him two hundred yards of protection and he went through it fast, half running and half sliding. When the shoulder faded away at his right Joe was windmilling desperately, running too fast for the slope, trying to get ahead of him. Watchman just kept moving, concentrating on his balance.

Now he was less than a hundred yards from the wickiups and the rider in the black hat had stopped, dismounted, and was standing by the corral watching all this with baffled interest. Joe was still three hundred yards out, upslope a little way, coming along awkwardly.

Then Joe settled down to shoot and this time he meant it. Watchman skidded prone into the grass and the bullet whacked the air overhead.

He gave it ten seconds before he even lifted his head to look.

Joe had used the time to get closer to the wickiups. As soon as Watchman's head appeared Joe whipped up the rifle and Watchman slid back down into the grass.

Joe was moving but still watching; this close to escape he wasn't going to let Watchman stop him even if it meant a killing. Watchman put himself forward on his elbows and knees, sculling through the wet grass but Joe was getting there ahead of him.

Watchman scoured the automatic out of the holster. It was a two-hundred-yard shot and conceivably you could make that kind of shot with a pistol if you held it in both hands with your elbows braced but neither his eyes nor his nerves were in good enough shape to make it count and anyhow he wasn't ready to kill Joe. That wasn't the point of all this.

He put his eyes up high enough to catch the vague movement of Joe's shadow against the farther hills; he poked the pistol out in front of him and snapped off the safety and pumped two bullets off, shooting well behind Joe.

It only made Joe run faster. Watchman scrabbled forward.

Joe was in line with the wickiups now and he quit shooting. He had the inside track to the Land Cruiser and it was all he had wanted. He ran straight down toward it while Watchman got up clumsily, wavered on rubber knees and then stumbled downhill after him.

‡ 260 ‡

Joe dodged past the wickiups and Watchman pumped his protesting legs. He knew he wasn't going to make it but there was always the chance that the starter wouldn't catch on the first push. . . .

The Indian in the hat made a motion toward Joe but Joe waved him back, waggling his free hand; Joe yanked the Land Cruiser door open, threw the rifle inside and climbed in.

Watchman was close enough to see Joe's terror. The starter was grinding and Joe's shoulders moved with stress, willing it to turn over. Watchman reached the side of the wickiup and panted along it.

The engine caught. There was the grind of gears and the Land Cruiser lurched, almost stalled, revved up with the clutch in; it bucked and pitched and got itself rolling and when Watchman reached the road it was gathering speed away from him.

8.

Watchman jerked the door of the pickup truck open. Then he wheeled toward the black-hatted Indian.

"Where's the keys to this thing?"

The Indian only watched him gravely.

Watchman strode to him and plucked the reins right out of the man's hand. "I'll bring him back." He hauled himself into the saddle, using his arms because his legs wouldn't lift him any more, and he put his heels to the horse's flanks and neckreined savagely around.

The Land Cruiser had reached the first switchback and was coming back across below him. Watchman had wasted too much time getting on the horse and the Land Cruiser beat him to the point where their paths intersected: the road zigzagged along half-mile loops and Watchman was cutting straight across; he had to cover only a fraction of the Land Cruiser's distance to reach the same points. There was a chance to intercept Joe on the third switch-back unless the horse broke a leg first.

The Land Cruiser was four-wheel-drive. Joe could get off the road and make a straight run for it but his speed would be cut down both by the gearing and by the terrain, and on humpy slopes like this a horse could outrun the Land Cruiser. So Joe had to stick to the road where he could do fifty on the straightaways and hope to beat the horse to the bottom.

The wind slitted Watchman's eyes and put tears in them. He leaned well back in the saddle to help balance the roan against the steep downward rush of the earth. He gripped the horse with what strength remained in his legs; he laced the reins around the fingers of his left hand and brought out the pistol.

The Land Cruiser flashed across in front of him and he was sure he saw the glisten of Joe's eyes.

The Land Cruiser rushed away to the right and Watch-man drummed across the road and kept going straight down toward the next piece of road. A patch of loose rock; the horse skidded a little and pebbles rattled downhill. The speed was too reckless but if he didn't make that next switchback the game was lost because the road didn't turn back this way again.

The Land Cruiser's brake-lights flashed angrily as Joe went into the hairpin bend and the thing began to sway on its wheels; Watchman thought for a moment that Joe was going over but the Land Cruiser righted itself and he saw the spurt of exhaust smoke. The machine lurched precariously around the last of the turn, rumbled up on the rim of the road and then straightened out. Watchman heard the high whine of gears as Joe speed-shifted, flooring the accelerator; clots flew up from the back wheels and the Land Cruiser slid in the rain-muddled road, wheels bouncing side to side in the ruts.

Watchman flogged the pony with the pistol, yelling a cowboy's "Hey-*yaah*!"

The horse flattened out into its dead run and it was like skiing down a fast slope.

It brought him into the road, angling away from Joe; he wheeled the horse and it responded so fast he knew it had to be a top-trained cutting horse. The Land Cruiser was bearing down and Watchman put the horse squarely across the road and lifted the pistol.

Joe had three seconds to make up his mind and through the windshield Watchman saw him thinking. Go around to one side: but that would give Watchman a perfect shot with the pistol. Go straight through: but that could wreck the Land Cruiser. Stop and use the rifle: but at this range the two weapons were equal and Watchman's was already aimed.

Joe wrenched the wheel and the Land Cruiser plunged away to the right, skidding down along the grass. He was trying to bolt across the open country but Watchman had a good forty-yard shot and took it.

He scored on the fourth shot; it blew the front tire and the Land Cruiser lurched to the left.

Joe tried to keep it going on the rim but it was no good, the thing slowed to a crawl and Watchman came along on the horse, and finally the Land Cruiser stopped.

Watchman sat the saddle, training the pistol on Joe. Joe thought about the rifle but you couldn't maneuver a rifle inside the cramped cab of a vehicle and finally Joe ran a hand through his hair, showing his desperation, and stepped out of the Land Cruiser bare-handed.

Watchman stepped down and handcuffed Joe's wrists together, looping the cuffs through Joe's belt.

"You made a pretty good run, Joe."

"I sure did," Joe screamed in a whisper.

A 4559

Garfield
    The Threepersons Hunt

DATE DUE
